CONFLICT

Award Winning Short Stories Edited by Ted Stanley

HAMMOND HOUSE

CONFLICT
Award Winning Short Stories

Published by
Hammond House Publishing Ltd.
University Centre Grimsby, DN34 5BQ, United Kingdom.

2nd Edition: January 2017

ISBN 978-0-9955702-0-7

Compiled and Edited by Ted Stanley.
Manuscript Editing: Persephone Clearwater.
Publication Research: Toni Josefsen.
Proofreading: Steve Jackson; Shona Wall; Michael Edwards; Abi Thompson.
Marketing: Heather Buckby.
Technical Consultant: Stewart Wall.
Cover Design: Ted Stanley.

Cover Image from the series *Displacement,* by Deborah Geddes, first exhibited in 2010. Produced by permission of the artist. All rights reserved.

The opinions expressed in this book are entirely those of the individual authors and are not endorsed or supported by the publishers or their sponsors, University Centre Grimsby.

Contains language that may be considered unsuitable for a younger audience.

www.hammondhousepublishing.com

CONFLICT

Award Winning Short Stories

Enjoy the raw energy of emerging talent and the polished prose of successful authors in this eclectic collection of short stories that brings together writers from around the world, each with their own unique interpretation of the theme. *Conflict* is the first in a series of anthologies, each featuring a different theme and including the top stories from the Hammond House Annual Literary Prize.

Includes the winner of the 2016
International Literary Prize

'A refreshingly brilliant collection of short stories each cleverly crafted by hidden masters of the art. Quite literally something for everyone or, frankly, everything for everyone.' *Stuart Spendlow, Best Selling Author.*

'This superb anthology gathers some of the best in modern writing and demonstrates our need for Hammond House to share these talented and exciting writers.' *Hugh Riches, Estuary TV.*

'A thought-provoking, sophisticated and thoroughly reflective selection of writing. A new generation of talent is on its way.' *Nick Louth, Best Selling Author*

ACKNOWLEDGEMENTS

Heather Buckby, Sharon Dormer, Stewart Wall, Steve Jackson, Gemma Gilbert, Carrie Strandt, Toni Josefsen, Ruth Liddlemore, Deborah Geddes, Stuart Spendlow, Shona Wall, Andy Maughan and the team at Central Services, Hugh Riches and the team at Estuary TV, Abi Thompson, Leanne Doyle, Persephone Clearwater, Jonathon and Katherine Williams-Stanley, Richard Hall, Nick Louth and Michael Edwards. To Simon, Lucy, Carol, and Ella in the University Learning Resource Centre for their endless patient and invaluable advice and support. The University Centre Grimsby for sponsoring the 2016 International Literary Prize. Judges - Peter True and Anjali Wierny. Finally, all the writers who submitted amazing stories for this anthology. We are sorry we were unable to include more.

INTRODUCTION

With its origins in anecdotes, parables and folktales, the form that we now consider to be a Short Story emerged from the oral storytelling traditions of the late 17th Century. Many successful novelists honed their craft through this form, often continuing the practice throughout their career.

Collections of short stories, Anthologies, often have an overall theme or overarching story. In *The Canterbury Tales*, Chaucer was able incorporate a variety of genres, including farce, drama and romance, allowing the framework story of the journey to be the unifying force.

The unifying force in our inaugural anthology is the theme of CONFLICT, interpreted across a wide range of genres by individual authors from around the world, each influenced by their own society, culture and, of course, imagination. It celebrates the raw potential and emerging talent of students in the craft and the polished performance of experienced writers, including Award-Winning stories from the 2016 UCG International Literary Prize.

Short stories allow you to explore new authors or genres without investing your precious time in reading a novel that may ultimately disappoint. While compiling this anthology, I enjoyed stories in several genres which I would normally pass by. The skill of the writers in telling their tales convinced me to broaden my horizons and reminded me that a good story is a good story, whether its set in the epic drama of space exploration, the turmoil of young love or the frightening frenzy of a zombie apocalypse.

I hope you enjoy our choice of stories in this the first of our annual anthologies. We welcome any reviews and feedback, either through the retailer or contact page on our website, www.hammondhousepublishing.com.

Ted Stanley

‘A good short story crosses the borders of our nations and our prejudices and our beliefs. A good short story asks a question that can't be answered in simple terms. And even if we come up with some understanding, years later, while glancing out of a window, the story still has the potential to return, to alter right there in our mind and change everything.’

Walter Mosley

CONTENTS

WILDCAT IN ESSEX
Ruth Liddemore

WILDCAT IN ESSEX

IT STARTED VERY SIMPLY, as these things often do. Toby annoyed his neighbour.

He didn't mean to, but he did. He seemed to do that a lot, since his mother died. He'd thought for a while that the lady from Social Services might help. She'd been to see him before, and he'd shown her how good he was at cooking his own meals, working the vacuum cleaner, and all the other things his mother had taught him how to do. The lady had seemed really pleased, but she hadn't come back, and he wished she would, because the noises coming from next door worried him.

Toby didn't like noises. His mother had known this.

'It's the boiler,' she'd say. 'It's broken again.' Or 'Sally across the road is practising her violin.' And 'No-one's been shot - it's just a car backfiring.'

These noises, though, didn't sound like that at all. Toby couldn't work out what they *did* sound like: Bangs and clatters outside that woke him up at night; Hissing and yowling that stopped and started suddenly; A hollow sawing sound from behind the fireplace between the two houses.

Then there were the other things, the things Toby sometimes saw when he looked out after a noise woke him up: Something hiding behind the dustbins. Toby knew there was something, because of the big clawing shadows and small lights that were there – then weren't – then were again.

Now, Toby knew about asking. It was something his mother had insisted on, ever since he was ten years old, and had seen smoke from the garden three doors down. It had worried him, so he'd called the fire brigade. The neighbours hadn't been happy when their barbecue was interrupted, but he hadn't got into trouble. 'Just ask,' his mother had said. 'If you're worried about something, *ask* before you do anything. You promise me.'

Toby had promised, and knew he had to ask someone about the noises, but his mother wasn't here, and neither was the lady from Social

Services, so the only person to ask was his neighbour, Mr Powell. Toby was quite pleased with this idea. After all, the noises were coming from Mr Powell's house, so Mr Powell would know what they were.

So Toby asked. But the answers worried him even more. So he asked again. And again. And again. And each time he asked, Mr Powell got more and more angry, while Toby got more and more worried.

In the end, Mr Powell's answers worried him so much that he asked Mrs Potter's husband. Mrs Potter lived in the terrace on the other side of Toby's house, and had been a friend of his mother's. Toby knew Mrs Potter better than he knew her husband, but when Mr Potter was working in his garden, Toby plucked up his courage and asked him about the things that Mr Powell said.

Mr Potter looked at Toby, looked at his watch, and decided, 'I need a drink. Come on.'

The pub was quite full, but they found seats with Mr Potter's friends, and Toby told his story. Everybody looked at everybody else. A stranger at the next table asked Toby questions about the noises, and how long he'd been hearing them, and what he'd seen. So Toby told him, and repeated what Mr Powell had said. Mr Potter and his friends were very helpful. They nudged each other and reminded Toby to 'Tell him about the teeth, Toby. Don't forget the teeth.'

'And the cage in the kitchen.'

'Oh, yeah. Can't forget the cage!'

The stranger was very interested, and wrote it all down in a notebook. When he'd gone, Mr Potter and his friends all started laughing. Toby was hurt and confused, but they explained it to him. It took a while, and Toby didn't really understand. After all, why should Mr Powell say things one way, when he meant another? And why would he be angry about Toby asking questions? No-one else was.

But they'd said he needn't worry about it, so he felt better when they left the pub, even though he still didn't know what the noise was.

But it carried on. And two days later, it was even worse. But now, there were angry voices, too, and then more banging; this time on his door. So he opened it, and looked out.

Toby didn't know why people always looked at him and sighed. Mr Potter had, and now PC Harris did.

'I might have known,' he said wearily.

'Known what?' asked Toby, puzzled.

'Have you been talking to a reporter?' asked the policeman.

'No,' said Toby. 'But I've been talking to Mr Potter.'

'Right.'

'Yes. In the pub. And there was a gentleman with a notebook. He was very interested. He asked a lot of questions.'

'I bet he did'.

'Yes. About what Mr Powell said.'

'And what did Mr Powell say?'

Toby tried to remember.

'He said, 'Yeah. What do you think? We keep a man-eating tiger in a cage in the kitchen.' He said it was to, 'chase off bloody stupid idiots asking bloody stupid questions!' and went in and banged the door.'

'So you asked Mr Potter?'

'Yes,' said Toby. 'But it's all OK, now. He explained about...' Toby thought about the two new words carefully '...sarcasm and irony, and I'm not worried any more.'

'Oh, good,' said PC Harris. 'I just wish someone had explained it to the gentleman in the pub.'

'Why?' Toby was worried again.

'Because he put it in the local paper, where it was picked up by a national paper, and the TV stations, who called the R.S.P.C.A., who called the zoologists. Who called me.'

'Oh.' said Toby. 'Am I in trouble?'

'No,' said PC Harris. 'But I think you ought to see this tiger, don't you?'

Toby didn't, but PC Harris was already dropping something into Toby's hands: a small, marmalade kitten.

*****

THE BEEKEEPER
Joe Fuller

*2ND PLACE in the 2016 University Centre Grimsby
International Literary Prize*

THE BEEKEEPER

J OHN FELT HIS BRITTLE BONES creak and crack as he eased himself from the pinewood rocking chair.
A chair so beautiful.
So, delicate.
Adorned with the shapes of long horned buck and birds still desperate to fly.
But the birds would never fly...
And the chair was indeed spoilt.
'Shaw?'
His voice had been liquorice last night.
Sweet.
Suave.
Like an ode to Sinatra.
As John sang himself to sleep atop a mound of money and cocaine.
He could now only manage a weak, winded moan.
A hiss of breath.
'Forgot to feed the goddamn dog.'
He disregarded the notes and powder which coated the floor: shuffling beyond them.
A green dollar stuck to his forehead.
John didn't notice.
'Shaw you miserable bastard, where are you?'
The kitchen should have been full of dog crap.
Perhaps ripped bags and violated containers?
But he emerged to the golden Labrador - with its button eyes.
Trusting grin.
Like it was feeling his pain also...
Even without food, Shaw lay.
A cool, calm golden rug.

Spreadeagled on the tile floor.
'Good boy.' John grunted, locating the sink.
Subconsciously knowing.
Brain foggy.
Head pounding and pulsing.
He bolted to it, running the icy water over his bald scalp whilst vomit poured out of his mouth.
Sickly.
Lumpy.
Vomit.
He came up for air, only to enjoy the freezing embrace of the water once more.
Shaw simply looked on…
For there was a man at the rear window.
A man who had ugly intentions.

Who and why was John Hampton?
An ex Vietnam veteran with a tendency to howl racist remarks?
Just as a wolf to the moon.
Perhaps, but as everybody knows, character is only skin deep.
Like yin.
Like yang.
There is always more, so long as you scratch beneath the surface.
Mister Hampton lived in a bubble…
Situated on an isolated farm in a stretch of English countryside.
His friends were animals.
His lovers were strippers.
And his pub meats were enjoyed without company.
His card games, however, screamed the stuff of legend.
The war effort and this lucky sleight of hand had combined.
A beautiful concoction.
To create this gorgeous thing called money.
To give John Hampton a slice of the good life.
He'd been abusing it for thirty years…

A knock at the window spurred John out of his nauseous daze.
And flashes.
Constant flashes as he spun around to face the disturbance.
'Smile Johnny boy!'
In-between these bright lights, the intruder was caught.
A beaky nose and greasy black hair peeked out from behind the camera lens.

His accent, laced with heavy cockney.
A reporter.
'Piss off!'
'We just wanna talk mate. Grab an interview. It's in your best interests.'
We.
That ugly word.
'I don't play well with others,' John said through gritted teeth. 'Nor do I owe your country any fuckin' thing!'
'If you only knew…'
And the greaseball was gone.
A whisper in the wind, a possible dream, a drifting demon.
John would check later.
To see the mud encrusted footprints and a gun half buried in the sludge.
The 'nam flashbacks would run thick.
They would run fast.

Days passed for John Hampton: hellish days wherever nightmares were concerned - those screwed into his skull. Ducking away from gunfire and imagined explosions which still saw to burn away his flesh.
Every waking moment gave way to crippling anxiety.
Hallucinations.
The works.
Nights were liquid alcohol - it consumed his veins.
But also, did they consist of vices… pounds of pot, credit cards stained white, needles drained and hookers who drained him.
If the body is a temple, John's temple was dangerously close to collapse.
Shattering.
Unrelenting.
Collapse.
Yet his bees continued to buzz and thrive as if mocking him…
After a shot.
A line.
A ride.
Who cared anymore?

The company that night was a French doll: 'Cheree' or 'Celeste' somethin'.
A petite girl with crimson lipstick, diamond eyes and flowing blonde hair enriched with tints of colour.
Orange.
Purple.
Blue.

She was a painting.
So, delicate in the way she danced, seemingly porcelain as if one knock could break her.
The girl even dove into the coke, as if it was snow.
John simply left the girl to her acrobatics while he watched, almost disinterested and sparked up a cigarette.
She lasted two hours…
Swinging and pivoting in that tight black shirt, it clung to her as the sweat poured and the throb of 80s disco music reached new hypnotic heights, the skirt even began to ruffle.
Smoke hung heavy in the air.
'Honey?'
It was returned with a quizzical look, still so high.
'Your dance is a beautiful picture of violence and delight. You are fantastical. Angelic. But is that what I pay you for?'
Her eyes dropped, just as a mutter escaped those cherry lips:
'No.'
His own lip quivered, a telling sign of anger.
John chewed it until fresh blood poured…
'Money?' he hummed 'You have to earn it.'
The girl saw the flash of money, although well aware that she now smelt of ungodly perspiration.
Crispy packets of cash awaited… Tucked away in this old man's jacket, under the floorboards perhaps? Upstairs in a safe?
If she wanted, she'd have her way with it all.
But those usual thieving habits were null under his stare.
'C-can I have a glass of water?'
'I'll think about it sweetheart.'
The girl dared not to step on this tiger's tail, fearing that it would only infuriate him.
Instead, she squelched forward.
Pores dripping.
Bare feet sticking to the boards below.
All to the faux comfort of
'That's it.'
'Good girl.'
It made her repulsed.
Nevertheless, she advanced and plucked the fresh cigarette from his drooling mouth.
Inhaling.
Exhaling.

Forever calm.

As John only watched dumbly: the girl took a drag, blowing the smoke ring back into his face.

It stung.

But it stung good.

She proceeded to weave an elegant lap dance - a spider web of mystery - hopefully masking the dreaded odour.

Yet, when she sat, entirely comfortable in her ability to mystify.

Well, that proved to be her undoing.

It came with a rush of static.

A gloss of the eyes.

Shaking hands.

A low snarl.

And a grip too fierce.

'You're worthless Hampton! A fuckin' mook. You kill these Vietcong! You kill them! They ain't people, you need to stop viewing them as people. Torch. Shoot. Stab. Any order you like, you inept, renegade piece of shit.'

John's grip tightened around the girl's neck.

He was away in orange forests, flames licking his heels and silver scraps of shrapnel cutting apart a wrinkleless cheek.

All the while chasing these savages as friends fell around him.

Thurston Rivers disappeared into the tall grass and erupted in a fountain of blood.

James Yates caught the napalm, it engulfed him.

Like a swarm of ants, it ate away at his flesh until nothing was left but charcoal bones.

John Hampton however, got caught in a bear trap between the two warring factions.

Click.

He felt the razor teeth catch his right leg, digging deep into the skin.

'Son of a-'

'Bitch!' the girl bore the brunt of the insult… It was getting increasingly difficult to breathe.

His mental struggle continued on.

The flames began to lick and lust after him, feeling like boiling whiskey or a damn vodka shot. Where heat was concerned - this was palpable.

John dug out the knife from a left boot, trying to pry the metal monster loose.

To no avail, for a man, streaked in mud popped from his hiding place.

Beneath twigs and bamboo shoots.

And proceeded to swipe at John's leg - perhaps to tear it off? Maybe to hold him in place whilst the fire did the dirty work.

He howled.

He punched.

He screamed.
Yet for the life of him, this murderous cave dweller could not secure a clamp on the
American soldier.
The pain.
Searing.
Brutal.
Raw.
Real.
John pulled at his leg which resembled something of blended meat - wincing, letting the tears
fall and add fuel to his movements.
He dragged the bear trap towards the bear in question… A Vietcong with feral eyes and a
natural grunt.
Who welcomed him, taunted him, helped him…
This particular den dweller was sadistic and cocky.
So, when John Hampton fell into the hideaway, implementing a vice strangulation and a
narrow dodging of death.
The cocky sadist fell into the welcome embrace of darkness.
With a smile.

At first, John laughed demonically.
Then, came the realisation.
Pretty little mademoiselle lay snapped in his arms…
Even more gorgeous, even more dollish.
Nevertheless, she was a broken doll.
'Shaw!' he cried 'Get an ambulance.'
He bobbed in that rocking chair for minutes.
Approaching hours.
Nearing days.
Cradling her body with the only true emotion he'd ever felt.
In years, in fact.
Like a lover.
Like a Juliet.
A pure, red rose petal whom the owner would come to find.
Dead.
They stayed that way, preserved statues, as the music faded and gloom set in.
John occasionally fed - unsure on what… All he knew was, his little Cherie
started to miss fingers.
Toes.
And despite his initial spot of grief, he felt nothing now.

'Mister Hampton? A dog lies outside here Mister Hampton… Anorexic or at least in a bad way. Is he truly yours? We wish for an interview but don't you worry! Nothing too tragic, nothing condemning. We are your friends John.'
The voice was a woman's - all fresh and hunky-dory.
She sang her swansong from the bullhorn of the news truck.
A big, ugly plastic purple box with wheels… it had been chugging there forever.
'We'll send the broken guy to hospital,' she continued, sickly sweet, 'if only you'll come and join us… Then poor Fido may not be staring down the barrel of a gun. Not my words.' A chuckle. 'But seriously, this concerns your bee population John. We'd only harm the dog. But those damn youths and fanatics will hunt down and burn your liquid gold. You don't want that now, do you?'
The woman's name was Jane Flatley and she hung the bullhorn up with a smug smile, yellow bitten fingernails - down to the wick.
An air of superiority.
But also of anxiousness began to seep in.
Aaron held the gun.
Rodger drove the van.
Tom watched from the shadows…
They didn't have to wait long.
For a scruffy-looking man stumbled from his home looking dazed and confused, dressed in flats. A musty shirt. A beard big enough to hide secrets.
The shotgun drew their attention though: a Remington double barrel.
He held it aloof but determined as he wobbled towards the van.
Towards Shaw.
Towards the filthy dog killer.
'I've got no qualms about shooting you John.'
'If you hurt my boy-'
'Wouldn't dream of it.' he chuckled 'Assuming you play nice, of course. If you play nice, you get a fighting chance. You get… Enlightenment.'
'Sounds like fire and brimstone.'
'It is, for all of us.'
John thought he detected crazy hocus pocus but his intrigue got the better of him.
Blurred judgement made him lay down the firearm.
Crazy.
His eyes locked with Aaron and with the poor fluffy shape of his canine.
Those eyes were filled with madness.
Hocus.
Nevertheless, he followed the orders given to him by the rifle.

Which silently screamed:
'Get to the van, don't do anything stupid.'
Pocus.
Back turned.
Exposed.
Vulnerable.
John marched towards his meeting with Jane Flatley... and a revelation.

When John Hampton came face to face with the old crone, he was surprised.
Jane lay on the back seat of the vehicle dressed in a rainbow poncho,
clutching a cup of coffee and watching her precarious cigarette as it burnt its
way down.
The news van was just a knock off.
A cheap facade.
Next to her, a man sniggered, barely a boy.
John decided... he didn't like this smug bastard one bit.
He was young and ugly.
She was gracious and aging.
Much like a fine wine, he'd later reflect.
Still a crone, nevertheless.
'Take a seat sir.'
He obeyed her curt words, sidestepping the sweeping black wires and
electronic boxes which spewed out sparks and smoke.
To sit, to perch on the couch.
But never comfortably.
'We thank you for your cooperation, Mister Hampton. It's a pleasure. A
privilege to meet someone so skilled in the act of war. We'd have hated for
this to end in blood, sweat and tears.'
Jane drew her cigarette inwards - letting the ash creep towards her mouth.
'Even though, you yourself may be accustomed to that ending-'
'Wipe that grin from your entitled, lopsided face.'
Flatley and company recoiled as the venom poured from his mouth.
But the boy - the target in question, dropped it.
Even so, the gleam of a troublemaker rested in his eyes.
Whilst Jane's pupils boiled in excitement.
'Cut to the chase.' John grunted, adamantly.
'Um...' she was thrown, if just for a moment 'Are you aware of the flying
menace? The bee, Mister Hampton. Of course, you are! Once such minor
annoyances and honey spinners. They've evolved. Or at least are in the
process of this evolution. In short, they sting. People die. Injecting a poison

into the bloodstream that saps one's will to live. Due to this, as I'm sure
you've realised. Millions are extremely upset.'
'Millions will have to stay upset.'
'I take it, you've no intention of giving up the bees?'
'Nope.'
Jane Flatley caused her cigarette to splinter now, she bit her lip until a red
welt formed.
The boy-man hybrid and certified creep Roger tensed in his seat, hands
disappearing under the cushions.
All was crushing silence…
'We will reimburse you.' Jane cracked an unnatural smile. 'Find you a nice
home in the hills. New threads, New companionship. New you.'
'The old me is suited just fine.'
'Then I'm afraid Mister Hampton, your time is up.'
Roger unearthed the hidden pistol as if it were simply an extension of his
arm, with demonic reflexes he spat three shots where John resided.
And Jane didn't even flinch as the elderly gentleman leaped, boiling soldier
blood, into the bullets.
Two grazed his shoulder.
One hit home.
Crimson sprayed into her eyes and coffee but she simply watched the old
'nam veteran go to work…
A vicious right hook.
A knuckle breaking left.
Shots turned to breaking bone.
To screams.
To muffled cries.
To nothing.
John left the corpse a pulpy mash of skin and bone, he smoothed his beard,
took the discarded weapon.
Aimed it at Flatley.
'We can protect your bees, John. Think about what you're doing… Any
shots you make today will be heard around the world.'
Endless crap.
Torture.
Manipulation.
Jane was but a Vietcong now.
'You'll bring armed fools to your door!'
'Let them come.'
The trigger was squeezed and Jane Flatley became but a memory.

She is a mop of blonde hair in a sea of blood.
He is a mess of pulp fiction in a bad noir comic book.
Both lay like they lied… Sporadic and hopeless.
Leaving John with a grim determination.
Pulse pounding.
Racing faster.
A thermometer.
He bolted through the door like a thief in the night.
Tearing up grass.
'I'll kill it, you son of a bitch!'
But he could see: Aaron didn't have the cajones.
The fanatic facade had faded.
Perspiration and doubt were setting in.
Mistakes.
The lot of them.
Before he could shoot the mutt - John leaped onto his prey.
And felt his bones shatter as they tumbled together.
'You ain't killing my boy!' he howled with a purple ribcage 'You ain't hurting
my boy!'
The gun scattered without a shot.
John frothed at the mouth, a rabid animal laying crunching punches once
again.
Aaron's face concaved… yet still he fought, screaming for backup that would
never come.
An unrelenting beating that ended in warm, salty tears and a barely conscious
man about to face his judgement.
Hampton composed himself - leaving the body beneath him, as a vulture
might.
'What happens when the drugs don't work Mister Wolf?'
A manic chuckle to top the silence…
Whilst the mist creeps in.
All encompassing.
A deadly white shadow.

'We should've burnt you while you slept! Thought an old fella couldn't be so
much trouble… We know about the hooker. We know. We reported it. And
believe me, they're on their way. The mobs. The guns. The knives. You'll
hang for whatcha done!'
'It's by my understanding, England don't hang anymore.'
'They'll make exceptions, John. Cultural collapse and all that. We'll be
massacring the nation and it will be a thing of beauty!'

'You won't be around to see it.'
John continued to drag the vile enemy through fields, helped by a few syringes accrued from the house.
Sedatives or heroin?
He had need of a heroine to save him now.
The mist bit at his ankles but it felt comforting.
He could feel.
They were at the golden grasses now.
Home of the hutches.
Bees.
Honey.
Flowers.
Existing in a yellow utopia.
'If I jab you again, you got no chance. Stay quiet.'
John propped him against the hive without much remorse…
'The bees won't sting me. They love me,' sang his merry brain.
But anything more than a whisper and this stinking, swearing trespasser became insect food.
'We're gonna see if this little theory of yours holds any merit.'
John was met with pleading eyes.
Orbs like moons in those dying light sockets.
That just sent the rock soaring faster…
That just invited the first wave of yellow fuckers.
They devoured Andrew until his howls became muffled under yellow hides - hides that eventually shrivelled and died.
Miraculously alive, albeit a swelling lump, he took his own life on that cold summer morning.
And John watched him.
Rip.
Choke.
Claw.
At his throat until the pained air stopped flowing and he became man no longer.
And the blade pierced the watcher's throat.
Thomas was a sly devil.

*****

AFTER THE FALL
Jemma Hough

Highly Commended for the 2016 University Centre Grimsby International Literary Prize

AFTER THE FALL

RAIN FELL IN A SHEET OF NOISE, harsh and unyielding as the young girl continued to run. Her short hair was beginning to curl around her face and her clothes; felt heavy against her skin. As the gunshots sounded off in the distance, she could only imagine how much longer it would be before others arrived – and the others were not always human.

Ena ducked into an alley between two tall buildings, falling back against the wall and desperately trying to catch her breath. The sky above was flooded with clouds, dark and merciless, and as she heard the pounding of footsteps amidst the downpour, her fingers wrapped around the handle of the blade sheathed at her side.

She crouched behind a dumpster, hidden by shadow, her breath held – the voices seemed to be trailing off into the distance. A mixture of raindrops and sweat trickled down her neck, and for a moment, she closed her eyes, relief washing over her as she let the machete relax at her side. She would take this time to calm her nerves and steady the thudding in her chest.

Shouts echoed out through the desolate city and Ena wondered whether she dared betray her hiding place to see what was happening. They sounded panicked – a few desperate pleas cut short with the resonance of a gunshot.

She heard rushing footsteps coming closer and tightened her grip again on the blade in her hands, praying that nothing would find her – human or otherwise. There had been too much noise already, and if any of the infected were nearby then they were surely alert to the commotion by now. So far, all seemed clear of them, but she waited, squeezing her eyes shut again.

To her left the footsteps grew louder, slower than before, and as a hand gripped her arm tightly, she spun, weapon raised. She was able to stop herself from lashing out just in time to recognize the man's pale face.

'Vincent!' she breathed a heavy sigh of relief, her heart still pounding as she dropped her arm. 'Where have you been, old man?'

'We have to move,' he said, lifting her from the ground. 'They're comin'.'

'Who?' she asked.

Before he could answer her, a distant screech swept the empty streets, piercing the rain. It was inhuman, but familiar enough to chill even the bravest of men to the bone, striking fear and desperation into their hearts.

Ena felt her eyes widen in panic.

Vincent grabbed her hand and pulled her into the alley, running in the opposite direction of the increasing wails and screams; anything to put as much space between them and the infected as possible. But as Ena kept her head down, she could feel her legs begin to ache. She had been running for so long already that she wasn't sure how much more she could take.

She slowed, almost to a stop, causing Vincent to let go of her hand. He ran a few paces ahead before looking back over his shoulder, water droplets dripping from the rim of his hat.

'Ena - c'mon!'

She placed the flat of her hand against the wall and shook her head. 'I can't.'

Vincent looked into her eyes, and she knew he could see the barely concealed weariness there. He breathed slowly, squinting upward and around for any sign of a rooftop escape – but to no avail. Tall buildings and barbed wire fences covered the alleys, and they couldn't double back without being in danger of the infected. They couldn't afford to remain stationary for too long, either – their only chance was to keep moving forward.

From the corner of her eye, Ena spotted something and as she pushed herself away from the wall, she stared at the worn metal door. She grasped it with both hands and pulled, heaving it open with a grunt before pushing the matted hair back from her cheeks.

'In here,' she waved Vincent over.

He stepped towards her cautiously, and as she made to step inside he grabbed her arm and pulled her back. She refused to let go of the handle.

'We don't even know what's in there,' he hissed.

There was a shout then, the pained scream of a mercenary somewhere close by, causing them both to turn their heads towards the direction they had come from. Ena was suddenly aware that her body was trembling, a mixture of the cold and fear. She glanced at Vincent as he instinctively placed his fingers over the hilt of the gun in his belt.

Empty glass bottles clinked together just around the corner and they both stiffened, rooted to the spot as one rolled out from behind the wall. They watched as it landed in a puddle of dirty water, rocking back and forth. A hand slammed against the wall - Ena jumped, but Vincent covered her mouth. The long, bony fingers of the hand at the corner dug their broken nails into the bricks as it dragged its body into view, so forcefully that it caused them to crumble.

She could feel the drumming in Vincent's chest, and as he held her close, she tightly gripped the sleeve of his trenchcoat.

The Biter had its back turned away from them. Its shoulders twitched and its head jerked. The lower jaw continuously clicked open and closed, covered in what appeared to be stains of blood and dripping saliva. All of its limbs were on auto-spasm as it lurked by the dumpster.

Vincent kept his steady gaze focused on the infected, and as he lowered his hand from Ena's lips, she tightened her grip on the handle of the metal door. The gap where she had opened it moments earlier was not nearly wide enough to slip through unnoticed.

Placing the palms of both hands on the inside of the door, she held her breath and pushed. It groaned at the hinges, loud and heavy, and the Biter immediately whipped its head around. With bent knees and twisted fingers, its mouth dropped open and a high-pitched cry tore from its lungs. Just as it prepared to lunge, Vincent hauled the door open with a mighty pull and shoved Ena through the gap, almost sending her to the floor. She cried out in surprise and looked back just in time to see him slip inside after her.

Vincent tried to slam the door closed behind him, but the Biter was already wedged into the gap with one arm flailing towards him hungrily. He fumbled at his belt for his gun as the creature growled and screeched only inches from his face. Ena rushed over, the sharp blade of her weapon falling down on its head, cutting into the skull.

She raised the machete to strike a second time, but with a swift kick to the Biter's chest, Vincent booted it backwards as it wailed in pain and swiftly banged the door shut.

They stood for a moment, panting into the darkness.

'That was too close,' Ena murmured, clicking the button on her flashlight and shining it towards Vincent.

He shielded his eyes but he didn't respond.

Ena sniffled, turning away to direct the light around the room instead. She began making her way through what appeared to be a kitchen, possibly to what used to be a bustling restaurant, searching for a way out.

'Where are you goin'?' she heard Vincent call from behind her.

Without turning to face him, she said, 'Well, I don't want to stick around here. Do you?'

He let out a sigh, his feet shuffling along the floor behind her, reluctant to follow. She glanced over her shoulder at him – he was adjusting his fedora and wiping the sweat from his forehead with the back of his glove.

She rolled her eyes and swept through a pair of swinging doors, her boots crunching on broken glass as she went. 'Let's go,' she muttered, pulling her scarf up over her mouth and nose as her voice echoed lightly through the musty kitchen.

The flashlight beamed over the array of tables and chairs, all tipped on their sides, lying in ceramic shards and torn tablecloths. The place was filthy and reeked of rotting … everything.

'Did you ever come to a place like this?' Ena asked curiously, nudging something small and tattered with the toe of her boot. As it turned over, she could make out the features of a rat – dead. Her lip curled into a grimace.

'I don't remember,' Vincent spoke, his voice somewhat distant and distracted.

Ena pointed the light upward to the ceiling. The light bulbs were all broken, or gone completely, and the fancy shades that once enveloped them were all scattered around the decaying carpet.

'Looks like there's another room back here,' Vincent informed her.

As she turned the flashlight to him, he was already rounding a corner into another hallway.

She followed quickly, skipping over a toppled chair – she didn't want to be left alone, and she didn't want Vincent to be, either. She spied him in the room at the end of the hallway.

'Take a look around,' Vincent told her.

'What are we looking for?' she flashed the light on a desk drawer that he was rummaging through.

The beam of light faltered, flickering as Ena banged it against the palm of her hand a few times. She shook it, turned it off and on again as she ambled over to the other side of the room, until it finally burst back to life.

'You got it?' she heard Vincent call.

'Yeah,' she almost chuckled. 'This stupid piece of crap always does this.'

But, as the light stretched towards the far wall, she wasn't prepared for the sight before her. She jumped back a step, a shocked yelp escaping her, and held a hand over her heart.

'Jesus,' she breathed, closing her eyes for a moment to calm herself.

Quick footsteps came up behind her until Vincent was by her side. 'What happened?'

She touched his arm and raised the light again. 'Look,' she said quietly.

Vincent followed the bright glow until he could see the body bathed in it. A man, possibly middle-aged and withered from death, was propped up in an office chair, his arm outstretched across the desk. His cheeks were gaunt, jaw slack, and his eyes were rolled into the back of his head.

Vincent winced at the display in front of him. By the looks of the shredded, decaying skin it was clear that a Biter had torn him apart.

He dropped his gaze and his jaw tensed.

'Do you think he died alone?' Ena asked quietly.

'Yeah,' he replied, and turned away. 'I don't think we're gonna find anythin' here. Let's go.'

Ena opened her mouth to speak, but thought better of it. What would she even say? She watched as he left the room swiftly, and took one last look at the body before clicking the flashlight off and hurrying to fall into step behind him.

Ena glanced at the tall man walking beside her, his gaze fixed on the outstretched road ahead of them. He had been silent for a long time.

'We need to find somewhere to stop for the night,' she spoke, her voice bored. She scanned the buildings around her. 'How about over there?'

Vincent didn't answer, but she wasn't paying much attention until she almost slammed into him. He had come to a stop, his expression worried.

A chill crawled across her skin and she watched him closely. 'What's wrong?'

'We've been followed,' he said, listening for something that she couldn't hear.

Ena grabbed his wrist. 'What?' she blurted. 'How is that possible? We've been clear ever since we left that Biter a mile back.'

He didn't speak, nor did he look at her as he continued to scrutinize the buildings for any sign of life, and it dawned on her then that it might not be more infected – the Biters were predictable, but the same couldn't be said for humans.

'Vincent,' Ena urged, quiet but forceful, bringing his attention back to her.

He took her hand, lacing his fingers through hers, and headed left down a shadowed side street. Rounding the corner, he picked up the pace, almost breaking into a run as the soft, diffused light from the sky fell down on them once more. As it turned out, their path was blocked.

Two mercenaries stepped out from behind a burnt-out car, and another two flanked them, each with a pistol gripped firmly in their hands. They appeared worn and rugged with frayed holes torn into their sleeves and dried mud caking their military style boots. One man, standing in the front, held a smirk that etched up one corner of his mouth as he casually scratched his dirty fingernails across the unkempt stubble of his chin.

Ena felt her eyes widen slightly at the sight of them and her hand instinctively sought the reassuring cold steel of her weapon tucked into the hem of her cargo pants. She knew that her gun remained holstered at her right hip, but the blade gave her a comfort that no firearm could. Beside her, she could sense a shift in Vincent's demeanour as he took a slow step forward to cover her. He pressed his gloved hand against her arm to push her behind his tall frame, and he raised his chin slightly, his jaw set as he clenched his teeth together.

'Word amongst the survivors all across the edge of this here city is that somethin' of value is on the run,' Stubble spoke as he picked at his yellow teeth, his dark eyes flickering between the ground and Vincent. 'And somethin' tells me it's standin' right behind ya, my good man.' He gestured to Ena with a lazy wave of his gun and she felt herself shudder.

Vincent stayed rooted, focused and unflinching. 'I'm not sure I understand what you're talkin' about.'

Stubble snorted, taking a quick glance behind him to the others, who all shifted in response, knowing grins sitting smugly on their faces.

'Listen, I don't wanna have to do this the hard way,' he spoke again, taking a step forward. 'So let me make it easy for ya. Rumour has it that there's some kinda cure for this hellish nightmare we've been livin' – in the form of a person.'

Ena kept her eyes on the merc, but felt the space between her brows crease in confusion. There was still no change in Vincent.

'Now, I'm willin' to bet everythin' on that little girl you seem so keen on hidin' from us.' This time he fixed his eyes on Ena, and there was some kind of hunger resonating like fire as they bore into her. 'You did already take out some of our guys, after all.'

Her heart gave a great thump against her chest and reverberated through her ribcage; her nerve endings jolting and the hair on the back of her neck beginning to stand on end. Vincent still did not move.

'They attacked *us*,' he said stiffly, but Ena could already tell that there was no reasoning with these men. 'What do a bunch of smugglers want with this ... so called 'cure', anyway?'

Her hand gripped the back of his coat desperately, clasping the fingers of the other around the hilt of the hidden machete, letting its familiarity encompass her.

'We don't much care for the details,' the merc shrugged indifferently, 'but they're gonna need someone to thank when balance is restored to the world.'

So, they're only in it for the fame, Ena scowled to herself.

'I'm sure that girl don't mean a damn thing to ya, stranger,' Stubble continued to grin as he stepped forward, both hands raised, feigning surrender. 'What d'ya say we make this easy on all of us and you can just hand her over. We'll take good care of her, no need to worry 'bout that.'

Vincent tipped the rim of his hat between forefinger and thumb and let out a short breath of a laugh, and the mercenary stopped in his tracks, an expression of growing impatience on his grubby face.

'I'm afraid I can't do that,' Vincent told them, his voice calm and collected.

'So, I guess that means ya choosin' the hard way.,' The merc's fingers gripped his gun tighter as his face began to contort into an ugly expression of displeasure. Although, Ena noticed, there seemed to be some sort of satisfaction mixed in for good measure. These days, it seemed, no man was as honest as he made himself out to be. 'It don't have to go down like this, friend.'

For a moment, Vincent remained silent, and Ena waited as the bitter wind carried the loose tendrils of his long, dark hair as it passed. She couldn't see his face, but she wanted to. She stayed hidden behind him, taking in their surroundings.

To their left was an abandoned apartment complex, the entrance barricaded by wooden planks. The window appeared smashed through – but they could easily follow them that way.

To their right was the back of an unfamiliar looking building with an exit door –there was bound to be a stairwell on the other side, if only they could make it. The burnt-out, moss-covered cars would have to do as cover.

She looked back towards the mercenaries. Two against four – it was not impossible.

Ena could hear the pounding of her heart in her ears.

'I'm not your friend,' Vincent finally spoke, and just as the mercenary raised his gun to fire, he drew the 9mm pistol from beneath his trench coat and fired off two shots. One bullet pierced Stubble's left thigh as the other embedded itself in the space between his clavicles, causing Ena to recoil as the man's body hit the ground in a lifeless heap.

As expected, the men that accompanied him moved into action and open fired as the two flanks ducked for cover. In one swift movement, Vincent turned to wrap his arm around Ena's waist, covering her from the hail of bullets, whilst his other hand proceeded to draw the second gun hidden beneath his coat and take a single shot to the third mercenary's skull. With a loud *crack,* the bone split and the bullet pierced its way through the back of his head. The man hit the deck beside his friend.

Ena, having buried her face in Vincent's chest, looked up only to realise that they were now hiding behind one of the wreckages of a car. It had all happened so fast that, somehow, he had managed to pull them both to cover.

'Come out ya coward!' one of the men yelled, which only received a short laugh from Vincent.

'We need to make a run for that door,' he informed her, his voice low as he gestured to the building on the right with a curt nod.

Ena huffed. 'And you couldn't have hidden us on that side?'

Vincent gave her a look of disbelief. 'I was kinda in the moment, savin' your ass and all!'

Ena rolled her green eyes in annoyance.

'Look, just wait here while I go distract 'em,' he instructed, holstering one gun and checking the magazine clip in the other. 'Avoid usin' your gun if you can help it. No point in wastin' bullets, got it?'

'Alright,' Ena nodded and unsheathed the machete from her belt. 'What if there are more of them on their way?'

'Another reason to do this quickly,' he replied, and clipped the magazine back into place. With that, he dashed out from cover towards the opposite car.

Ena watched in anticipation as Vincent kept his head low and his gun by his side, Machete gripped tightly in her right hand, she waited, only to whip her head to the side at the sound of crunching gravel behind her. As she turned, she realised that one of the bastards had managed to sneak up on her unaware. He raised his gun and cursed when she noticed him, but with a swift turn on her heel, Ena swung the blade against his arm, knocking the firearm to the ground. She lost her balance and fell back onto her hands, dropping her own weapon.

The mercenary let out a painful scream, the sleeve of his worn, brown jacket now stained red with blood. With a grunt of anger, he lunged forward, pressing his knee into her abdomen and wrapping his fingers around her neck. Ena clasped her hands over his, attempting to prize them away as she choked for air.

A shot rang out and the man above her immediately went slack, his hands around her neck now loosened as blood spattered across her cheeks. She gasped, both in shock and in gratitude at the rush of air returning to her lungs. The oxygen burned as it cleansed her throat. With a heave, she pushed the body off her, taking a second to notice the bullet hole in the crown of his skull. As her hand reached out for the machete that had fallen beside her, Ena rolled over to look in Vincent's direction.

'C'mon,' he urged as he ran towards her, holstering his gun. Ena took his outstretched hand quickly and hauled herself to her feet as he dragged her towards the building.

It took a mighty heave for Vincent to force the solid door open ,before he ushered her inside. It was pitch black and she grabbed the flashlight from her belt to beam the light on the broken latch. Vincent picked up a heavy wooden plank and shifted it into the metal slots on the door. He stepped back, breathless.

Ena rubbed her reddened neck and turned around in a slow circle to get her bearings. She pointed the light ahead of her. 'Stairs,' she croaked.

A resounding bang sounded somewhere below their feet and Ena pursed her lips shut as they both froze in place; there were large office cabinets and desks barricading a stair route downward.

Slowly, she glanced at the man beside her and nodded silently, following him upward with light footsteps.

Dust and darkness clogged their senses as they made their way up the seemingly never-ending stairwell. Any sounds they had heard before were now fading into the abyss several stories below their feet.

'Does it exist?' she asked suddenly, a twitch of hesitation in her voice.

Vincent slowed for a second. 'Does what exist?'

They turned into the next set of stairs. 'A cure,' she replied.

He stopped, but he didn't turn to face her. She shone the torch over his shoulder.

'Do you think it's possible?' she pressed. For all she knew, those mercenaries were liars.

Vincent sighed deeply. 'I don't know.'

He finally peered over his shoulder at her, and then moved aside to allow her to take point. Ena averted her gaze from him, and they continued their flight upward until, finally, she shone the flashlight over a sign that read EXIT in bold red letters. The door was already slightly ajar, and with a less forceful approach than the door downstairs, Vincent pushed it all the way to reveal a set of rusted, metal stairs that led to the roof.

'Up we go,' he murmured, raising his face toward the sky. The clouds were beginning to darken above them again, threatening rain to accompany the bitter wind. As Ena began to ascend to the rooftop in contemplative silence, turning off the flashlight, Vincent shut the door behind them and followed.

At the top, they paused, and as they gazed out over the landscape, the city was awash with colourful rays of orange and pink. The sun was setting, creating the false impression of serenity and calm. They knew what really lay beneath the surface, and as Ena held out her hand, palm up, the first few raindrops of the night fell.

*****

DUTY

Peter True

DUTY

ERIC'S LIFE WAS SO HARD. It was a never-ending toil of doing this and doing that – and always, now; right now! Take this morning for example, he had been awake only minutes before he had to go outside and patrol the perimeter.

He'd checked all around, to make sure there had been no intruders in the night, and marked all the places that had to be marked; so that everyone knew just whose place this was.

He was rewarded of course. By the time he got in – after doing a great big poo in the middle of the garden – there was his bowl, full of lovely meat and jelly. And some of those nasty, boring biscuits too, but they were no bother to push out of the bowl with his nose. Eric didn't know why they wanted his poo so much but that was the deal – that was his duty; he'd give them all the poo he could muster and they'd give him food as payment, which also allowed him to make more poo – the perfect working relationship.

Then it was time to guard the family inside. This he did primarily from on the big chair under the front window. Vigilantly he lay in a half doze, making sure no intruders pounced on the small boy human and the slightly bigger but still small girl human.

It was not easy. There was all the jumping up and down thing he had to do. It was part of his job that, when the biggest girl human came into the room, she would make loud human barks and he would have to jump down from the chair, make his eyes look wide, look at the floor with his head low, wait until the biggest girl human went out the room and then jump back onto the chair. He would have to do this all day until the biggest boy human came home, and then Eric could lay on the sofa next to him. It was a physically demanding job. But it seemed to be very important to the biggest girl human.

Now it was evening and time for one of Eric's most important jobs of all. This was the hardest work and the most punishing. However, he would endure, because he was a good boy, and that's what good boys do.

The humans got ready, clattering about the place, opening and closing cupboards. Then, when they finally finished doing this, the biggest boy human took the choky string down from the wall in the hallway. Eric didn't like the choky string. It made him choke.

Then they'd all go outside and Eric would be on guard patrol again, only, when they went out together, and out of the front door, they all went on patrol together. Eric always tried to patrol the front, as was his job, but it was always made difficult by the stupid choky string. If only Eric could talk, he would explain to the humans that it was very difficult for him to patrol out front with the choky string round his neck. Eric was sure, however that if he kept on pulling the choky string really hard they would eventually figure it out. Sometimes his humans were a bit slow on the uptake.

Then they got to the field and Eric's first job was to do more poo – as much as possible – so that the humans could pick it up in a bag (a bit gross, Eric had always thought) so they could take it home with them. Eric often wondered at this job and thought it would save everyone a lot of trouble if he just did his second poo at home, that way the humans wouldn't have to carry it back with them in a bag.

Eric was again rewarded for his pooing job; this time by being allowed off the choky string. When he was let off that he was allowed to run about. This was lots and lots of fun. Especially when there were puddles about: great big muddy puddles!

Of course there was a downside to puddles. Whenever there were outside puddles, there would be the inside human puddle when they got home. Eric felt a little bad for his humans. They obviously saw him enjoying the puddles outside and this was their way of trying to treat him; by putting him in a really big puddle inside the house. But the inside human puddle was a rubbish puddle. The humans had missed the whole point of puddles all together. There was no mud in the inside human puddle, it was warm (whoever heard of a WARM puddle!) and smelled really really weird. In fact, they had got it so wrong that the human puddle made him CLEANER instead of dirtier.

Also done outside was the fetching job. This was a frustrating job; pointless and repetitive. The humans would take it in turns to throw the bouncy thing. Then – and you won't believe this – it was Eric's job to run after the bouncy thing, grab it in his mouth, take it back to the humans, whereupon they would throw it away AGAIN and he'd have to run after it AGAIN, grab it in his mouth AGAIN and take it back to the humans – AGAIN! Eric thought that human's would never understand how hard it was for him to work so hard, every day, at such a boring job. And did they have any idea how gross it was to keep picking up that bouncy thing when it was covered in slobber?

But Eric enjoyed his work, overall. And, for the most part, he was treated well. Which was why he thought he'd go above and beyond the call of duty. This day, he thought he'd give the humans a little something extra; to show how much he appreciated them and to show them just how much of a good boy he really was.

So, in the middle of the night, he got up extra early – he sure did hope they'd appreciate him putting in the extra hours – and did them an extra THIRD poo! And what made it even better for the humans, thought Eric, was that he did it right there in the middle of the kitchen floor – that way, they wouldn't have to pick it up in a bag and carry it anywhere.

Eric was pretty pleased with himself. He thought it was a brilliant idea. And it was an extra big poo too. He'd made sure it was a big one by nosing open the cupboards and eating everything he could find inside. He even – and this was REALLY going the extra mile, thought Eric – tried to eat one of the biggest girl human's shoes; now how's THAT for dedication!

In the morning, Eric sat next to his masterpiece, wagging his tail and awaiting his hugs and kisses. And here came the biggest boy human now... Eric wondered why the biggest boy human was making the human barking and why he was waving his front paws about. Then he wondered why the biggest boy human was picking up a magazine. Didn't the human realise that dogs can't read, thought Eric, and, even if dogs could, he thought, there was no way he could have read it all rolled up as it was...

*****

THE DATING GAME
Carrie Strandt

THE DATING GAME

'MATTHEW YOU ARE A SANCTIMONIOUS PRAT, do you know that?' I spat the words out with more venom then I had intended.

'No, no don't answer that! It's a rhetorical question. I can't believe you're standing there with such audacity lecturing me on relationship advice, you of all people!'

How on earth I put up with him for the best part of ten years, god only knows. Today Matthew was naively relentless:

'All I was saying, Gracie…'

I disliked it when he called me Gracie, the pet name he used for me during our ten long, often bumpy, years together as a seemingly happily married couple; at least to the outside world anyway. Gracie implied his intimacy toward me, an intimacy that had deceased the day he left for 'Double D Denise' from Humberston.

'All I was saying,, Gracie, is that you don't have to rush into these things, it's only been three years since our divorce and these things take time.' Matthew spoke his 'words of wisdom' obviously forgetting his past transgressions.

'Really Matthew, well, you didn't take your time when you buggered off with Denise an hour after Sasha's tenth birthday party!' I threw the hurtful truth in his face and relished the embarrassed grimace it provoked. 'Do I really have to remind you of your actions? Or shall I carry on acting the dutiful subservient wife who will put up and shut up?'

'Before you even begin a feeble attempt at trying to deny it or do your usual sugar coating over your selfishness, remember I'm not the naive impressionable twenty-year-old girl you married. I entered our marriage a young girl and came out of our divorce a woman scorned and everything that goes with it.' He hated to think he had hurt me, but was always oblivious to the consequences of his actions. 'You are completely clueless to who I am now, the woman I have become, so I will live my life, raise our daughter as the loving competent mother and woman I am and I will bloody well date who I like, when I bloody like, comprende?'

My words hit Mathew like a punch to the stomach leaving him breathless, and he took on his usual countenance of an injured puppy seeking sympathy, but my sympathy for this man had run out three years prior.

'I'm sorry Grace, I am really sorry, I know what I have done to you and Sash and I have to live with that for the rest my life.' For the first time in such a long time I saw sincerity in his eyes; warmth I had not seen in some time and I knew it was heartfelt and real. 'It's not easy Grace, I'm not asking for understanding I'm not even asking for forgiveness, I know I don't deserve it, but please can we make our peace for Sasha's sake?' He knew my Achilles' heel and struck for it like an anaconda.

I knew I had to let the past go so I could now move forward however difficult that was going to be, my journey had to start, I just needed to take that first step. I had to rediscover who Grace was, what she wanted and ultimately what she needed.

Sasha would always come first, that goes without question, but I knew that life was going to be different; very different in fact.

The sound of the front door shutting brought us both back to the present: it was Sasha.

'Mum, I'm home,'

Her voice brought a smile to my face, she was the centre of my universe and all things revolved around her including my happiness and hers.

'Hi love, Dad's coming tonight to take you out for tea, then a sleepover at his house: your overnight bag's ready.'

'Thanks mum.' A sweet, innocent smile beamed from Sasha's face and I could feel all the tension from the furious tongue-lashing I had given Matthew melt away. Sasha ran to me and threw her arms around me. 'Love you, mum.'

Sasha was the double of her father and inherited his raven hair that spiralled in loose curls half way down her back and framed her perfect porcelain complexion, making it appear ethereal. The only physical trait she gained from me was my eyes. Large green eyes shaped like saucers. She might be the spit of Matt but she's my girl alright.

'We're off now Gracie.' Matt's words brought me back from my wondering mind.

'OK, have fun, see you tomorrow, love you Sasha'

It's not often I get a couple of hours to myself, but I thought I'd make the most of it anyway, be rude not to. Go to Morrison's, get the shopping done and out the way. Then I'll head to the beach for a walk along the seafront, I enjoy the sound of the gulls as they swarm and swoop with their chorus of cries over me. It also gave the much-needed opportunity to clear my head and recharge my batteries before Kim pops round for Sauvignon Blanc and a chit chat tonight. 'Not all that bad being single is it?' I thought to myself.

'What have you got to lose, Grace?' Kim asked.

'My sanity,' I shot back without hesitation.

'Grace, it's been three years since you separated from Matt, you can't keep yourself shut away under lock and key forever you're only thirty-three, go out on dates and have a bit of fun for God's sake woman.' I had to laugh at this remark, maybe because I know it sounded all too familiar and I knew it was the truth.

'You know Kim, I can put the bravado on for Matt, although not for his sake, for mine, but…'

'But what?' Kim interjected.

'The longer I leave it, the more scared I get, the more stuck in my ways I get'.

'Well let's just see about that!'

Kim was headstrong and always thought she knew best for me. Within an hour my profile (or so the dating website calls it) was uploaded along with a couple of choice photos. I found it rather odd to be describing myself in so few words and showcasing what I'm potentially looking for in a man. This all seemed rather detached and quite frankly nonsense. Kim, however, wouldn't take no for an answer and the second glass of Sauvignon Blanc sealed the deal. By that point it was too late and I had already pressed the button.

I could always rely on Kim; she had been a pillar of strength to me after Matt left. With her direct, tough, no-nonsense approach, she didn't allow me to wallow in self-pity for too long in our numerous heart-to-heart conversations. She made me believe that I could and would get through my divorce. That I could raise Sasha as a single parent and do a bloody good job of it, hold the fort at home, and my job and work life would take care of themselves - she also made me eat when I couldn't and didn't want to and she was also right!

My laptop suddenly pinged.

'Oh my God, Kim, I've got a message.' I felt slightly surprised and curious at the same time.

'Go on, quick, open it,' Kim responded.

We both looked at the picture uploaded with the message and it was from Leighton.

'Oh god Kim, it's Leighton, the office Lothario, saying he was surprised to see me on here and would I like to go out for drinks and a meal with him next Friday?' I felt lost and out of my depth. 'What should I say?'

'Tell him yes, next Friday is fine and that you look forward to it. You have nothing to lose, girl, it just might help loosen you up a bit, it's just what you need.'

'I guess you're right, it's a case of now or never,, and Sasha is away for the week with her dad. Oh, by the way, did I tell you Matt has roped me into dog sitting for the week. Not that I mind, Ruby is a gorgeous little Westie and she will keep me company while Sasha is away and she's better house trained than Matt ever was.'

The two of us laughed like drains for the rest of the evening and polished off the second bottle of wine between us. I knew deep down I needed this and Kim was right, I needed something to look forward to other than looking at the shelves in Morrison's. I was certain Leighton was not going to be the love of my life but what did I have to lose?

Friday night came with a tummy full of butterflies and a giddy head through adrenalin. I was feeling excited and nervous at the same time, knowing that this was the ice-breaker for me. I decided on a navy wrap-over dress teamed with my nude slingbacks and purse to match, my hair in an up do. I felt and looked like I had made an effort, albeit mostly for my sake and not for Leighton's.

The taxi beeped outside and I was all ready and set to go apart from a spritz of Lancôme, then I'd be ready to face the dating world for the first time in three years.

The Bistro was busy and Leighton was already at the table and stood up to greet me as I approached him.

'Hello Leighton, good to see you.'

'Hi Grace, good to see you too, you're looking hot tonight babes.'

Oh dear God he called me babes! I detest that word, it's so patronizing.

'Can't believe I'm actually on a date with you. Gaz and Dave at the office both think you're the office totty, much nicer then Bev in accounts and Amanda in dispatch.'

I didn't know whether to laugh or cry, to take it as a compliment or an insult. Did that mean I was in the top three?

'Oh right, thanks, I guess.' I had no qualms about hiding my displeasure at his attempt at flattery.

'Right, shall we order, I'm starving. And if we order in the next five minutes we can still have the two for one offer on the meals!'

I rolled my eyes and shrugged.

'We can go halves on a bottle of wine - I like red full bodied just like I like my ladies.' He gave a cringeworthy wink to match his equally cringeworthy remark.

'I prefer a dry white actually.' Dry and acidic, I thought, exactly how my temperament was heading whilst in the company of this clueless buffoon.

It went from bad to worse; not only him talking and behaving like a chauvinistic womaniser, but a skinflint to go with it. No doubt he squeaks when he walks too. I was already thinking of what excuse I would make to leave early.

The meal couldn't have arrived quickly enough. How the hell this man earned the title of 'The office Lothario' was beyond me. He certainly didn't know how to wine and dine a woman and clearly needed to learn the basics of how to converse and behave with the opposite sex correctly. The evening ended with me going more than Dutch on the meal, trying to hotfoot it as quickly to the taxi as I could before Leighton, more letch than Lothario, tried to make a beeline to kiss me and share my taxi home.

Before I went to bed that night I deleted my profile on the dating website and breathed a sigh of relief. Good riddance to bad rubbish, I thought. What a horrid man, but at least I had dipped my toe in the water.

Kim reassured me in the morning, although I didn't share her confidence or enthusiasm for that matter.

'Oh it was awful Kim, just truly awful!' I recalled the evening to her bit by bit. 'And he wore faux cream leather snakeskin loafers and do you know what, you can never trust a man who wears those kinds of shoes.'

'It shouldn't be allowed; ban the slip-ons I say.' Kim snorted in mock gesture.

'Don't give up yet, Grace, it's only just begun.'

'That's what I'm worried about!'

Later that day I decided to take Ruby out for a walk on the pitches. I had to reassure Matt several times on the phone earlier that she was fine and dandy, eating well and was not off her food or drink due to being in different temporary surroundings whilst her neurotic owner was away. If only Matt had been as attentive towards me in our relationship-who knows eh!

Ruby was proving to be great company whilst Sasha was away with Matt for the week: it was just him and Sasha in the south of France. 'Double D Denise' was at a hair and beauty convention in Birmingham. I knew Denise was not the kind of woman to tolerate child friendly holidays and anything less than five-star high maintenance would have been unthinkable torture to her, but Matt had chosen his bed and now he would have to lay in it, nails and all.

Ruby had a great run on the pitches and was friendly towards others dogs and their owners so at least I didn't have to contend with any showdowns with any other canines whilst taking her for walks. I quickly realized that taking your dog out for a walk is not just for exercise but a social gathering for the owners. I was soon speaking to the other dog walkers and having brief but pleasant conversations en route. I was quite enjoying this for a change from my only other frequent social gathering-the supermarket shop!

I enjoyed the walk until my inexperience caught up with me and Ruby did her business. I suddenly realised I had no bags to pick it up with. I stood stock still staring at Ruby's handiwork, not knowing what to do, I couldn't leave it there, but I certainly wasn't going to pick it up with my hands.

'Looks like you could use one of these'.

I turned and saw a man in a Lazy Jacks rain coat, jeans and bright red converse trainers holding a plastic bag towards me. His salt and pepper hair gave him a certain mature look, but his boyish grin showed he was a child at heart.

'Don't worry, I forget them all the time, had to scrape one up with an old newspaper last week.' Even this slightly disgusting story couldn't detract from his charming manner, but I suddenly became aware that I had not said anything and was stood staring in dumb silence.

'Oh, erm, I am new to all this.' I tripped over my own tongue in an atte,mpt to break the silence.

'Yeh, me too, though I am kind of growing to like it.' Again, he cracked his grin showing off perfect white teeth. 'I'm Dan by the way.'

'I'm Ruby,' I blurted then realised my mistake, 'Sorry I'm Grace, my dog is Ruby.'

Dan chuckled and got down on his haunches.

'Nice to meet you, Ruby.' He stood and looked into my eyes. 'Nice to meet you too, Grace.' He extended his hand and I shook it. His hands were warm, and his grip felt soft yet firm and comforting, and I could smell Chanel emanating from his clothing.

'Anyway I better go and catch up with the dog, he's so impatient.' He turned and strode away, leaving me in a daze staring after him. After a few paces he cast a glance over his shoulder and I felt my heart skip a beat and all I could do was meekly wave at him. Who was this man? Who could reduce me to feeling like a schoolgirl again when I would stare at Simon Le Bon on my 'Duran, Duran' posters with nothing more than a glance and a smile.

Once back home I picked up a message on my mobile it read *'7.30pm tonight Laceby Waterloo pub speed dating I'll pick you up at 7.15pm Kim xx. PS beware of men wearing 'slip-ons!'"*

After a quick shower and a couple of changes I opted for an emerald green jersey dress with tights and suede black ankle wedge boots, with a small black tassel bag and a teal neckerchief. One last slither of pink lipgloss and a spray of Chanel Allure; even if I didn't feel that alluring tonight. I couldn't let the side down, Kim had opted to come with me rather than accompany her hubby Steve to the quarterly anglers do at the fishing lodge, and I knew how she really enjoyed that evening! You wouldn't put Kim and fishing in the same sentence. Kim would argue that angling has saved her marriage as Steve is away on frequent fishing trips and she is a married woman who needs her space and after 18 years of marriage I can quite agree, but I do admire that woman's honesty.

'SPEED DATING NIGHT.' The huge sign stood out like a sore thumb.

Oh Christ, it's like the Winter Gardens, but at its worst. You stuck to the carpet a bit more and the glass beneath your feet crunched a bit louder. Kim reinforced the fact that beggars can't be choosers-charming!

As we headed to the bar I gave Kim a nudge and said,

'You will never guess who's here - look over to your right, two-o'clock.' Kim and I chuckled.

'We're not secret agents on a spy espionage night out down the local boozer, the Cloak and Dagger!' she retorted.

I shyly looked over at Dan and quickly relayed the encounter to Kim who dubbed him - Dan the man. He stood at the far right of the bar; I caught his eye and he managed a slight embarrassed nod of my acknowledgement and a wry smile, then I saw that heart-melting grin appear on his face.

'A large dry white wine and one for my mother!' Kim bellowed to the barman over the noise of Cindy Lauper's 'Girls Just Wanna Have Fun' that blared in the background. I rolled my eyes at her cheek and the young barman blushed and gave a nervous laugh at Kim's old age joke. If she was a single woman she would have eaten him for breakfast, dinner and tea no doubt.

'So after some Dutch courage are you going over to the Dan the man?' She was attempting honest curiosity, but it felt more like a schoolyard dare.

'I doubt it Kim, he could have a girlfriend or wife for all I know.'

'No wife Grace, I already checked his ring finger - absent of a ring and a tide mark!' I laughed at that comment, trust Kim to be so observant and as if she read my mind, she, said, 'Well somebody's got to check these things out, you're too backwards in coming forward my girl.'

Before I could compose myself, Dan was walking over to us. He cut a handsome figure, taller than I remembered six foot two. He wore a smart white shirt and jeans with laced tan suede boots; the shirt showed off his broad shoulders and lean waist. His salt and pepper hair was roughly styled, but still managed to look smart. I had never considered his age before, but he must have been around forty, give or take a couple of years. Our eyes locked and I noticed for the first time the incredibly long, thick lashes that framed those ice blue eyes.

'Hi Grace, it's a nice surprise to see you here.' Before Dan could go any further Kim nudged me and gestured to Dan's boots.

'Not slip on, I think he's a winner,' she whispered. Then, without missing a beat, began talking to Dan in that boisterous, strong woman manner that both terrified and intrigued men.

'I had to drag her here, Dan. So are you here speed-dating yourself?'

'No this is my local, and to be honest I didn't realize what was going on in here tonight until Alan behind the bar told me I was brave coming in.' He gave a nervous laugh and looked as though he felt a tad awkward being in this scenario. It made me warm to him even more, his genuine coyness that matched my own. 'My brother and his wife are due any minute, that's whose dog I'd been walking when I met you before, Grace. I don't think I got that chance to tell you they were back late last night so I probably wouldn't see you on Bradley pitches again when you walk Ruby.' I was flattered he remembered my dog's name, and mine of course.

'Oh that's a shame.' Before I could go any further I was hauled away to table red, so I was told, as my speed dating experience was now beginning, led by a blousy tall blonde lady wearing a large red love heart badge that read 'Cupids bow' that was complemented by her siren red lips and nails.

Oh my God, what have I let myself in for? I chastised myself and as I did, I cast a glance over my shoulder to look back at Kim, all big smiles and giving me the thumbs up and a rather shocked Dan, who had the same expression as watching someone being thrown to the sharks.

With a name badge sticker stuck on me and now seated, apparently, I was ready to go.

'Hi Grace, the name's Bullock, Craig Bullock; builder by day and secret agent by night.' Craig proceeded to laugh at his own joke, which was good because I wasn't. I knew what he was full of and it wasn't Bullock although that was close. Hold your tongue Grace - mother would say you're being uncouth.

I gave a little smirk, 'Hi Craig, nice to meet you, too.' Before I could go any further Craig very kindly took the lead and went on to tell me he ran his own successful building company, his words not mine. And that he was a divorced father of four and that juggling four kids, four ex partners, four times child maintenance, he wasn't looking for any kind of commitment or monogamy and that after four kids he felt he had done his bit for queen and country and so had got himself 'the snip' and felt it was only fair to tell me. He was clearly presuming that I wanted to procreate with him: builder, entrepreneur, commitment phobic and general 'cock of the north' as my Nan would say in that south-westerly lyrical twang she had gained after sixty-two years up north. Thank goodness she never lost it, I always found it comforting and reassuring, unlike Mr Bullock who, in one brief encounter, had soured the whole idea of this night.

When the buzzer sounded I stood, tore the name sticker off and walked back to Kim. She cast me a bewildered look.

'What a waste of time this is,' I proclaimed. 'The only people I'll meet here are the dregs of the barrel, the sort my mother told me to avoid. Then I heard the sound of a man clearing his throat and turned to see Dan with a mock hurt expression on his face and a big pair of puppy dog eyes. I blushed and began blathering.

'Oh God, no, Dan, I didn't mean you.' I began tripping over my own words again. That seemed to happen a lot in Dan's presence and he began to chuckle.

'Grace, how about we go on a date and maybe less of the speed part?' Dan suddenly looked serious for the first time since meeting him. 'There's an Indian a few minutes away, I'm sure we can get a table for the three of us.'

'What now?' I squeaked.

'No time like the present and you're both dressed up to go out.'

Dan's smile returned with a cheeky edge to it. I smiled in return, grabbed Kim's arm and whispered 'Grab your coat, we've pulled.'

*****

42

DIALOGUE
Ian McDonald

Editors Choice

DIALOGUE

A - Well, hello there. I haven't seen you for literally ages.

B - Oh, hello. Sorry, I didn't see you there, I was thinking about something.

A - So, what have you been up to all this time? I can't believe I haven't run into you before now; have you been on the grand tour?

B - Of the universe, do you mean? Well, yes, as a matter of fact, I have. But...

A - You didn't find it very thrilling?

B - Not really. Oh, it was exciting at first, being able to go to all the stars we could see in the night sky and find out what was <u>really</u> there. But after a while it started to feel just like jumping from one rock to another.

A - Because there's no life.

B - Yes, that's it. The planets and the stars and nebulae and all that are very impressive but somehow, because there's nobody living there, they're just not very interesting.

A - I know what you mean. Do you remember those people who used to say that, because the universe was so vast, the laws of probability dictated that there had to be intelligent life elsewhere than on earth? Even back then I used to think it was a half-baked idea because nobody really knew what the probability of life arising on any planet really was. It could easily have been infinitesimally small, but just seemed more to us because <u>we</u> were alive.

B - And now, of course, we know that the probability of life arising spontaneously is zero.

A - Ah yes, not too many physicists were willing to take Big G into account back then. Come to think of it, that's another reason why the grand tour disappoints; there's nothing to find out, all you have to do is ask Big G. It's funny, when I first got here I was chuffed to bits that I could see him whenever I wanted. I felt ever so important. It took me a while to realise that everyone can see Big G any time - it's just a sort of conjuring trick.

B - Steady on! It might be, as you say, a trick, but it's a very good one.

A - Yes, it is. And he'll explain all the secrets of creation in a way that you can understand, but have you ever tried to ask him any important questions?

B - Like what?

A - I asked him once what he was doing in the infinite amount of time before he created the universe.

B - Good question - what did he reply?

A - He said that he created time when he created the universe and so my question had no meaning.

B - That sounds fair enough to me.

A - Yes, but when he explained about fundamental particles when I first got here, even though I knew nothing about physics beforehand, I could immediately see the truth in what he was telling me. I didn't feel that about the answer about time.

B - Superstrings.

A - What? Ah, I'd forgotten that you used to be interested in that sort of thing.

B - Yes, I used to be. It was just a bit disappointing to find out that superstrings were the basis of all matter - it was around as a theory back in the 20th century. Come to think of it, I once asked Big G which of the old Earth religions was closest to the truth and I didn't get a very satisfactory answer to that.

A - What did he say?

B - "All belief systems lead to me and so all of them must be true. Truth is an absolute value, something is either true or false, one thing cannot be more true than another."

A - Hmm. Weren't you a Christian when you were alive?

B - Sort of.

A - So, were you put out when you found things weren't the way you expected here?

B - Not really. I was never that sort of a believer. I didn't get worked up about the fine details of the faith, it just seemed like a nice thing to be involved with the church; and sort of comforting. All the people I knew looked down a bit on the evangelicals, the "happy clappies", we used to call them.

A - There are plenty of them up here.

B - There certainly are. You were an atheist, weren't you?

A - Yes.

B - It must have been a bit tough when you first got here.

A - I had to be forgiven a lot.

B - Ah, yes.

A - Of course, I don't suppose I had to go through as much forgiveness as some people.

B - What do you mean?

A - Have you ever wondered if there's anywhere else apart from here?

B - There's the whole universe.

A - You know that's not what I mean.

B - You're talking about...

A - Hell. Think about it, is there anyone who isn't here, anyone who could be there.

B - Hitler?

A - You <u>have</u> been out of touch, haven't you? Yes, he's here. At first he kept a low profile, no moustache, different hairdo, but these days he's almost back to his old self - even taken to going around in a sort of uniform. Everyone's here, the mass murderers, all the villains of history. Even Richard Dawkins is here, although he's mightily embarrassed about it.

B - So there is no...

A - Hell - you're allowed to say it. If there is a hell, then it's empty.

B - I hadn't thought of it before, but I suppose you must be right. It's funny, I reckon that there's not anyone here who guessed exactly what it was going to be like when they died.

A - And not everyone's ecstatic about it.

B - Oh but surely, this is heaven, after all. Although...

A - Yes?

B - I was thinking about someone I met, far out on the remotest edge of the universe.

A - Who was that?

B - Jesus, of all people. He was sitting completely still on a dark little planet, not much more than an asteroid really. He didn't even look up as I approached him, he just sort of groaned and then said, "Look, it's not my fault, I never so much as thought half of the things that people claimed I'd said. I certainly didn't pretend to be anything special and I didn't have any idea it would be like this." I tried to tell him that I didn't blame him for anything but he didn't seem to be listening. I sat with him for a while, but he didn't speak again. It was very strange, I didn't think I'd ever again meet anyone so unhappy, and certainly not him.

A - I heard that he was pretty much mobbed by new people arriving here in the old days. The first person everyone wanted to meet when they got here was him; and mostly they wanted him to explain why everything here was different to what they expected. After a while he must have got fed up, and he disappeared.

B - You seem to know a lot about everything.

A - I like to keep in touch with what's going on. Unlike you, apparently. Just what have you been doing for all these millennia?

B - If you must know, I've been before the throne of god.

A - Ah!

B - Well, meeting Jesus like that depressed me a bit. I started wondering if there really wasn't anything else to all of this. Was it just going to be hanging around for all eternity? So I made up my mind to go before the throne. I knew that's where all the devout people went and I wondered if maybe they were right after all. Maybe that's where the <u>real</u> heaven was.

A - And was it?

B - You've never been?

A - No, but I've heard a lot about it.

B - Well, it was actually a bit weird. All the happy clappies were there, of course, singing, praising and looking ecstatic. And there's Big G sitting up at the front and seeming to enjoy every minute of it. But it just went on and on: century after century of the same thing.

A - So why didn't you come straight out as soon as you realised it wasn't for you?

B - The thing is, no matter when you go in, and no matter how many billions of souls are already there, you always get a place right up at the front close to Big G himself.

A - Another of his clever tricks, eh? I suppose it's a bit awkward to just stand up and walk out if you're right under his eye.

B - Exactly. I'd still be there if one of the happy clappies hadn't got a bit overexcited.

A - What happened?

B - He must have forgotten for a moment that everyone here understands all languages: he started speaking in tongues. Of course, all the others could tell immediately that he was just babbling and the whole place went quiet. It was almost funny; as the truth slowly dawned on him he sort of slowed down gradually to finish in an embarrassed silence. Anyway, while Big G was forgiving him I was able to slip away - and bumped straight into you, as it turned out.

A - So, what are your plans now? You must have thought a lot about what you were going to do when you got away from the singing and praising.

B - Do you know, I haven't the faintest idea. I don't seem to be able to summon up much enthusiasm at all. I can do anything I want to do, pretty much, and I'm not sure I can even find the will to stir from this spot.

A - There's a world of meaning in your "pretty much"...

B - You haven't changed, have you? You're still sharp at picking up on things, and I can see from the look on your face what you think I mean. You're right in one way, I was thinking about sex, but I don't want it.

A - None of us do.

B - Quite. And that's what I miss, the wanting.

A - That, and perhaps also the uncertainty? Not quite knowing how things would turn out?

B - Yes, I think you're right.

A - Did you ever run into Shakespeare by any chance?

B - That's an odd thing to ask.

A - Bear with me, there is a point to it. Did you?

B - I've never met him personally. I went to quite a few of his plays when I first got here. They were all the rage then.

A - Indeed they were! Every one a triumph and, as the bard himself might have put it, therein lay the rub.

B - What do you mean?

A - Well, in life even Will Shakespeare wrote the odd turkey. And that was OK - it made him strive all the harder on the next and made his successes, when they came, taste all the sweeter. But, of course, things aren't like that here. Mind you, he might still have been happy enough if it hadn't been for the others.

B - Others?

A - It must have started after you embarked on your grand tour. You see Shakespeare was so successful and popular that very soon lots of other "playwrights" were having a go for themselves. And because this is the sort of place it is their plays were also triumphs. Poor old Will got into a right state about it. It wasn't that he begrudged other people success and he certainly wasn't jealous, you couldn't wish to meet a more generous minded man; I think it was that his sense of himself was undermined. He told me once that he didn't find it hard to write, in fact once he had an idea he could be starting rehearsals in six weeks. I got the impression that was how he thought of himself. For most people what they do is incidental to their "real" lives; but for Will he didn't just write to make a living, he wrote because he had no choice, because that was who he was. When he found that everyone, absolutely everyone, could do what was so special to him, and do it as well as him, then I think it left him without a reason to continue to exist.

B - What happened?

A - He disappeared. None of his friends have seen him for centuries.

B - You know something else though, don't you?

A -I do. Just before he vanished, Will told me he was going to ask Big G for the one thing he wanted and couldn't have - oblivion.

B - Death!

A - "Eternal, dreamless sleep" was how he put it, but it boils down to the same thing. Yes, death.

B - And do you think...?

A - Oh, hardly! Big G's not going to go to all the trouble of gathering all these souls into heaven just to let them dribble away into oblivion. Apart from anything else it makes him look a bit foolish – but there might be another reason. No, my guess is that Will is sitting on a rock somewhere, just like your Jesus.

B - Aren't you worried about talking like this? What if Big G finds out?

A - He knows! He knows everything we say and do and think. Why should I be worried? What will he do, kill me?

B - Is that what this is all about? You want the same thing Shakespeare asked for?

A - Let me ask you this - say you're watching one of Will's plays, when do you understand what it's all about?

B - Look, you've got me a bit scared and now you're asking me about going to the theatre. I don't understand.

A - Well, do you know what a play's about after the first scene, at the interval or at the very end?

B - At the end, I suppose, but I don't see...

A - And if the play just carried on? If new characters kept coming on stage and the action continued forever?

B - Well, then you'd never be certain what it was about.

A - Exactly! And it's the same with a person's life. How can it ever have a meaning if it doesn't have an end? We spend our time thinking that death is our enemy when, in fact, the reverse is true. Death brings a completeness to our lives in more ways than the obvious one: you might say that death makes life worth living.

B - You said something about "another reason" for Will Shakespeare not getting his wish.

A - Have you heard of Pliny?

B - There were two of them; Pliny the elder was a Roman scientist and the younger was an author.

A - Well, one of them once argued that God couldn't be omnipotent because he wasn't able to take his own life: I have a feeling that he wasn't far from the truth. I also have a feeling that, at least sometimes, it's what Big G wants as well. Incidentally, Pliny also said that the ability to end his life when he chose was the greatest advantage that God had given to man.

B - But Big G hasn't really given it to us, has he?

A - We might still harry him into it, nip at his heels and make such a nuisance of ourselves that he's glad to be rid of us.

B - Rebellion in heaven? The dark angels rising up against their lord?

A - Nothing so grand. I'm more of a talker than a warrior. Perhaps I can just spread a little discontent, get people to think a bit more deeply about an eternity spent like this.

B - As you've done with me. When Lucifer had failed with force of arms he tried to gain his ends by seducing men.

A - That's only a story. I'm no devil and you're no Eve. I'm your friend not your tempter: I can see from your eyes that you desire death as much as I do, I've merely shown you how you might hope to die.

B - It is, as you say, only a story, but death wasn't the reward for Lucifer's rebellion. Aren't you afraid of the alternative?

A - Of being sent to hell, you mean? I can't pretend I haven't thought about it, and yes I think I am afraid, both of success and failure. But it seems to me that nothing could be worse than this bland sham of an existence.

B - I can never tell with you, you are quite serious about this aren't you?

A - Deadly serious, you might even say.

B - In the story, the forbidden fruit conferred the knowledge of good and evil. That's not so very different from what you've had me bite into today.

A - So why not come and help me sell some apples?

*****

THEO KASIUS
Natasha McLellan

THEO KASIUS

I SWUNG MY HEAD IN TIME with the loud drums that vibrated through my bones. Each strike was making my blood boil with anticipation of what was to come. The air became cool and still as I closed my eyes and released all my morals and fears. I could feel them silently fall away from me and drift away into blackness like a child drifting away into slumber. The cheering crowds vanished so the slow beat of the drum was all that surrounded me.

I opened my brown eyes and looked at my opponent who was poised for battle, his axe held across his chest. I could see the well disguised fear that filled his blue eyes and the way his hand shook at the mere sight of me. I smiled softly and raised my axe high above my head and swung it to the beat of the music, earning a loud cheer from the crowd.

This was the final stage I had to complete before I reached my goal. The goal I had been working towards since I was five years old. I had gone through every class, from survival to earning popularity, given my all during battles with my fellow finalists and now here I was. Only one opponent stood between me and my place as a champion. I had been taught well and in every battle, the most I walked away with was a bruise or a slight cut, but I wasn't big-headed. My opponent was here for a reason. Like me, he had destroyed every contestant he had been given in the final, and it only took one slip up for me to end up in a bloody heap on the floor.

'Five…four…' My breath became calm as our trainer started counting down. I lowered my axe to my side, the tip of the handle facing my opponent and the blade facing the crowd of younger trainees. I smirked as I heard a few snigger at the way I held my axe but what to them was a dumb mistake, was the reason I had got this far. I didn't fight the old-fashioned way and put my own twist on moves I was taught. Using the same moves as everyone else never did anyone any good, and it looked like I would have to be the one to teach them that.

'Three...two...ONE!' I moved forward the second my trainer bashed the gong behind him. I charged at the boy who held the axe in the regular position with the blade facing towards me. By the time he had swung his axe far enough back to gain enough momentum to be deadly, I was already on him.

I turned quickly but gracefully when I reached him, my axe swinging with the movement of my body. It cut through the air and struck him above the elbow, scraping bone as I pulled my blade across his muscular arm.

He screamed out in pain and swung his axe towards my tall frame. I saw the quick flash of silver and dropped my right leg to the ground and crouched down, just below his swing. He grunted in anger as he brought his axe back round and swung it down towards me in a straight cutting motion. I leaped to the side and swung my leg round, making him lose his balance slightly, earning a loud shriek from him as his foot slipped from under him. Twisted ankle. I had had enough of them to know they were painful as hell and could affect your performance.

I swung my axe towards his legs and struck his kneecap, and with a blood-curdling scream and crack, he fell forwards, his axe raised above his head. As he fell forward, his axe struck my hand, cutting my index finger free but he quickly fell to the ground as his axe slid across the floor away from him.

I watched as my opponent let out another scream as his hands grasped his caved-in kneecap. My breath was heavy and pained as I tried to stop the blood spilling out my hand, but judging by the river of tears falling from my opponent's eyes, I was better off. I looked at my forefinger and started to feel better about it. My index finger was nothing but a stump now and the pain was horrendous, but I had completed the first part of my mission. I quickly calmed, and rose to accept my victory.

I deserved it. I am Theo Kasius after all.

*****

MEETING YOUR MAKER
Olivia Waelde

Highly Commended for the 2016 University Centre Grimsby International Literary Prize

MEETING YOUR MAKER

Christie's Auction House, 1905
Sale; 'Assemblage of Items of Unknown & Unexplained'
Lot 332
'A collection of writings on pieces of worn parchment, supposedly produced from the mouth
of Teresa Yearnet at birth (Wyoming, 1823) and held in possession of family since.'

THERE MUST BE A BACKLOG on today's order. The wheeze and groan of the Vivifium suggests the ominous possibility of a shutdown. The last time so many orders came through was international chaos, as I recall. A national outrage, a mad whirl of blame and urgency to find someone to point the finger at, politicians scarpering left right and centre in a desperate bid to shift any question of their own faults. Terrorists were an unlikely choice as the perpetrator in this case. Unfortunately, global warming provided an equally unsatisfying option. You couldn't string Global Warming up in public and give him a good lashing. You couldn't pierce Global Warming's ankles and drag him around the city, leaving pools of ashen cloud in his wake. Global Warming couldn't be hung, drawn and quartered on national television, in front of the faces of millions of wide eyed viewers, kipped back on sofas across the world with a cup of tea and a plate of biscuits. Fists would curl, biscuit paste momentarily forgotten beneath the pallet as the executioner drew closer. The people wanted bloodshed. They wanted pain, the pain of others, to pay for the pain of their children and the pain of their mothers and fathers and semi forgotten aunts who - as they were alerted to by delayed airmail - had suffered an extensive and prolonged death when trapped beneath the falling rubble of a three story flat in some far off country. Reduced to the misery of starvation from the barren, dry fields of the East and the rising supermarket prices of a loaf of bread in the West, the people wanted to objectify something tangible, a name spat with anguish over the dinner table discussions, a face plastered with crude graffiti slurs through central cities. This barbaric witch hunt, the striking of torches and savage idealisations was always the more appeasing option against blame on their own shoulders.

Now where was I? My mind's constantly slipping. Everything else operates like the machinery I'm surrounded by. The smooth slip of the cogs and bolts on a low order day, allowed to lean back and appreciate coherence of the machine. Everything fitting together in unification, moving slowly and smoothly in a way that humans could never possibly fathom. Like I said, today doesn't seem to be a low order day by any means. The machine already groans and heaves with the weight of the souls being poured through to the left. My heart aches a little for the lost critters. On the quieter days they can float through, the transient and peaceful experience narrated in picture books for the young in a bid to educate them on life after death. The gift and curse of eternal vitality means that I'll never personally float through the Earth and this place myself. I've contemplated asking to experience the ride, perhaps as a late birthday gift or raise, perhaps? I've studied the teeming office buildings clogged with corporate humans, the conflict and rivalry in desperate bids to reach the top, feeding of office bonuses to find the newest car model and weekend getaway pool house. He might find my request amusing, endearing even, and let me float through the tubes for a few peaceful moments in reward. He might also double the orders and jack up the heating in scorn if I asked, so I relent. You see, the journey doesn't always seem quite so peaceful. I pity the souls, the impermeable vapour-like substance which constitutes their half time bodies packed together like goggle eyed sardines. They wriggle and inch along the tubes, looping through the last section of my bureau, mouths stretched in wretched open O's. He hasn't given them eyebrows, not for this section of the journey, but if they had they would most certainly be downcast, furrowed in fury or quivering in blinding fear. Occasionally, one will end up wedged right against the glass of my bureau, jammed into position while a steady stream of souls drift on behind it. I'm not entirely sure why I was given the small section of viewing glass into the pipes. An aquarium of my own, I can watch the listless life drift by. Perhaps the glass section was installed in case of emergency, a blockage of some sort. I suppose my role would include the part-time plumber, ready to leap in and usher the half-dead along. Thankfully his technology has proved flawless thus far, for which I am grateful for heaven knows what I'd find to use as a plunger.

It takes the souls a while to wind round the tubes, up from the resting places of their material vessels and into the skies. The matter of time has always puzzled me; whether the looping tubes provide a ride lasting only seconds or thousands of years. Although I've no need for sleep, he's factored in shifts for my working schedule, giving me a generous amount of time in each day for my own affairs. I've considered requesting a companion for my lonely little office, something to rub itself around my legs and curl up under the generators, but I've never asked what happens of the animate pets kept and mollycoddled by humans; whether or not there's a bureau somewhere else, some other chamber with someone like myself returning them to the living. I suppose it would be rather a lot of hassle, having one little furry soul set aside to inhabit my office. My working hours are busy, endless. The duty of an entire hive of honeybees performed by one little tired bluebottle. Turning on all the generators is an issue of its own. He must have overlooked the height of the series of knobs and levers when creating my sturdy little legs, for I hardly reach up to half the height of many. Fortunately, my little bureau comes with a sturdy wooden stool. Convenient, perhaps he placed the stool there intentionally, and amuses himself at my scrabbling around, balancing on rickety legs to wake up the machines. Or perhaps just coincidence, for the stool matches the scarred wooden table in the centre of the room. On it sits a fist-sized paperweight depicting a jolly panda bear wearing a festive hat, inscribed with 'Happy Birthday Emily – Detroit Zoo'. God knows how it came to be here, the only possible solution I can think of is it somehow being dragged along by someone in the tube and deposited here. I hate to think of the blockages it might have caused for my predecessor.

Paperweight aside, I haven't seen another soul – bear with me, I see plenty of souls but not necessarily of the living variation – since I was installed in the bureau. Since my own creation. The creation of the creator. By the ultimate creator. It all gets terribly confusing if you try and differentiate us, to 'meet your maker', so to speak. One could conclude that I run the real business around here, up all hours sorting out the souls and defining their features before posting them back down to the Earth. However, one could also ascertain me as a mere employee, though I'm hardly paid beyond the salary of my existence. I've pondered what happens when my time runs out, my wages finished. The average lifespan of a human may be 71 years but I don't think I fall into the Homo Sapien category and I'm sure I've already been around over ten times that already. I've had all sorts of peculiar fantasies about my demise. The tube might split open and suck me into the flow of souls. I've never checked the ceilings in my bureau, so maybe those will open and I'll be plucked out from the room by some gigantic hand. It tickles me just thinking of the possibilities. No need to brood over what is to come, however, I have far too much to focus on at present. Like I said, today's orders seem to be particularly overdriven. The last occasion on which there was such a huge number of souls passing through was the result of three earthquakes and a tsunami within the space of a week. Natural disaster galore, I worked day and night to get the souls in shipshape condition for their return and rebirth. It was exhausting, both physically, for my little hooves tearing up and down between screens, and mentally. It's awfully disconcerting knowing that you sent a soul back down to the living missing an earlobe just because you were a little tired that day.

My task is an arduous one, but generally consistent and wholly rewarding. I stand as the main pilot for the Vivifium, the largest (and only) life generator I've ever seen. In the hours of running, the machine rumbles and groans as if alive itself. It pulls the wayward souls through the tubes by methods of extreme suction, drawing them all the way up from the Earth to my workshop. The rest is up to me; wipe clean whatever physiognomy the living world left behind, and work with the clean-slated soul left in its place. You could call it a form of art, if you like – although I've never been much of an artist. My creativity wasn't encouraged with brand spanking new sets of crayons and felt tips, and the glorious freedom of being able to colour outside of the lines. I'm not sure I was privy to any form of childhood. I don't appear to age and wrinkle like the human colonies below. Whoever made me just installed me in my prime, thinking it witty to mix my genetics with something strange and faun-like. Provided with no mirror in my little abode, the glass panels of the soul tubes provide a dappled reflection, bristly hairs running down my legs and furled horns on my forehead. I suppose having an actual human up here running things would be slightly perverted. Anyway, my artistry is an unusual one. In fact, I'm not entirely certain you could call it art, but I like to think of the creative flair I bring to my job. The Vivifium stands studded with multiple screens, with hundreds of buttons and levers jarring out from the wall, over five times wider than my menial height. Now you probably understand the conundrum involving my little hooves and the stool. The main screen is placed in the centre of the beast, an interactive display which allows me to ferret through possible features and physicalities and install them on to my soul.

You didn't think you were just born naturally did you? Goodness gracious no. Someone laboured away up here to make sure that your heart-shaped face has slightly slanted eyebrows. The trill of your laugh, why I could easily have granted you a hoarse cackle but I was feeling pleasant that day. One blue pupil, one green – why, maybe my fingers slipped, or I was feeling a little adventurous that day. I made you tall. I made you small, I gave you those slender legs you thought you inherited from your mother's side, and widely bridged nose which I know you hate, and have decided can only be a curse from a distant great Aunt. The Vivifium displays indistinct silhouettes of the parents to whom the next soul is being delivered, which I make effort to incorporate in my creations. I can't help it, though. Sometimes my little fingers run astray. God knows how many marriages I might have broken up, sending an albino down to dark-haired parentals. The expression 'gingers don't have souls', is in my eyes really the pinnacle of human wit. Of course they have souls! I installed the damn things. I watched the little quivering soul on the screen take shape and form, the transient particles of whatever they're made out of up here take form as I flicked through the hair colours on offer, deciding on a darkish russet red with a few streaks of gold. Every being has a soul. Or humans, as far as I know of, I'm not personally responsible for the mammals, or the fish, or the plants, but I'm sure someone around here is putting in the work to differentiate each and every being.

Some will demand my method of choice and selection highly unfair, but I do try my best. That little girl in the playground will descend on her classmate during break time, cornering her and yanking her white-gold plaits in frustration. Those glossy curls that all the little boys keep an eye out for in kiss chase, dainty little fingers and a high-pitched trill of a voice she pulls out for morning hymns, the little nightingale. Little do they really know that gifts often come accompanied by a variable curse. In this case, I have the little nightingale the most vicious temper imaginable to man. The sort of horrifying temperament that goes off like a shot at the slightest irritation. A hot fired disposition, one that will cause a wave of apologetic glances round the monthly dinner party table to the occupational parents, after the shrieking and the hurling of a plate of peas at the wall. Doors will be slammed all through her teenage years, and young suitors might be frightened off by her orchestra of insults upon ordering the wrong bottle of house red. Her temperament may even be her downfall; where her beauteous voice might carry her career, her temper may well be her undoing, as she flounces off stage from an early performance after someone admittedly turned up the air con a little high.

Whom shall be granted the greatest gifts, and who shall be born with a fated curse? That is a question which drapes itself over the Vivifium, a great weighted cloak of death in its own right. Whereas the decision is ultimately left to my own bristly little fingers, I was left an ambiguous set of instructions. Sitting on the table you see, beside Emily's paperweight, stands 'Percival's Guide to the Formation of Souls; a Guide to the Course of

Creation'. Quite a hefty hardback, I doubt it scooted along the tubes and rather like to think that someone left it here for me. My predecessor's hand's probably brushed the worn pages, following the minute cursive writing. It all comes out fairly formulaic in the end. Once every so often we have to ship out a great man – distinguished from the 'common herd'. Seneca seemed to know what category he had been folded into. You didn't think that Achilles just happened by chance? Although that wasn't entirely of my era or creation. My predecessor favoured the philosophical gifts, and I assume can be thanked for the likes of Pythagoras, and Plato. Who made Herodotus, well I'm not entirely sure. The guide presents a keen link between gift and curse, so, like my little songbird, no human will appear too blessed. Glorified, but to a conservative level. Achilles, for example… well, we all know the tale. A stroke of genius for whoever worked the Vivifium before me. I would never have thought to incorporate the tendons. I'm a little less creative in my intertwining of gifts and curses. Stevie Wonder, for example; I swapped everyday sight for a flair with lyrics. Cruel you might say, but look where it got him.

Of all the gifts I could give, you might very well question why I choose music. It's a little lonely up here, you see. Percy's handbook and my paperweight make for listless compatriots. A little furred friend to keep me company, now that wouldn't go amiss – I do wonder who takes care of all the little souls of the cats and the dogs of the planet. Probably a little gremlin near here, in a bureau very much like my own. Surely redirecting one animal soul along the pipes and dropping it off in my office wouldn't be too much to ask, but then again I'm not sure how I would care for the creature – if it needed care, unlike myself. In the absence of companionship, I do yearn for music. Sometimes, a little humming noise can be heard transcending the glass panels of the soul tube. A music festival having jacked up the speakers a little high, or a concert upon which the police have not yet descended in a desperate bid to turn down the volume and for heaven's sake let the locals sleep. If I can't be granted a phantom feline friend to curl around my legs and get in the way of day to day Vivifium runnings, I would wish for a set of pipes. Isn't that how the folklore runs? A fawn and his pipes. I could yodel and jig, and send out a stray accordion of notes whilst keeping the Vivifium running at a smooth pace, sending out my allotted souls. It sounds wonderfully romantic, don't you think?

Of course, there is the small question of human error when it comes to the creation – and recreation – of souls. Or not human, shall I say, but *fawn error* if we're being precise. Percival's manual unfortunately offers little assistance as to what to do in the event of natural disaster. The more the world seems to turn against its inhabitants, the higher the tides swell and the mountains shake. In turn, the more souls flood my walls, anguished faces pressed up against the walls. Terrorist attacks contribute to this, of course. I didn't stop to sweat after 9/11, issuing out warm shades of skin tone against flighty characters against those with fat knuckles and almond eyes. All this palaver led the machine to shudder and groan, grinding to a halt. The central screen upon which I filter through all possible traits and qualities flickered and turned an alarming shade of blue. They don't call it blue screen of death for no reason. Of course I dived into the depths of full-blown panic. 'Turning it off and back on again' doesn't really work up here since there's no magical switch powering in through the backrooms and fuelling the reincarnation of my souls – I'm honestly not too sure how this place is powered. God-currents probably don't need to be piped in through wires. Anyway, the threatening blue screen of death resulted in quite the anticipated outcome. I'm moderately grateful for the blue skinned gene to have turned out a dominant and inheritable factor, and must say I quite enjoy applying a washy shade of blue to my new-born souls whenever Kentucky pops up on the screen.

The humans can't seem to blame themselves for the ever-rising strain of the dead heaved upon the Vivifium. As I said, rather have the local deputy hung drawn and quartered. Splay the faces of the revolutionaries on live TV and blame them for the ever-rising death roll. The shame of slowly polluting your own planet seems too true to bear, so like all of us, even the less-human residing in our little offices somewhere high in the sky, they shirk around the issue. Why, more might be dying but let's have a round of applause for the *birth rate* now folks. One in one out would be a fair system I concede. Unfortunately, Fair and Square rarely turns up to Churchill's meeting table on time – he's always preoccupied with Vegas' casinos, trying to keep the tables running at a marginally lawful rate. Ashes to ashes, dust to dust, all that must die does pass to the ground below – the tangible composition, at least. I don't suppose anyone has to supervise the slow degradation of the skin, the fingernails and those pretty gold locks I opted for on that little girl. I don't like to think too much about material death, the wasting away of my masterpieces. Would Gaudi like to see the Sagrada Familia sink to the floor? Ashes to ashes indeed, or a great big pile of rubble. Or Vermeer's Girl with the Pearl, how would he appreciate his paint-strokes going up in flames. Let's hope she would put up her dainty hands in defeat and flee off into that dark canvas before the flames really took hold. The art and effort I put into each of my souls, sculpting them, defining them. Even the everyday human, the

Steves and the Plain Janes, the blank faces that slide out from under umbrellas on rainy New York sidewalks. Or the indistinct faces rolling past on the subway – did someone once say that all these strange faces make up the characters in your dreams. Praise be to *my* creativity, my ability to throw together a smattering of freckles, a stubbed nose and a tendency to inquire into overly personal beliefs, but you didn't think yourself capable of matching and making and binding together a whole set of personas surely? You lot have far too much to worry about down there as it is, with getting your articles in by Monday morning in fear of your new boss, you daren't comment on this nouveau hairstyle for what have you to know about the ebb and flow of fashion tides. Plus, the young ones always bite quickly, swift in sacking those old enough to cluster round the desks at lunchtime and cluck over the best current deals on washing powder. What else is playing on your mind… let's see, I should know after all, I decided to give you a fear of sudden loud noises, and an aversion to raspberries. You have to worry about the world blowing up on Thursday, according to the tabloids, and the price of tea in China would be a more tolerable woe than the rising oil costs. The everyday fear of having not turned the hob down after cooking your porridge, and the whole house having burned down to embers by the time the evening bus rolls into your road gives enough stress as it is. Quite overwhelming really, it's lucky you have me to sort your dream faces out and give you one less thing to twiddle your fingers over.

I'm not entirely sure why I'm writing all of this, or who will come to read it. It's not like I can post it off down the tubes in a bottle. Nor can I stuff it down the mouth of some unsuspecting soul, to ferry it down to Earth for me. Can you imagine the horrors, pulling out a wad of my scribblings from the mouth of some unsuspecting newborn. They would be heralded as the new Jesus, I've no doubt, the son of… well the fawn in the sky. They need something in which to place their faith, you see. Something to carry them through the dark days and someone to thank at tea time, and I just know that the Vivifium and my little hairy legs don't exactly fit the bill for the saintly position. Imagine my face, splayed and worshipped on every street corner. I'm sure my unidentified master would have crafted in some form of communication with the world below, if he so willed it. A string phone, for example. Why, I could bestow my wit and witticism upon the population through the quaint connection of two rusty old cans. Soup, even. Although I'm sure my master's technology is a touch more dexterous, considering the size and scale of the Vivifium. I'm assured means of communication would have been installed, had the broadcast of my voice to the people below been of necessary consideration. Thus, my job remains a quiet one, uncharted to the thousands of souls I let slip and slide back down to the world below.

*****

THE POWER OF BEING YOURSELF

Macauley Marshall

THE POWER OF BEING YOURSELF

'COME ON, KELL! It isn't like I'm asking you to shave your head.'

'No, you're not, but I've told you thousands of times that I like my hair as it is. And don't call me that.'

'Fine, *Kellen*, but your hair would look so much better this way!'

The round of agreements following the last statement caused the tall, longish-haired eighteen-year-old to frown in disagreement, but if they all thought that his hair would look better in the popular style then surely they must be right?

He - Kellen - sighed, his eyes scanning his group of friends to find them all awaiting his decision. With a small nod, he relented and set a date to get the haircut that they were pushing for.

Kellen stared in disbelief at the pile of clothes in his arms - clothes that his friends were pushing him to buy. He was happy with the clothes he had, though he would admit that he often lacked colour and stuck to black and white, with varying shades of grey making appearances. But his friends wanted him to look more 'stylish'; they wanted him to buy brands and bright colours.

They seemed to be finished, now pushing him to the checkout to make his purchases, not that they felt like they were his at all; more like theirs, for him.

'What's wrong with my Vans?' Kellen exclaimed angrily, his tall frame adding to his look of alarm with its tenseness.

'They're just not cool, man,' his considerably shorter friend replied, the rest of the group once again nodding in agreement.

'I don't care if they're cool, you guys know that I prefer Vans!' he replied sourly, the now common, uncomfortable frown making its way to his face.

'But we do, man. We just want you to look good, yeah?'

The Vans had been the latest in a long line of his things to have been shelved by his friends.

'Hi!' There was a short girl with bright green hair and shining blue eyes sitting next to him, smiling shyly and staring intently at him.

'Er… Hello?'

'I'm Cassidy! Prefer Cass though, sounds more chill, y'know?'

'Uh… Yeah… And I'm Kellen. Not Kell though, hate that name.'

'You know, your 'friends' don't really care about you, they just want to change who you are.' Her tone was light, but Cass seemed absolutely certain of what she was saying.

'Really? Nah. Besides, you don't really know them, they only ask me to do things that help me out.' He was being defensive and knew it, yet his gut was telling him that she was right, that they had made him change a lot recently.

'Whatever you say, Kellen, but from what I've seen of you, it seems like you'd really enjoy hanging around with my friends and I think they'd really like you. Anyway, bye Kellen!'

The murmured reply was vague and distracted, with Kellen lost in his thoughts and doubting himself for the first time ever.

Really, he felt completely powerless at that point.

The confrontation between Kellen and his 'friends' was loud and widespread, with everyone in the group seemingly getting involved in the argument, each having their opinions - almost all of them against him.

The aftermath of the argument was immense, leaving Kellen with nobody and tempting him into going to Cassidy for companionship.

Three Years Later

'Babe, can you get a towel for me? I kinda forgot to grab one!'

'Sure, Cass, and how do you even forget to grab a towel when you're going to shower?'

'Because, *Kellen*, I was on the phone to my mom and she wouldn't shut up about you, her *darling future son-in-law*.' The last part was said with a teasing tone that left Kellen grinning.

'Well, I haven't proposed yet, she knows that as well as we do.'

'*Yet?*'

'Yeah, *yet*. You might need to call your mom back later and give her the good news though.' The now green haired, soaking wet missile that collided with him was presumably naked and without towel. Her state of undress something he hadn't seen ever - with her or anyone else - and he knew nobody ever had seen or ever would see her other than him.

'So, you're gonna ask me to marry you? Of course I will! Wait, you need to ask first! Oh my God, I love you so much!'

'Yeah, Cass, I love you too.'

They'd come a long way from being the awkward teenagers they were when they met. Now living together, soon to be engaged, then married, they were still very much enjoying life together and would do so until they couldn't any longer.

But that could all wait. Right now he felt like the strongest, happiest man in the world.

*****

WHILE SHE SLEEPS

E C Robinson

WHILE SHE SLEEPS

'URGH! THAT AMY BITCH! I cannot stomach her!' Jessie shouted to her friend Lucy.

Lucy laughed in her face. 'Oh, you hate everyone, Jess!'

'I know but her, *her* I hate with a passion.' Jess rolled her eyes at Lucy and made a motion like she was going to vomit. 'I'd make her disappear. Poof! Gone!' Again, using sign language. As always it was loud, loud, loud in the club.

'Ignore her, the band's almost finished. Let's just enjoy the rest of the night?'

'Okay Mum!' Jess laughed and flung an arm around her best friend's neck. Together they pushed their way to the front of the stage and watched with adulation at their beloved unknown, unsigned band, Black Spiral, to Hell. *These guys are gonna be huge, especially if I've got anything to do with it*, Jess would tell herself, and with her job at Circle of Metal, the heavy metal magazine, she would make sure of it.

After successfully pissing off Jess and Lucy, Amy walked away, unaware of the hate she caused to rage in Jess. It was too noisy in there tonight. The smoke machine was spewing out some god-awful stench. She squeezed through the leather-clad crowd and pushed one half of the double doors open.

Freezing cold air hit her face; she took in two refreshing lungs-full then wobbled down the eight steps to the pavement. She had drunk more than she thought. She held on to the banister for a moment.

A cheer came from the club behind her as the band finished a song. She was ready for home. Instead of phoning for a taxi, Amy decided to walk back to her house. It's not far after all. She walked into the blackness of the night to the end of the road. There was a taxi office around the corner if she changed her mind.

It seemed to be darker than usual tonight. The noise from the club faded with a startling quickness. Round this corner and two more streets and, she thought to herself, *nearly home.*

Behind her arose a large black mass. It solidified up out of the ground with great speed. Amy was almost around the corner when she got a sudden feeling of being followed; very closely.

'I've got a knife.' She hadn't.

As she turned to see who was behind her, the mass engulfed her. Two colossal arms grasped her head, and with a sharp snap, broke her neck. The essence engulfed her body. Then both it and Amy disappeared.

Jess woke herself up with a stifled scream, her tee-shirt, wringing with sweat, clung to her body. She touched the lamp base, the light was blinding. Squinting from the brightness she fumbled around on the bedside table to find her phone. Jess saw the time: 3.33 a.m. She'd only been asleep a couple of hours. Her hand was still shaking from the dream that had disturbed her sleep. It was about Amy. Jess shivered. Not just from the coldness because she was soaking. The nightmare had given her chills.

Jess' dream had been really vivid. In it she saw Amy, strutting out of the club and swaying as she walked down the street. Then the blackness rising from the ground, the smoke-like hands round her neck and a single thrilling twist. Her neck broken before the cloud consumed her.

She got to the bathroom and opened the cabinet, took two Ibuprofen from the shelf, filled a glass with water and closed the mirrored door. She stared back at her own image. *Just a nightmare! Go to bed.* She took the pills then switched off the light.

Jess climbed back in to bed after changing into a dry shirt, leaving the light on to keep the nightmares away. It didn't work. She dreamt of one of her bosses at work; the woman who she'd had an interview with for her job. Her name was Marge. She had been dubbed 'Metal Marge' and everyone laughed when they said it because it was the most un-metal name they'd ever heard. They were on the top floor of her office building. There was an atrium in the centre that meant that if you looked over the edge you would see the reception area below. Marge and Jess were arguing. Jess had got the feeling at her interview that Marge hadn't liked her much. She had no idea why, but then again, you don't have to like everybody she supposed. Marge scolded Jess for something that she wasn't quite sure about, but she was mad. The more the anger rose, the clearer it was to her that she would have to throw her over the edge. Jess woke with a start by her alarm going off, just as Metal Marge was falling over the Atrium. It was time to go to work.

Jess was sitting at her desk busily working when she heard a scream from outside her office. She got up from her desk and looked through the glass wall. She couldn't see anything, until she looked up and spotted three of the male members of staff peering over the railing on the top floor. Their faces drained of colour, just staring down to the reception area with horrified expressions. Jess dashed out from her office. What she saw left her cold. Lying in an expanding pool of bright red blood was Metal Marge.

After the coroner had left. everyone was sent home for the day. Jess waited in the nearest pub for Lucy to finish work, as they had arranged to meet up. Lucy ambled in to find Jess just sat staring at her shot of Jack Daniel's.

'What's wrong Jess?' asked Lucy. Jess hadn't told her in her text about what had happened at work with Metal Marge.

Jess had decided that for her 21st birthday she would treat herself to her first tattoo. She had known for a while she'd wanted a piece, but wasn't sure what she wanted. They were going to go to the tattoo parlour that had been recommended by colleagues.

'Did you see on Facebook that Amy's boyfriend was asking if anyone had seen her? Jess. Jess! What's happened?'

'Something horrible.' Jess whispered, 'I was busy writing a review and trying to sort out press passes. Then all hell broke loose. Marge is dead, Lucy. Besides, Amy is not someone I tend to want to hear anything about. You know that. Last I saw of her was when she left the club.' Jess thought about the dream she had the night before. She decided not to mention it to Lucy, especially after what had happened with Marge today. Feeling she'd sound insane if she told her friend about her dream. Jess thought that she was going a bit bonkers, made a mental note to herself that she should phone her mum to see if there were any cases of mental illness in the family. She also pondered about her father. She knew she would have to ask her mum about him too. It wasn't a conversation she really wanted to have, but now she needed to know. They left the pub for the tattoo parlour after some intense cajoling from Lucy. She stressed to Jess that she needed something to take her mind off what had happened.

'Look Jess, what about a unicorn?' Lucy said with an awkward laugh.

Jess pulled a face. 'What am I? Twelve?'

Lucy peeked over Jess' shoulder to see what she was looking at. Inverted pentagrams, animal skulls and ornate devils with pitchforks and Satanic looking symbols. 'Jeez Jess, are you a Satanist or something?' They looked at each other and burst out laughing. It was a nervous weird laugh from Jess. Everyone in the shop turned to look at them. They stopped laughing.

Jess decided on one of the horned goat head designs she had been drawn to and took it over to the heavily pierced and tattooed girl who stood behind the counter. 'I'd like to make a booking please, and this is what I want.'

'Good choice. Are you a fan of Anton LaVey then?' The girl asked whilst flicking through the appointment book.

Jess looked confused.

'It's a great read.' With a flourish, the girl produced a pristine copy of The Satanic Bible from under the counter. 'I keep mine with me all the time,' she said with a grin.

Jess and Lucy said their goodbyes after a quick pre birthday/first tattoo celebratory drink and Jess thought she would walk home. It was a lovely evening, considering the day she'd had. She'd always enjoyed the Autumn/Winter months more than the rest of the year. She was in deep thought about her dreams, her father and, of course, whether she was having some form of psychosis. Suddenly she was jolted out from her contemplations when a cyclist whizzed past her, far too closely, and almost knocked her off her feet.

'Fucking idiot!' she fumed. She really wasn't in the mood for this tonight. 'You should be on the road not the pavement!'

The cyclist laughed over his shoulder at her and sped across the road.

Shaken and still seeing red, Jess noticed that a strange lump formed in the tarmac right in his path. A car was speeding towards him. The rider didn't see the blackness. He rode towards it. His bike hit the bump. The man flew off his bike and soared head first into the windshield of the oncoming vehicle; loud screeches of brakes frantically being slammed on and then the thud of his body hitting the car.

Time froze for a second. The protruding road was now flat. The driver frenziedly exited his car to aid the injured man, taking out his phone to call for an ambulance as he did so. Jess ran over to the scene knowing that she would have to stay until the police came. She wouldn't mention the shape-changing road.

At home, still shaking as she held the phone to her ear, Jess called her mother. 'Mum?' There was panic and confusion in Jess' voice.

'Jess, what's wrong?'

'Oh, I've had a hell of a day. Marge from work fell off the top floor, and then on my way home I saw a man on a bike go smack into the front of a car. Then I had to stay with the police for ages to tell them what I saw.'

'Oh god, was he OK? Are you OK? What about Marge?' Virginia was having a bit of a panic.

'I don't know, but it wasn't looking good when the ambulance left. Marge is dead, Mum. I really didn't need this today. I wanted to ask you something; it's about my dad...'

Silence from the other end of the phone told Jess she needed to keep talking. 'I need to find out about his family, Mum. I know he's not alive, but his family is. I've got to find out their history. Mum, I think there is something wrong with me'.

'What do you mean *wrong with you?* There's nothing wrong with you Jess. You are just very intelligent and have a vivid imagination.

Typical Mum answer, Jess thought.

That night after she had got off the phone with Jess, Virginia thought about all the times that Jim had come home and abused her. She remembered the night that she had decided he had done it for the last time – Clack! That familiar sound of metal on metal as her husband tried to find the keyhole. It took him a good five minutes to finally unlock the door, all the time she lay there, petrified. She knew what was coming. It seemed to take Jim forever to make it up the stairs and exhausted, she had dozed a little. She didn't hear Jim collapsing in a heap at the foot of the stairs. Virginia's eyes sprang open when she heard the door creak, but she laid still, frozen on her side of the bed, trying hard not to make a sound, trying to not even breathe. She felt her husband's side of the bed depress, felt every muscle in her body tense as his putrid breath warmed her ear. His hand touched her thigh and her stomach turned. This was the last night she was going to let him do this to her. She had decided enough was enough.

Virginia cried as she looked at her photos of Jess as a child. She'd never noticed before but the majority of these snapshots had an unnerving black smudge on them.

Jess hung up from the very emotional conversation with her mum and decided to check on her social media sites. She thought it would give her something good to focus on. She knew that her mother's married name had been Lincoln, so she searched for that name in the North East of England. She would concentrate on that fully after she had got through the deluge of social media responses. Having a large amount of followers on Twitter and Facebook, it took a while to get all the replying done. People would share photos with her of the gigs they had attended and would recommend bands for her to keep an eye on. She loved her job so much; music was her life.

Tonight though, she half-heartedly trudged through it all. After the messages were answered, the tweets re-tweeted and friend requests accepted, she continued with the search for her father's family. Astonished and stunned, Jess found a Facebook profile. It was her dad. He *was* alive. Upset and furious that her mum had lied to her, she sent him a message. An hour passed and Jess was still sitting there looking at the message she had sent. A faint *Bing* noise snapped her out of her daze and she saw a reply.

Dear Jess,

Thank you for getting in touch, but I have to tell you that I am a little unsure about why you contacted me. I do not have a daughter with anyone else but my wife. Yes, I was married once to the woman you say is your mother, but we didn't have any children. To be honest we didn't part on very good terms and I haven't heard from her since we split. I do hope this helps you with your search and you seem to be doing very well on your own without having had a father in your life. For the sake of my wife and children, please do not contact me again as I don't want to upset them. I wish you well in your search and all the best for your future.

Jim

Jess, shaking and bewildered read the message through teary eyes. How could he deny her? She needed answers, but she needed to calm down first. *I'll have a bath and call Mum again in the morning* she told herself. Her sleep was plagued by nightmares of her mother being attacked by a large black mass like the one that she'd dreamt about attacking Amy. It pulled her heart out through her chest. She woke up again at 3.33 a.m., soaked and jittery. *This is getting ridiculous!* She thought, to herself this time.

Jess had finished getting ready for work: she made herself one last coffee before she set off and then prepared herself for the phone call to her mother. She was still fuming from the discoveries of the previous night, but knew that she had to be calm when she talked to her. She knew that if she went full throttle she would get nowhere. She had definitely got that trait from her mother, where accusatory tones just sent her on a belligerent train of stubbornness.

'Morning Mum.'

'Morning sweetheart'

'Mum.' Jess paused for a moment. 'I found Dad.'

Silence.

'Mum?'

'I'm here, Jess.'

'Why did you lie to me, Mum?' Jess was trying to keep her cool.

'Sweetie, it was better that way. You don't know what he was like...'

Jess cut her off quickly.

'He's re-married with a whole other family. He, he said I wasn't his daughter.' Jess broke down.

'Don't cry Jess. I will tell you all about it when you come home at the weekend. I promise. I will tell you everything. You won't like it, you probably won't believe me now, but I'll tell you the truth, the whole truth. Honest.'

Without answering Jess ended the call. She didn't want to hear anymore and besides, she had to go to work. She wondered how the hell she was going to concentrate with all this crazy stuff going on in her life. She ignored the phone when it rang. It was her mum calling. She'd heard enough.

'It's tattoo day!' Lucy smiled at Jess and was giddy with excitement.

'I know Luce, but I'm really nervous.'

'Oh you'll be fine, it doesn't hurt, honest.'

Honest. *There's that word again.*

'Seriously, it's like a load of pins tickling your skin. I bet you'll enjoy it. I know I do.' Lucy winked at Jess, she was trying her hardest to cheer Jess up, trying to get her to smile. 'Come one Jess, you need this right now, it'll take your mind off everything. Even if it is only for a couple of hours.'

Sitting on the train, headphone buds in her ears and listening to some Mozart to calm her down, Jess stared out the window watching the green flat British countryside whizz past. Her mind racing, dreading what horrors her mother would be divulging to her when she got back home.

Jess gathered her things as the train slowed down and arrived at the station. She sighed a bit too loud and the ticket collector said something in her direction. She didn't hear as Mozart's requiem was at a crescendo, but grimaced a faint smile in his direction. The cold North East Coast wind stung her face as she walked from the station to her childhood home. Her stomach churned. She felt sick with anticipation.

As she turned the corner to walk down the dimly lit street to her mother's house, she noticed blue lights flashing. *Is that outside Mum's?* Her pace quickened and as she got closer she saw it *was* her mother's house. She started to run.

'What's happened? That's my mother! What's going on?'

'She had a heart attack,' the paramedic told her. 'She's conscious, but we need to get her to hospital quick.'

'Can I come with her?' Jess had tears filling her eyes, but managed to keep them from trickling down her face. She had to stay strong.

'Of course,' said a different paramedic, 'We're just about to bring her out.'

'Jess?' A muffled, faint voice called to her from the doorway of the house that Jess was just trying to get in to, 'Is that you, Jess?'

'It's me Mum, don't worry, I'm coming with you. I'll dump my bags and lock the door. I'm here Mum, just don't worry,'

Jess held Virginia's hand all the way to the hospital. To Jess, it seemed to take an eternity to get there, when in truth it was only ten minutes.

Jess had to wait outside while the doctors and nurses got her mother settled. She walked out into the cold air and promptly gagged at the smell of cigarettes. She saw a spot, a little way from the smelly doorway and headed over to it. Looking around, confused, Jess could have sworn it was getting darker and darker. Suddenly, she wasn't outside any more, she was in what she thought was a cavern of sorts. It was stifling hot; she found it difficult to breathe. She stopped dead in her tracks.

'Jessica,' said the very tall, extremely handsome man coming into view right in front of her, 'it's about time we met.' A huge warm smile spread across the man's face. She wasn't scared. Jess thought she was just hallucinating. 'I'm very real my dear,' Jess looked at the man with confusion on her face, 'and I have waited a long time to meet you.'

'Who the hell are you?'

'Why Jessica, I am your real father.' He smiled again.

'No you're not! My father is living with a new family and doesn't even realise he *is* my father...'

'Let me stop you there, my dear.' He walked towards her; behind him black inhuman shapes formed and dissipated in the darkness. Disbelief and tiredness made her rub her eyes when Lucy, her best friend for quite some time now, rose from one of the black billowing masses.

'Lucy?' Jess spoke past the man who was still on a trajectory towards her, 'What *is* happening?'

'Jess, I am your best friend and I am sorry but I haven't been entirely honest with you. I know how much you hate being lied to; especially given recent events, but you know you can trust me; you can believe me. This man, he is my King, he is the King of Hell and yes Jess, he *is* your father.'

The man motioned for Lucy to stay where she was and to be quiet.

Jess, a pained look on her face, was having an internal meltdown. She thought her head was going to explode with all of this.

'No! None of this is real; I must have passed out with shock when I saw that ambulance at my house. No. No. No!' She was shaking her head violently, fingers gripping her hair, squeezing her eyes tight. She felt a warm hand on her elbow. The touch seemed to soothe her. She calmed immediately and opened her eyes, her arms fell to her side.

'It is real, Jessica. Sit with me, I will tell you what you need to know,' her father said to her with a surprising softness to his voice.

Jess looked around and he was sitting on a large black carved chair which sat atop a pile of human skulls. She felt her knees buckle. As she collapsed, a chair, smaller than her father's but just as ornate, appeared under her. She saw that Lucy was stood to the right of *his* seat. He spoke.

'The night you were conceived, your mother thought that I was her husband. He wasn't a good man back then. He would beat her and rape her whenever he wanted to. I saw she had a tormented soul but, she also had a good soul and I knew, I knew Jessica that she would be the perfect mortal parent for my child. I chose her because I knew she would take care of you. She would, she *will* do anything for you. She has done well and she will be OK, I can promise you that. But it was you, Jessica, you were the one that put her in the hospital. The dreams you have been having; the ones you have had all your life, it's you Jessica. You are the one who made things happen to those people. You are my daughter and you have my powers.'

He rose from his throne and offered Jess his hand. She took it as he led her towards the edge of where they had been sitting. Below them fire bellowed, screams rose to her ears and he smiled.

'This is your destiny Jessica. You are my child and you can rule here. My time is running out. On your 21st birthday, all your powers will come to fruition, but you will have thirteen years after that to decide. Rule in Hell with me until I die, or be a mortal and die when you reach thirty three years of age. The decision is yours Jessica.'

Jess looked up at the man, the demon that was her father. The King of Hell!

*****

DIVERSITY

Ted Stanley

DIVERSITY

J OE WAS DRAWN TO THE GLINT of bright plumage hanging in the window. Scrawny brown chickens scratched in the shadows of a yard across the road.

'Can I help you?' asked the barrel-chested man with the bloody apron emerging from a room behind the shop counter, irritation falling from his face to reveal a customer-facing smile.

Joe had to be careful, he didn't want to reveal the real purpose of his visit. Not yet.

'Err … sausages,' he decided.

'Pork? beef? ostrich? alligator?' enquired the butcher.

'Alligator? any…vegetarian ones?' asked Joe.

The reply that was forming on the butcher's lips had already been communicated by his expression, when Joe's phone beeped: it was Jessica.

'Hey Joey,' she chirped, as if addressing a pet budgerigar.

'Oh hello,' Joe responded without much enthusiasm.

'Where are you?' she asked.

'Norfolk, I'm up for the weekend.'

'Great, I'll come and join you. Book a room at the Hoste in Burnham Market and a table for dinner.

There were times when Joe would like to organise his own life for a change.

'I'm not in North Norfolk, Jessica.'

'Well where are you then,' she demanded.

'Cawton,' he responded. 'It's a village in the boring bit we drive through after Thetford. Could be a new weekend destination.'

'Now you're my piquing my interest. What's going on?

He hadn't piqued her interest, or anything else recently.

'Can't tell you,' he gloated. 'It's a secret; no one knows I'm here.'

The butcher smiled.

'What's the name of that pub in the village?' Joe asked, turning to the butcher.

Joe gave Jessica directions to The Slaughtered Lamb, promising to find suitable accommodation before she arrived.

'Sounds charming,' she said sarcastically. 'Find a nice place to eat tonight and wear something smart, not those scruffy jeans and jumper.'

Joe looked down at the offending articles lurking under his grey windcheater.

'I'm not a fashion accessory,' he bickered.

'I just like you to look nice darling,' she soothed, 'see you later.'

Joey wondered whether he would be a keeper, like her Birkin Handbag, or a passing fancy like her UGG Boots; trampled and discarded.

Turning back to the butcher, Joe asked for bacon.

'Wife?' enquired the butcher nodding at the phone.

'Girlfriend,' responded Joey, showing the butcher a picture on his mobile of Jessica on a good hair day.

The butcher nodded approvingly.

'Strict vegetarian, but can't resist the occasional bacon butty. Smoked and streaky,' said Joe nodding at his choice.

The butcher turned to slicing the bacon.

'So where's the best place to stay around here?' Joe asked.

'Try The Firs,' advised the Butcher. 'They say royalty stayed there once.'

'Sounds perfect for her majesty, how do I find it?'

'Follow the Swaffam road for two miles then take a left turn opposite the lavender field. Follow the track and you'll come to it.'

'Lavender field? Unusual crop for this part of the world.'

'Diversification,' explained the butcher. 'We've all had to diversify since Brexit. Didn't get the subsidies the government promised when we left the EU.'

'Ah!' said Joe. 'What else have you diversified into.'

'Oh, all manner of things,' said the butcher, wrapping Joe's bacon. 'You'd be surprised.'

'Thanks,' said Joe, paying. 'Off the Swaffam road you say: The Firs?'

'That's right; no point going now though, the Harpers won't be back from the market before 3.00. You can get some lunch at The Lamb if you like.'

On his way to the pub Joe browsed the traditional shops in the high street for something to wear. Jessica's going to love this place, he thought.

The ploughman's lunch was excellent. His enquiries, with the landlord and customers, however, drew a blank: no one was talking. The sound of a passing tractor broke the stillness of the summer afternoon. The Landlord smiled. At 2.45 Joe returned to his car and set off for The Firs.

As he turned off the Swaffam road by the lavender field he noticed a dark car following him. Perhaps this was the Harpers returning, he thought. The next bend revealed a stationary tractor blocking the narrow road. He sounded his horn but the tractor didn't move. Getting out to investigate he noticed two men emerging from the car behind.

'Everything OK?' he shouted up to the cab. The driver stared straight ahead.

'Have you broken down?' he called.

He felt a movement to his right as a sack was rammed over his head. Strong arms held him tight as the chloroform began its dark work.

***

Intrigued, Jessica put down the phone and headed to the editorial meeting. Travel and fashion. Fashion and travel.

'So what's happening out there that our readers are desperate to hear about?' asked Jessica.

'Well, Chief,' began Pam, one of her two staff reporters, 'Radley are launching a new accessory range, handbags and purses.'

'Hardly Louis Vuitton is it,' sniffed Sophie, Jessica's other staffy.

'They're launching in Paris,' continued Pam, ignoring Sophie. 'I could pop over and cover it.'

'We've no budget for staff jollies,' said Jessica. 'See if any of the stringers can pick it up.'

'So what have you got for me?' Jessica asked Sophie.

'Benjie's getting an award for the Syria documentary at the BAFTAs. I can work it from the inside and pick up on all those little indiscretions that our readers love.'

Changes were looming, and it would be a difficult choice. Pam was loyal and reliable. Sophie, with her perfect grooming, well-connected family, and celebrity boyfriend, brought in the stories. Bitch! thought Jessica, everything comes easy to her. She doesn't have to struggle with a mass of unruly red hair, boring middle class family or feckless boyfriend. Joey was going to have to shape up, she thought, or I may need to make some changes there as well.

'Sounds great Sophie, get me some scandalous gossip, they love it.'

Sophie nodded. 'You bet.'

'OK guys, that's a wrap. Next Wednesday for the final meeting before we go to press with the August issue.'

The Friday evening escape from London was its usual nightmare of motoring mayhem, but Jessica's mood brightened as she turned onto the road for Cawton; the flat landscape giving way to rolling hills. Grassy meadows were interspersed with fields of bright yellow rape and blue lavender.

The Slaughtered Lamb turned out to be a charming old coaching inn nestling in a street of traditional shops. You could be in the Cotswolds, thought Jessica.

Seeing no sign of Joey she settled in a window seat with the menu, the rising bubbles sparkling in her Prosecco. It was nearly nine o'clock by the time she had finished the surprisingly good vegetable bake. Where the hell is he, she thought.

'Are you sure you haven't seen him?' she asked the landlord showing him a picture of Joey on her phone. He shrugged and shook his head.

Too tired to search for a decent hotel she took a room at the inn. Drifting off to sleep, she wondered where Joey was and what other surprises the village might have in store for her.

****

'… and if you thought standing me up was funny then you seriously overestimated my capacity to appreciate a joke,' fumed Jessica.

Slamming down the off key on her phone, she finished her muesli, before wandering down the high street to check out the shops.

Smart Boutiques; a Deli, coffee shop, Gambles, the little jewellers, a charity shop resembling a smart dress agency. Exclusive! she thought, smiling.

By mid-morning her anger towards Joey had turned to concern.

'I'm worried about you, sweetie. If you're tied up with your secret assignment just give me a call so I know you're OK.'

She called his paper but no one manning the news desk had heard from him or knew where he was.

By lunchtime she'd given up on Joey and headed back to London. He's probably sulking about being told what to do and wear, she thought. He'll be in touch.

'The Boss wants to see you,' said Pam when Jessica stalked into the office on Monday morning. She went to find Steven.

'Circulation figures for the last issue,' said Steven, the magazine's Editor in Chief, pushing the report across the desk. 'Down another 5%. Something has to be done Jess; we need exclusive stories, something different, the next big thing.'

'We're working on it Steven, I've got a lead on an exclusive UK destination, and Pam's working on the new Radley ...'

'That's all very well, Jess,' Steven interrupted, 'but it's hardly Front Page. I need results, Jess, and I need them fast. Get Sophie on it, she's always rubbing shoulders with the great and the good, let's see what she can come up with. I'll drop in to the editorial meeting on Wednesday, see how you're getting on.'

'I've got things under control Steven,' replied Jessica, flushing.

'All the same...' he said.

'About the redundancy situation...' started Jessica, pausing at the door. 'I've decided to let Sophie go and keep Pam.'

'Let's hold fire on that for the time being,' Steven responded, studying the papers on his desk.

Dismissed, Jessica returned to her own office fuming. She hit the phone to everyone she knew, pleading, threatening, pulling in favours where she could. She realised this was now about survival, and she wasn't about to let Sophie or any other well connected bitch push her out.

By lunchtime her thoughts returned to Joey. He had his faults but he always listened patiently to her worries and ideas. Where the hell was he when she needed him most.

She called his paper again and this time spoke to his editor, Brian.

'No, not heard a thing from him,' said Brian. 'Should have been in the office for a meeting today. Secret assignment?' he laughed. 'Don't know about that, said he'd had an anonymous tip and was off up to Norfolk to investigate. No, don't know what it was about, maybe they've changed the menu at Morston Hall,' he chuckled. 'OK, Jess, well if you hear from him, tell him to report in asap.'

Jessica replaced the receiver. She had a bad feeling about this. Her father, a retired police inspector, would know what to do, but she'd not spoken to him for four years: she couldn't just ring him out of the blue asking for help. Her carefully constructed life was falling apart and there was no one to turn to for help.

***

'I'd like to report a missing person,' she said to the enquiry clerk on the phone at Norwich Police Headquarters and waited.

'Yes, that's right Detective Inspector, a missing person. You see…' Jessica explained the circumstances to Detective Inspector Ian Mason who just happened to be passing the phone in the incident room when the call came through. He was now regretting it: he had a massive caseload and bad toothache.

'So let me see if I've got this right, Miss Jameson. Your boyfriend stood you up after you had a row on the phone and now he won't return your calls.'

'It wasn't a row,' responded Jessica, 'just a difference of opinion on dress code.'

'Does he have a medical condition?' asked Mason.

'Not that I'm aware of, although he's very untidy,' responded Jessica.

Mason sighed. 'Why don't you try his friends and family; I'm sure he'll turn up,' he reassured Jessica. 'Call us again tomorrow if you're still worried about him.'

Wincing from a new wave of toothache, he returned to the genuine missing person case his team were working on.

Jessica reflected on the conversation: it did sound silly on the face of it, and Joey could just be sulking, but her instincts told her he was in some kind of trouble.

***

She hadn't come up with anything new by the Wednesday editorial meeting. Steven dropped in for long enough to gush with enthusiasm when Sophie mentioned the BAFTAs.

The phone was ringing when Jessica got back to her office.

'I understand you were looking for a young man who disappeared near Swaffam last week,' said the male voice with a soft country accent.

'That's right, who is this?'

'Ever eaten alligator meat?' asked the man, ignoring her question.

'Alligator? Off course not, I'm vegetarian.'

85

'You can buy it in the butcher's shop in Cawton, except it may not be alligator,' the man continued.

'Well what is it then?'

'You're a journalist, why don't you check how many people have gone missing around Cawton recently and draw your own conclusions.'

'That's preposterous…' started Jessica, but the line went dead.

Oh, Joey, she thought. She had to find out the truth. The magazine would have to wait.

***

It was late afternoon when she arrived in Cawton. Leaving her car at the pub, she headed straight for the butcher's shop passing a van marked Hollingbrook Farm that was pulling away. Wrinkling her nose at the smell of raw meat, she made her way in, colliding with the elegant woman, glossy dark hair and smart business suit, coming out. Mumbling an apology, she waited for the bull-of-a-man behind the counter to notice her.

'Can I help you?' he asked with a warm smile, turning from the joint he'd been filleting.

'Yes,' said Jessica. 'I think …I'll have some bacon please. Just a few rashers.'

'Anything else?' he asked, slicing the bacon.

'I'm tired of chicken and beef; do you have anything different?'

'Kangaroo? ostrich? game?' he suggested, nodding at the brightly coloured pheasants hanging in the window. 'The ostrich is local.'

'I was told you might have alligator.'

'Ah well,' smiled the butcher, 'we usually do but we're out at the moment. Try again on Friday.'

Paying for her bacon she turned to leave.

'I don't suppose you saw my boyfriend here a couple of days ago,' she asked. 'Tall, sandy-coloured hair.' She showed him a picture on her phone and watched his reaction carefully.

'Can't say I did,' he responded looking up at her with a frank expression. 'You lost him then?'

'Misplaced,' corrected Jessica.

The butcher smiled and nodded.

Jessica's phone rang.

'Where are you?' asked Pam. 'Steven's looking for you.'

'I can't say; no one must know where I am for now.'

The butcher smiled.

'Tell Steven I'm following up an exclusive and I'll be back in the office tomorrow.'

'OK, but I'd get back as soon as you can,' warned Pam, 'Stephen's taking Sophie to lunch.'

Shit, thought Jessica.

'Oh, and that PR agency rang for a meeting again,' said Pam. 'They claim to have an exclusive on a new fashion range.'

'OK!' said Jessica. 'We need exclusives, book them in for early next week.'

'No problem, Chief,' she replied.

Pam was definitely a keeper, thought Jessica.

'Staying here long?' asked the butcher.

'Oh, maybe overnight,' replied Jessica.

'The Firs is nice on the Swaffam road if you're looking for somewhere to stay. Turn left by the lavender fields and you'll find it down at the end of the lane.'

'Thanks,' said Jessica,

'I'd give it an hour or so,' said the butcher looking at his watch. 'The Harpers won't be back from back from town till after 6.00.'

The butcher followed her to the door and nodded to the man tending the chickens in the yard across the road. The man nodded back and disappeared. A few minutes later the growl of a tractor engine was heard from behind the house.

Jessica glanced into the shop windows on her way to the pub. A Philippe Patek watch in Gambles caught her eye. It was identical to the one she bought Joey for his birthday. Tan leather strap, cream face. Her heart pounded. Resisting the urge to go in and ask about it, she continued towards the charity shop. A tractor drove passed, laying a muddy trail on the road.

On the rail of men's clothing she spotted a light grey windcheater. It had a dark in stain on the lining where Joey's pen had leaked. Oh, Joey, she thought, what's happened to you.

The evening was still warm so she took her Prosecco to the tables outside the pub, and began to mull over what she'd found. Something was bothering her about the conversation with the butcher but she couldn't put her finger on it. He seemed to be genuine, but she knew he was lying.

Two old men at the next table were discussing the problems caused by Brexit.

'What do you think about all this diversi'cation malarkey,' said the one with the flat cap.

'Ah well, lavender fields is one thing,' said the second, 'but the goings on at Hollingbrook Farm is another. T'aint right and t'aint proper, that's all I'm sayin'. That sort of thing shouldn't be allowed.'

'Excuse me,' interrupted Jessica. 'I couldn't help overhearing your conversation. What goes on at Hollingbrook that bothers you?'

'You'll have to ask them,' said the man with the flat cap. 'Tis none of our business, but it'll lead to nothing but trouble: you mark my words,' he responded, as they drained their glasses and got up to go.

Hollingbrook? She remembered the van pulling away from the butcher's shop. She also remembered what had been bothering her about the butcher: the bacon. She opened the pack of bacon: smoked and streaky. How did he know?

As she left the village on the Swaffam road heading for The Firs, a dark-coloured car pulled out of a farm track and began to follow her.

What she had discovered was overwhelming, and Jessica needed time to think. She slowed down by the left turn to the Firs, then, changing her mind, continued on her way to London. She would do some more research before contacting the police and be in the office first thing tomorrow to fight for her job. The dark car was no longer behind her.

I was nearly midnight when Detective Inspector Mason's phone rang. It had been a long day and his toothache was no better.

'DI Mason,' he growled.

'You've had eight people reported missing on your patch in the past six months alone,' said Jessica. That's four times the national average. As far as I can determine they're not locals, all visitors, and you haven't found any trace of them yet. Am I right?'

Mason groaned. The women with the missing boyfriend.

'That's police business,' he said. 'I'm afraid I can't comment.'

'Well perhaps I can help you.' Jessica told him what she'd discovered.

'Cannibalism!' he exclaimed. 'That's ridiculous.'

'Have you got a better explanation?'

He couldn't think of one offhand and she was right about the missing people, all visitors, vanished without trace.

'OK, I'll get a search warrant for Hollingbrook Farm and we'll interview the shopkeepers. I'll need you there to identify the items.'

'Get a sample of the alligator meat from the butcher,' suggested Jessica, 'check what it really is.'

Mason agreed they would do it on Monday; Jessica would drive to the pub and wait until she was needed.

Not bad, thought Jessica, admiring Mason's broad shoulders and chiselled features, spoilt somewhat by the pained expression on his face.

'The team are on their way to the farm now, and we should have the lab report on the alligator meat shortly,' said Mason, running his tongue over the offending tooth. 'Let's go shopping.'

'How will you know for sure it's Joey's watch?' Mason asked as they looked in the jeweller's window.

'Because it has his initials engraved on the back. J.P.'

'May we see the Philippe Patek in the window,' he asked the assistant.

'Mmm, not really what we're looking for,' said Mason, examining the watch. 'Thank you.'

'They must have replaced the back,' fumed Jessica when they got outside.

'Or it could be one that looks like Joey's,' said Mason. 'Either way it's not evidence.'

The charity shop wasn't any better.

'Yes, I remember the jacket. It must have been sold over the weekend,' explained the assistant.

'No, I don't remember it having an ink stain.'

'Sorry, no, we don't keep any records of cash sales or donations.'

Back at the pub Mason was finishing a phone call. 'That was the lab,' he said. 'They're not sure if it's alligator, but it's definitely not human.'

Jessica's face fell.

'Let's hope they've had more success at the farm,' said Mason, as a car pulled into the car park and the driver approached them.

'Well?' inquired Mason.

'Carcases, about half a dozen of them strung up by the legs in the barn,' said the DC.

'Human?' asked Mason.

'Birds,' said the man, smirking. 'It's an ostrich farm.'

Jessica looked dismayed. 'But the men said there was something not right at the farm. Look they're over there.' Sarah pointed to where the two old men were sipping pints of beer; making them last.

'Excuse me, gentlemen. Detective Inspector Mason,' Mason announced, showing his badge. 'I understand you're concerned about the goings on at Hollingbrook Farm?'

''Bout time someone did summat about it,' said the one in the flat cap.

'What can you tell me?' asked Mason.

The other one leaned close to Mason and spoke quietly.

'Ostriches,' he said. 'They're farming bloody ostriches. T'aint right and t'aint proper.'

'Thank you,' Mason sighed. 'We'll look into it.'

'Well, Miss Jameson,' said Mason sitting down opposite Jessica, 'looks like you brought us on a wild goose chase.'

'More like a wild ostrich chase,' chuckled the DC.

'There's something wrong here,' said Jessica. 'They must have known we were on to them and got rid of the evidence.'

'That's precisely the problem,' said Mason. 'I'm sorry about your missing boyfriend, but without evidence, hard evidence, there's nothing more I can do.'

***

Jessica was in her office on Tuesday morning when Joey's editor phoned to see if she'd heard from him.

'He'd better turn up soon or he'll be out of a job,' warned Brian.

He's not the only one, thought Jessica.

She tried to focus on her work, but she couldn't just give up on Joey. Her thoughts were interrupted by Pam on the intercom.

'Your two o'clock's here. I've put her in the meeting room.'

The tall well-dressed woman with the glossy hair looked familiar. They exchange pleasantries and Jessica gathered she was Katherine Gamble and her client wanted to make an exclusive arrangement with Jessica's magazine.

'Why us?' asked Jessica.

'I happen to be a fan and regular reader. You're small and exclusive, just like my client.'

'Does your client have a name?' asked Jessica.

'Diversity,' the woman replied, opening the box she had placed on the desk and taking out the most beautiful handbag Jessica had ever seen. It glowed with layer upon layer of iridescent colours each blending into the next in a perfect combination, constantly changing as it turned in the woman's hand. Jessica reached for the bag feeling the soft layers of translucent leather. Attached to the clasp that closed the bag was a perfect curl of sandy coloured hair.

90

Jessica only half listened as the women explained how the magazine would get exclusivity to interviews, pictures and the whole of the substantial advertising budget. She agreed to leave the sample with Jessica and collect the following day.

Back in her office Jessica buzzed Pam. 'When did the PR agency first get in touch?'

'Oh they've been trying to get an appointment for the last three weeks,' said Pam.

Just a coincidence then, thought Jessica, they haven't made the connection.

This could be a saviour of both the magazine and her career. Who cared about provenance, models and celebrities were wearing fur coats again. If it looked good, did their readers care what died to make it? It really was a no brainer.

Jessica eyes welled up as she curled the lock of hair around her fingers and picked up the phone.

'DI Mason? Jessica Jameson here. I think I've found the hard evidence you asked for. DNA evidence and a lead to the culprits.'

*****

ODE TO A LOVING HUSBAND
Amy Naylor

*Highly Commended for the 2016 University Centre Grimsby
International Literary Prize*

ODE TO A LOVING HUSBAND

I PULLED THE DOOR SHUT SO HARD that the already damaged handle ripped completely free. I'd done this one too many times before.

My left hand found its way to my head and started tugging and tugging at my hair. My right hand pulled it away. Stop it. Calm down.

I breathed. I breathed and I put the keys in the ignition. I put the keys in the ignition and put the car into gear. I put the car into gear and I drove home. My knuckles turned white. My hands left the wheel slippery with sweat. My tears blurred my vision of the road.

I breathed.

I hated it in there. The walls were too white. The corridors smelled of cleaning agent and the doors led to rooms full of illness and death. The stairs always went on too long and the nurses always rushed past, feigning busyness. They didn't want to deal with another crying woman.

When I'd made it to the room I only managed to catch a glance of him on the bed. Tubes up his nose, eyes closed, brows furrowed, face bruised. His sister held his hand and her head turned at the sound of my footsteps.

Her face was wet. She let out a cry and a nurse emerged from behind the door. She made excuses as she came into the hallway and closed it behind her, being all polite. He's asleep. He needs rest. He already has visitors. I know you're his wife but his family are already in there. We've no room for more people. Visiting hours finish soon anyway.

Nurses are full of shit.

If they didn't want me there, all they had to do was say something. Rick's family never did accept our marriage. They never stopped interfering with our lives.

Going home was always hard. It never used to be but when I lost my job and started spending more time at the house he became easily agitated, easily annoyed by my presence. Even after spending time back at home for a little while, things were still rocky. Men need their space. But he's my husband, and I couldn't bear to know he was hurting inside. I couldn't bear to know that he was fighting his battle alone. But when I tried to help, he pushed me away.

From day to day I didn't know what he would do, how he'd react to me. I hated that sense of unknowing. I hated the arguments and the heartache and the words that we threw.

But this time was different. This time I was returning to a silent home. A home without my husband, the man that I loved so dearly and so much. This time he was laid in a bed elsewhere. A hospital bed. Car accident. No seatbelt. Such carelessness. I wished he would take more care of himself. I wished he would let me protect him. But he never did and he wound up here. With stitches and wounds and a scar across his face and a cheating whore of a secret lover.

I flexed my bruised knuckle over the plastic of the steering wheel. Stupid nurses always getting things wrong. They're so caught up in their own little heads that they can't understand the world of others. That's the problem with life. We see it through tinted lenses and closed-up minds and we never get the full story, even if we think we have. Even when we think our husband is faithful. Even when we think that nice, innocent young lady is just a work colleague. How could he keep that from me?

I kicked the brake hard and screeched to a halt in front of the door. My home. No cheating husbands, no red handed lovers, no punches or bruises or pain. Just me.

I wrangled my way out of the car through the passenger side, the driver's side door well and truly broken, and walked up the driveway.

I opened the door. It was unlocked. He was always so careless.

I closed the door. I didn't slam it. Not today for there was no need. I was alone and didn't need to put up a fight. I was in control.

I breathed in deeply. That smell. The smell of home. The smell of freshly vacuumed carpets, laundry drying on the airer, meat and veg in the hot pot. He'd made enough for two. But only one of us will eat tonight.

I fought back the tears. I was trying to stay strong. For my husband. I couldn't break down while he lay there in bed so afraid and alone.

I walked down the long wide hall, skipping over that one creaky floorboard out of habit. I'd learned not to disturb him as he slept.

I walked past the little table with the phone he never used and the golf bag leaning against it with the little white glove laid on top. He had such tiny delicate hands and his putt was perfect every time.

I turned right into the living room. The carpet was immaculate. I hadn't left it that way; he must have cleaned it himself. I looked at the pictures above the fireplace. His teeth were so white. His smile was so perfect.

The TV was only small. He didn't watch it much anyway and the sofas were pointed towards each other, not towards the screen. My husband was very sociable like that.

I brushed a hand over the two golf trophies on the mantelpiece, cold and smooth. I had been so proud of him when he'd got those but he was never one to celebrate.

I sat in his spot on the sofa. He got so mad if I sat there.

Being there felt wrong so I stood up and left the room. I turned to my right and made my way past the stairs towards the kitchen. There was an open sports bag on the breakfast bar full of Rick's clothes. I brushed a hand across it as I passed to reach where the kettle sat between the toaster and the stove on the kitchen side. It was an electric stove. The switch on the wall that indicated it was on shone red. I switched it off. Safer that way.

I flicked on the kettle and grabbed a mug from the shelf above. It was a blue Yorkie Bar mug, given to Rick with a chocolate egg in it two Easters ago. I grabbed a tea bag and popped two sweeteners in with it. As I waited for the kettle to boil I had a rummage through the bag. His favourite shirt wasn't packed yet. I left the kitchen to find it.

When I reached the stairs at the end of the hallway I saw that the banister was decorated with fairy lights. It wasn't my idea but I was glad someone had thought of it. I flicked them on before I stepped onto the staircase and ascended. They were pretty.

The kettle stopped boiling.

The silence was long and beautiful.

Until I heard a creak upstairs.

A light that I hadn't noticed was on switched off in a bedroom upstairs. My hand was gripped tightly around the banister, my fingers turned white, and I felt the throb of my bruised knuckle. I loosened my grip to release the pain and suddenly realised the extent of my danger. I stepped slowly backwards; descending the stairs while my eyes stared straight ahead to the landing.

The door. It had been unlocked.

The silence was no longer welcoming. I wished for a sound. An indication. Something to let me know where I stood, how much danger I was in. But I heard nothing. Whoever was upstairs was aware of my presence and was, perhaps, hiding.

I contemplated my next move. Should I call out? Walk towards the intruder and assert my confidence or continue back down and wait?

In the movies the homeowners always went searching. But this was my husband's home, not mine. I didn't know how to defend it.

I stood frozen halfway up the staircase. I could feel my hands tingle as my heart pumped fear through my veins. It was all too similar to that feeling of anger, it rushes through you in a blast of adrenaline and suddenly you can't control your actions anymore. You just act on impulse and before you know it you're pulling your hair out and screaming at your loved one and wishing death on strangers and punching walls and digging into the old scabs on your knuckles and-

Another creak upstairs and I couldn't stand to wait around any longer. I turned and rushed back the way I had come, spinning around the bannister to walk down the hall towards the kitchen.

There on the breakfast bar was the open bag, still not completely packed. I zipped it shut and grabbed the handle, dragging it off the breakfast bar rather than lifting it. Doing so knocked a placemat onto the floor. I jumped at the sound.

My heart raced as I rushed back through the hallway and yanked open the door. I scurried to my car, fumbled in my pocked for the key with my one free hand and unlocked it.

Throwing the bag over onto the passenger seat I attempted to close the door, realising the handle was missing. I quickly wound down the window so that I could grab the door itself and pull it shut.

I breathed. I breathed and I put the keys in the ignition. I put the keys in the ignition and put the car into reverse. My left hand found its way to my head as I drove above limit to the hospital.

When my head started throbbing I stopped the car and punched the wheel. It beeped. I jumped. Then I cried at my own helplessness. Pathetic. Running away from my own home. Again.

I sighed and looked out of the window to see that I was pulled up outside the park. The golf range was on the other side of it. When Rick used to get stressed this is where he'd come. I remember him walking around the lake one night. There had been this swan that had appeared from behind the island in the middle. It swam towards him and he stopped and watched it, so taken by it. When it started to paddle away, following the line of the lake, he followed it right the way around.

I threw the bag into the back of the car and shuffled over to get out. Stepping over the low railing I walked into the park. The night with the swan

had been quiet, but today was busy. It was almost evening and so it was packed with school kids still in their uniforms. They sat on benches, swung on swings, gathered by the slide, much older than the children who actually wanted to play on it.

I walked past the play area, through the thick natural green smell of the stuff the kids were smoking, to where it became a little quieter by the lake. I stood for a long while and watched the corner of the island in the middle, hoping I might see the swan paddle into view. It wasn't the first time I'd done this, but the swan never came to me.

I breathed. I breathed and I waited. I felt calm here, calmer than anywhere else I'd been in my whole life.

I stood alone for too long and nothing happened.

I sighed. I sighed and I turned back.

I figured they'd let me in this time. They had to. I had his clothes and he was going to need them if he was staying for so long.

I didn't bother buying a parking ticket when I arrived at the hospital. Instead, I pulled the bag out of the back of the car and sauntered with the best confident stride I could muster towards the hospital.

Fake it 'til you make it.

I stood tall as the automatic double doors opened before me and strolled into the building without making eye contact with any of the few staff that were present. I veered right in the direction of Rick's room. Nobody stopped me.

As I approached the open door I heard a booming male voice. It stopped me in my tracks.

'I swear to god Doreen if I get my hands on that-'

A quieter voice of reason cut in, 'Jack calm down, you don't know that she-'

'I know that she was there. She was right fucking there, going through his things. The bag was gone. I dread to think whatever the fuck else she's taken.'

'Not in front of Rick.' The voices were his parents. I recognised them from the family barbeques that he used to host and the times they argued about mine and Rick's relationship. I'd heard Jack raise his voice too many times. The man had a temper. I took a single step back, my knuckles turning white against the handle of the bag that I held.

'What the fuck does Rick care, he's a fucking vegetable!'

'Jack!' Doreen yelled and a chair scraped across the floor. I saw shadows move in the light coming from the doorway. My mouth went dry.

'I can't do this any more Doreen, I can't see him like this.'

There were footsteps and the figure emerged from the doorway. A tall figure. Jack's figure.

He stopped when he saw me. I remained planted in my position in the hallway. His body remained solid but I saw as his eyes moved from mine down to where my arm hung. Down to where I held the bag.

I couldn't swallow.

I had as much right to be in that house as he did. And he had the nerve to-

'And you have the nerve to show your face *here*.' Jack spoke through gritted teeth.

My fingernails dug into the palms of my hands.

I breathed. I breathed and I dared to speak. 'I came to bring Rick's bag of clothes that I-'

'That you stole from the house that you broke and entered into.'

'The door was open and I can come home whenever I like to!'

I caught myself. I'd learned the hard way not to get defensive around this man. This man that could not be controlled. This man that was so full of anger and hate. This unstable man. And then I realised. '*You* were the intruder.' I accused.

He snorted and shook his head.

'You broke into your own son's house just to get in my way. Why can't you accept your son's marriage? Why can't you accept that we are in love?'

He stepped forward and reached out. 'Give me the bag.'

'No.'

'Give me the fucking bag!'

'I don't want to.'

Doreen appeared behind him, 'Jack?'

'Shut up Doreen!'

Nurses scurried towards us from either end of the corridor but none had the courage to interject.

'Let me in,' I said, 'Let me see him.'

'You fucking freak!' He took a sudden leap towards me and I swung on impulse: on defensive impulse. Fight or flight. It was nature, not me.

The bag connected with the side of his head at considerable force and my arm carried on swinging round even after he'd fallen to the side. Even after he'd hit his head on the wall on the way down. Even after a burst of oxygen pushed his lips into a horrendous sound. Even after the wall was stained red. My whole body swung round, carried by the weight of the bag, and I almost lost my footing. Almost.

When I recomposed myself I turned to look for the support of those around me.

Doreen was white. The nurses were white. My knuckles were white.

The wall was red.

I looked around me. The speech that bounced off the walls was just noise to me. I heard words. Words like restraining order and thief and stalker and JACK!

The horrified scream broke me out of the trance.

I looked to the bag in my hand.

I looked to the man on the floor.

I dropped the bag.

The blood rushed back into my knuckles.

I ran.

When I got outside the noise was overpowering. People were yelling my name. Others dodged out of the way as I rushed past them. I didn't appreciate their stares, like I was some sort of animal. Why were they looking at me like that? Couldn't they even think to help me? I was being chased!

I made it through the car park and onto the street without getting caught or hurt and I began to feel quite pleased with myself for having such great survival instincts.

But then I heard sirens. And it didn't take long before they were on my heels. The police station was only around the corner; they must have been alerted.

It was as I reached the path closest to the road that I began to remember things.

The road.

It had been the road that had started all of this. He hadn't been wearing a seatbelt. Such carelessness. But he had swerved to save me. Such selflessness. He was so kind my husband. My... Rick.

No.

I shook my head. My cheeks felt warm and wet and my vision blurred. I collided with a woman's pushchair and heard the wail of a baby but it was distant.

Sorry. Sorry.

I heard myself speak somewhere far away.

Rick.

He had been going to visit her. That bitch from work. That bitch from the park. He thought I hadn't seen him sharing a picnic with her, watching the swans.

'The romantic thing about swans,' he had said, 'is that they stay with their partners for life.'

We'd had an argument. I never meant any of the words I said, I was sure that he never meant any of his. But he just jumped into his car and slammed the door shut before I could reach him. So I ran. Of course I ran, I had to stop him. But he was driving so fast. He was angry with me. And when I jumped out in front of him he swerved. Neither of us had seen the car coming the other way. Until it was too late.

I rang the ambulance. They took us both in. Separate rooms. They came in and told me my husband had been induced into a coma. So I rang his parents. I didn't want to but they needed to know. I knew that.

It was when they arrived that everything changed. The nurses treated me differently, like I was a child. They practically forced me out of the building.

And now, here I was again, running ahead of cars.

Rick. My husband.

No.

Rick.

My.

Rick.

My Rick.

No.

Rick.

He never loved me.

After all this time he had never loved me.

But I loved him. I loved him so much. Ever since the day I met him. Ever since the coffee shop, when he had given me that extra 40p so I could afford my drink. Such selflessness. He had been so kind to me. I wanted to return that. I wanted to care for him. To love him. But all I did was make things worse. I ruined everything. His life is over. My life is over.

The sirens came closer.

The flashbacks were making my head pound.

I couldn't bear it anymore. I didn't want to hurt anyone. I never wanted to hurt anyone.

I listened as the engine reached further towards me. As its pitch ascended.

I listened. I listened and I breathed.

I breathed and I jumped into the road.

My legs flew from underneath me. The sirens came to a halt.

All went dark. All went peaceful.

I woke up to the sound of beeping. I couldn't quite see. I couldn't quite feel. When I turned my head my neck smarted and I heard myself groan.

A voice.

Then another.

Doctors. Nurses. All moving around me. I fell away again.

When I opened my eyes a smiling face was looking right back at me. I tried to smile. It hurt.

'Good morning.' A woman's voice. Chirpy. It belonged to that smiling face. It made me feel warm. 'I'll get the doctors for you in a minute, let them know you're awake and smiling.'

So I was smiling.

'I'm Dr. Horton. But you can call me Jane.' She smiled some more. 'I'm your therapist.'

I felt myself frown.

'You've nothing to worry about; you've had a traumatic few weeks. I'm here to help you through it. I'm a friend.'

My face softened and as the tension went away so did the pain.

'I'll be right back.'

When she stood up to leave I felt the cool air hit my hand and realised that she had been holding it.

I smiled weakly.

In my moment of comfort I didn't at first notice the tall, blurred figure that appeared in the doorway following Jane's leave. A doctor? But he wasn't making any move to step into the room.

I squinted to stable my vision; I was still in a state of waking.

When I realised who it was, I wished I were still asleep.

Jack. Rick's dad. Tall. Wide. Arms crossed. On the defensive. But something was different. His hair was gone.

I met his eyes. He was staring into mine. There was anger there, I was sure of it. His face was tense, like he was in pain. His eyebrows were all contorted into an uncomfortable frown.

He didn't say anything to me. I couldn't speak. I didn't have the energy. We just remained locked in this intense stare, waiting for the other to make some sort of move. Or not. Maybe this was exactly how he wanted it to go. Maybe he just wanted to see that I was in a good amount of pain, that I'd gotten what I deserved.

Well I hadn't. I was still here. Much to his contempt.

Much to mine.

He took a deep breath. His shoulders tensed as he breathed in. His chest expanded. He became physically bigger.

His arms dropped down as he breathed out. I held my breath in fear and anticipation.

His eyes dropped to the floor. He turned around.

I saw the back of his head.

A large, freshly stitched wound ran from the top of his ear, into the middle of his head and down towards his neck.

My head pounded as images of before hit me. The bag. The wall. The swing I'd thrown.

That scar. That was my doing.

Jack walked away.

My cheek was wet.

That family had been torn apart. And here I was, confined to the very hospital that they were stuck in too. They were trapped with the woman that had ruined their lives. I was trapped with the man who wished to avenge his son.

We were stuck together.

I felt my heart quicken. My hands were gripping the sheet on top of me. My knuckles turning white. My head a thunderstorm.

But then everything was okay.

A friend walked into the room and suddenly I was calm. I was safe.

There was only one person who could make me feel like that. And here she was. Thank god.

Jane approached my bed smiling. 'The doctors are just going to run some checks and then we'll be moving to another ward. I hope that's alright.'

She sat beside me and took my hand again.

I nodded against my pillow. I felt joy. Actual joy.

'Good.' Jane beamed.

We were leaving. Me and Jane. She was getting me out of this place. She was holding my hand every step of the way.

Such kindness.

It was me and Jane against the world.

*****

BREATH
Shona Wall

BREATH

THEY WERE LIKE DOGS, and they were closing in, braying, panting, flanking, biting. Hot breath. Hot breath.

There was a moment when entrapment was inevitable. They celebrated their victory by spreading me open, splaying my limbs and pinning me to the ground, their grins wide and smelly.

I can't bear to hear a dog panting, and never have done. My friend, Emily has a dog – don't ask me what type, but it is a sheepdog-looking thing. Its shit is soft and bright orange and plentiful. She brings that animal to my house, without ever asking me if it's okay, and it lies beneath my coffee table with its long, pink tongue dangling and drooling. It has long hair and little clumps of it can be found for days on my laminate floor, days after each visit.

Emily chats non-stop about mankind's unimaginable cruelty to animals while I gaze at the choke chain that glints about her dog's throat. Then I touch my own throat, and I feel something that isn't there – rather like the way you see an entity when you stare into the window of a train and your own soft reflection dances on bushes and tunnel walls. The reflection is real but it can't be touched. It can't be healed or soothed. The reflection wobbles and weaves and splashes and jumps and ripples. It sometimes looks as if its mouth is curling into a smile while it is wobbling. But it is not a smile. It never smiles. But Emily's dog pants. Later it dreams, and its lips curl back over its sharp, ugly teeth like a grin – hot and smelly.

I remember my last day at work with the familiarity of hearing your own footsteps as you approach your own front door. It has replayed often.

Computerisation was so remote and clinical and safe and thorough. There was nothing upsetting about a computer. I could click a button and access that attachment. Then everything was there – all to be studied. Best done in pyjamas over a bottle of red.

Those plans should never have been discussed. Why were they discussed? We all knew what they had looked like.

I remember the room. Blinds at the window, lines of light and shade were tipped. Then the contrasts were gone, replaced by sanitised soft greys.

There was an Internet connection problem, so the tips were tapped. How eager was he to show again what was already seen? He had a scroll. He brandished it about as though with the authority of the ancients. It must have been trustworthy, if it merited a scroll. His brown hands brought it to the table and he opened it out, pinning down its edges with his long fingers.

My curtains always stay the same way; never quite closed, so that a slab of light bleeds over into the dark. They are plain chocolate brown; cotton, unlined, tab-tops. When the sun is shining you can put your face close and see little pins of sunlight through them, a glorious shimmer.

I cannot have my mother here. She *tuts* at my half light and briskly opens the cloth. Her fingers grasp it firmly with the strength of hundreds of thousands of accomplished household tasks. Her words of disappointment land like little stones. The stockpile is plentiful. I cannot explain to her; the woman stands unafraid of sunlight.

What-you-see is what-you-get with her. She is not afraid to open her thoughts to anyone. It unzips. But it's as though a tooth is missing, so it never zips shut again. Everything in her 'opinion box' tumbles out, through a large gaping hole, leaching continuously its toxic trail.

I don't need her to bring me things. I can order them on the Internet. She brings a pot plant anyway. It stands on the windowsill, competing with all those other unwanted things that she had to bring me: company, advice, a few food provisions and a word-search book.

The pot plant is forlorn and thirsty. She waters it and pulls off the leaves that were crushed in transit. She does it briskly, without mercy, for as any doctor will tell you, if these things must be done, it is best to do them quickly.

When she is gone, I dare myself to sweet torture, in the same way I soak up the exquisite presence of Emily's panting dog. The pot plant is violated, its innocence torn from the soil.

There must be dirt under my fingernails.

Bruises are the sweetest tangible proof of resistance. But there will not be enough of them. There would never be enough.

*****

THE DEATHS AND DEATHS
OF WINSTON WITHERSTONE

Marian Harrison

*WINNER of the 2016 University Centre Grimsby
International Literary Prize*

THE DEATHS AND DEATHS
OF WINSTON WITHERSTONE

AFTER TWENTY YEARS, there is nothing to show that he cares for me in any way. A convenient habit, that's all I am. I skewer the Sunday roast with a little more force than necessary and wonder how it feels to stab someone. Pink juices trickle down the leg of lamb. Winston Witherstone likes his meat rare. I increase the heat and set the timer for another forty minutes.

I have considered poison, always a popular choice amongst female murderers according to the book I borrowed from the library. In the living room I am greeted by a symphony of Winston's snoring. Knocking the two reception rooms into one was always going to be a big mistake; I told him that but he wouldn't listen. I scoop his dirty socks from the floor and briefly consider stuffing one into his gaping mouth. Wait. The crescendo peaks. He snuffles and snorts and smacks his lips together. On this occasion, he does not wake and look around **accusingly**. I study my husband, slumped across the sofa: unshaven, unkempt, one arm flopped over his abundant belly, with his hand still clutching a can of lager. I have long ceased caring about spills on the furniture: no point. I read a magazine article about sleep apnoea; it can be fatal. One day he might just choke to death in his sleep. I can be patient.

Several weeks pass and Winston returns from the office Christmas party, drunk. He crawls up the stairs but fails to reach the bathroom before the contents of his stomach spill across the landing. Dutifully, I help him to his feet and we teeter at the top of the stairs; it's a struggle to keep him upright. I am so tempted; it would be easy. I wouldn't even need to push, just let go. As far as I'm concerned, Winston's nineteen-stone body heaped at the foot of the stairs, with his head twisted at an odd angle, is a sight that could only mean a very Merry Christmas and a Happy New Year. I blink away the comforting vision and, with considerable effort, steer him towards the bedroom. *You're a coward Rose Witherstone*, I scold myself.

Christmas Day is here: perfect for a memorable murder. I debate my options. Salmonella in the turkey? Warfarin in the brandy sauce? Anti-freeze in the champagne? No! I have read more books and articles and now consider myself far too adventurous for soft options; when I kill, I am going to kill in (what my latest criminology book describes as) the manner of a man. Unfortunately I don't have the strength of a man, certainly not a man the size of Winston. I need time for careful planning and Winston receives, unwittingly, a stay of execution as a Christmas bonus.

The early signs of spring are creeping into the garden and I take to sitting in the conservatory.

Good idea! says Winston, *We don't appreciate the garden enough.*

He joins me, regularly, snoring to a chorus of birdsong as I pursue my new pastime: plotting the perfect crime. The new laptop I bought myself for Christmas together with an upgrade to Superfast Broadband makes my research much easier. I make and save notes as I go, all on one little machine. It contains my life and Winston's death and, as I work, I can even don headphones and allow the music of my choice to drown the sound of his snoring. *Drown*, that reminds me, I need to check out a couple of sites. A glass of wine, the World Wide Web, Mozart and my victim reclining in a chair, eyes closed and chin raised, I've never been so content. In a matter of seconds, I could grab a sharp knife from the kitchen and slice through all those chins, from ear to ear; it would be over before he knew anything about it. Of course, Winston is perfectly safe at the moment. I could never murder to Mozart; it would be all wrong. Mozart's music is motivational, inspirational and uplifting but homicidal, it is not. I add *murderous music* to my to-do list. I'm only going to kill this man once so I want everything to be perfect.

The blossom is falling from the trees and Winston has been stabbed, drowned, burned, poisoned, eaten by lions, frozen, starved, suffocated, hung, eradicated by the 18:31 from King's Cross, ejected from a light aircraft, crushed by a steam roller, dissolved in a bath of acid and even struck by lightning. There is, however, one thing that foils every single plot. Unlike many of my long-suffering friends, I have no real motive. I find myself envying those unfortunate women married to drunks, gamblers, wife beaters and adulterers. I struggle to turn the crimes of mediocrity and apathy into justification for all the terrible deaths I have contrived. There is limited satisfaction in killing a man, unless one can also feel vindicated by it.

As my conservatory evenings grow longer, I turn my thoughts less to murder and more to motive. I find myself gathering evidence of every misdemeanour: forgetting our wedding anniversary, farting in bed, dominating the remote control, all the little idiosyncrasies that, over the years, have become a plethora of irritating habits. I try hard but have to concede, they are insufficient to sanction Winston's demise. Ultimately, I reach the conclusion that my only solution is to *force* Winston to give me a motive.

Soon I discover that trying to bring out the nasty side in a man of such exceptional indifference is not easy. I nag excessively, write-off his car, recycle his childhood collection of *The Beano*, flirt with his boss at the office party and spend hours on the telephone to my childhood sweetheart, having tracked him down on Facebook. Winston remains the perfect sloth.

I have always looked forward to our annual holiday. Winston enjoys night fishing and sleeps for most of the day. This leaves my days free for shopping and sightseeing and my nights a peaceful, snore-free haven. I decide to take some respite from my quest for motive and my murder fantasies. I flit from romance, to historical novels, to poetry and finally several craft books and a paperback on 119 uses for yogurt. Why did I leave my laptop at home? I last for two days then find myself in the reference section of the local library making notes from a volume of Criminal Psychology. It isn't until I get back to the hotel in the evening, that I realise Winston has been missing all day.

The bloated corpse on the mortuary slab does not bear much resemblance to Winston. I try to blink the image away but it persists. It is so unfair; I'm not ready for this. It's just typical of Winston to skip the rehearsals and ruin all my plans. It's like being jilted at the altar – all that preparation, all that expectation, all for nothing. I'm sure I was close to resolving the issue with motive and then I only had to select an appropriate modus operandi from my thoroughly researched collection. Now I find myself without a victim; no merry widowhood for me.

The funeral is over and the dutiful attendees have respectfully gone. I am sitting in the conservatory wondering how to occupy the evening ahead. I flit through TV and radio channels but find nothing of interest. My shelves hold numerous books: fiction, non-fiction, hardback, paperback, bought, borrowed, old, new, in a range of shapes, sizes and colours, and every single one of them about murder, motive and means. A few remain unread. They were captivating, but now... what's the point? Without a victim, they are irrelevant. I turn on my laptop and check my emails; a few virtual mourners have sent digital condolences to Winston's cyber-widow. They hope I am coping. I click my *favourites* tab; almost every link is related to murder. I would never have believed I could miss Winston.

It is time to begin a new project.

Over the next few months, I try learning German, yoga, amateur dramatics, writing a novel, building my family tree, pottery and even experimenting with yogurt. All are disappointing. I consider buying a dog but when I see a neighbour, on an exceptionally cold November morning, bending down with a pooper scooper and then conscientiously depositing a little blue bag into a bin labelled: *dog waste only*, I consider the prospect of this daily ritual and buy a hamster instead. I call him Mozart.

I am visited by Winston's sister Antonia who, having first cooed over Mozart, broaches the subject of romance.

You're not getting any younger Rose, she says, *Winston wouldn't want you to stay on your own forever.*

Winston was far too apathetic to care one way or the other, but I go along with her; going on a date can't be any worse than struggling with German grammar or grappling with slippery mounds of spinning clay.

Mozart is cute, she agrees, *but let's face it, hamsters have their limitations.*

She tells me that she knows someone, who knows someone, who knows of a reputable dating agency, or there is always the Internet, if I'm feeling brave.

It's amazing how many unattached males there are waiting to meet someone just like me. I have dated several charming and eligible men but none of them really appeal as a long-term partner.

For goodness sake Rose, Antonia says, *I know Winston must be a hard act to follow but are you sure you're not being just a bit too choosy? What exactly are you looking for?*

Oh, I'll know him when I find him, I tell her. Hard act to follow indeed! But then, in some ways, I suppose he is.

It is my 13th date and I have high expectations. Antonia strokes Mozart and studies my date's profile.

He looks a bit dull, Rose, he doesn't seem to have any interests, she says.

Well that'll give us something to talk about, won't it? I reply.

I've got a gut feeling about this one Antonia; trust me... I say. Mozart supports me by giving her a little nip. She's a bit too heavy handed at times. I tell her not to make so much fuss; he hasn't even drawn blood. Blood? A moment of nostalgia.

I arrive; he's already here and he's halfway through a pint of beer. He recommends the *Daily Special,* chilli con carne, and suggests beer to go with it. I tell him I'm not keen on beer. He orders two specials (buy one get one free) and two pints.

Don't worry, he reassures me, *I'll drink yours if you don't want it.*

I ask about his interests; he likes football, cricket and fishing. I tell him I don't like any of those activities and, as we tuck into the Daily Specials, he talks about all three at great length. I listen attentively as he spends the evening talking about himself; he fails to ask anything about me. I manage to interject the occasional comment into his monologue but he doesn't appear to hear me. The bill arrives and he insists on paying a bit more because I haven't drunk as much as him. He places an extra three pounds on the table towards his five pints. He looks at his watch and apologises for having to rush but he doesn't want miss the snooker on T.V. Oh yes; has he mentioned that he likes snooker? No he hasn't and no I don't. He stands to make his exit and pauses; he tells me that this has been his best night out in ages and he really wants to see me again.

I wave to him through the restaurant window as he runs for his bus, then I settle the bill. The waitress tells me my taxi will be here any minute.

You look very happy, she says, *you must have had a good evening.*

Best in ages, I tell her. I feel a broad smile stretch across my face.

I was right to trust my instinct. This man is exactly the kind of man I've been waiting for.

He is the kind of man I will grow to loathe. Time: The Great Healer; in time he will make a highly deserving victim and the perfect replacement for my tragically deceased and greatly missed spouse.

*****

THE DOOMED SUCCESSION
Toni Josefsen

THE DOOMED SUCCESSION

THE WOODEN BLOCK LOOMED BEFORE HER. She fixed her gaze upon it, everything else losing focus. It was a surreal, dizzying experience, her vision swimming before her. Her breaths became short and ragged. She could see the crowd below her, nobles jeering like common people.

The Queen Mary sat rigid upon her platform; her countenance was unnerving, her face impassive. Jane closed her eyes: taking a deep breath. She shifted her feet forwards, brushing across the straw that rustled beneath her.

The crowd fell silent, waiting with bated breath, as a large raven cawed from atop its perch on the Queen's house, staring down with beady eyes.

She grasped the kerchief handed her; felt the soft material as she grasped it between elegant fingers.

'My Lords and Ladies! If you would be kind enough to do so, remember me as a good Christian woman who served her Lord well.'

**

'Sire, you know your sister, the Lady Mary, does not share your views. She will not uphold your beliefs when she becomes Queen,' John Dudley, the Duke of Northumberland, whispered,' despite not being able to see another soul in sight. Spies were everywhere. Enemies, under the guise of loyal subjects, lurking in the shadows to utilise any information to their advantage.

Edward turned to him, his eyes held an air of power even as his body failed him, succumbing to all manner of illness. Northumberland's worries mirrored his own. He was in turmoil. If his dear sister had any measure of respect for his authority, then she would follow him blindly. Alas, she did not, adamant in her own faith. Not for the first time a rift had grown between them, a cavern that grew more by the day. She had even attended mass. It was forbidden for her and any other, to do so. *'No,'* he thought *'Mary could not rule.'*

'I am aware of my sister's vehement denial of the Protestant faith, but there is no alternative.'

'There *is,* my Liege,' Northumberland stressed adamantly. 'My daughter-in-law, Lady Jane, *your* cousin, follows the ways of our religion. She honours her faith daily.'

Edward sighed deeply, his eyes became veiled, glazing over with the stress of such a troublesome decision and the strain of being unwell. His body grew weak. Coughs wracked his slender frame, his skin grew clammy and pale. He clenched his fists, puffing air from his nose when he could barely do so. He was the King; he had much left to give. He had so much to do.

*

The sound of marching echoed across the Tower's walls and into Jane's eardrums. Each stomp kept rhythm with the next; a wave of noise. Left stomp, right stomp, every man together. It overcame her, vibrating through her being, filling her with dread. It would be an almost calming experience in different circumstances. Men taking leave to defend their country; instilling hope in the people.

Perhaps it would be a relief to be free of her burden. She'd been Queen but nine days; already she grew weary. *What had possessed me to take on such a role? A role that is not rightfully mine!'* Jane pondered. She stood tall, awaiting her fate as the drum of feet on stone got louder. Then the force of the steps grew weaker even as they grew closer. The door swung open. The Lady Mary and several of her guards stormed in. Her presence was that of a Queen; she exuded grace and power.

The rich purple dress she wore swayed around her feet and across the floor, blowing up dust. She came to a halt as did the guards behind her. They stomped one last resounding clank, the metal of their armour rattling. Through the small slit in the men's helmets she could sense their powerful, threatening stares upon her; mocking and belittling her for trying to be Queen.

Jane lowered herself to the floor in a deep bow, signalling her allegiance. At her father's behest—after a change of heart—she had taken the lavish crown from atop her head. She felt all the lighter for it. Responsibility taken from her slender frame, passed on into Mary's capable hands. Her father beside her, knelt.

'My Queen, I—we, are gravely sorry for any treasonous actions taken against you. We wholly support your claim to the throne.'

Mary looked down, lip pursed but temper in check. Seemingly every bit composed, despite having marched tens of thousands of men across the Tower's flagstones in pursuit of the throne.

'Jane and Henry Grey, you are to be arrested on the count of treason. You are charged with obstructing the rightful heir from claiming the throne, in favour of your own gain.' Her voice was harsh and deep, it echoed around the room in the form of an absolute command. There was no room for objection; those in the room held no power to do so.

*

Jane shifted her weight as the floor creaked beneath her feet. A layer of dust had settled, showing the amount of time the lieutenant spent away from his lodgings. With pleasure, she noted the mahogany writing desk situated in front of the room's only window. She could read her prayer book in the adequate lighting and write to her sisters— whom she had not seen since the night of her wedding.

The bed was almost as large as her marital bed, not quite as ornate, but satisfactory, with a sturdy wooden frame. The silver drapes hung from the bed's four posters. At least she'd be afforded some privacy. She waited on the lieutenant to leave. When she heard the clunk of his heavy footsteps stop on the last step she sat upon the stiff mattress. *'Better than the hard stone flooring of a prisoner's cell,'* she thought.

It seemed so long since the moment she was told of her ascension in the line of succession. It was a moment that would be ingrained in her mind for as long as she lived.

The pounding of footsteps rang throughout the room as Guildford's sister burst through the door and launched herself towards Jane.

'The King! The King is dead!' yelled the Lady Dudley unable to keep her composure, losing all decorum. She attempted to calm herself and regain some of her grace.

'Jane! Jane, you are to be his successor!'

Unable to comprehend what was told to her, Jane fell upon the cold stone tiles. 'Queen. Me?' She shook with the shock of such news.

'I am insufficient! I am unworthy!' she wept. She couldn't control the fury of the sobs that wracked her body, overwhelmed.

Her husband, Guildford, soothed her, whispering how great a Queen she could be, that she was worthy. She steeled herself for the difficult journey ahead. Rising to her feet, she looked upon those that were bowing before her. She was humbled.

'If it is true, if it really is to be, rightfully and lawfully, then I shall rule by God's will and govern the realm to his glory and service,' she announced.

How she wished now that she had never said such a thing. To rule? She had no claim to the throne, she knew that now. She had been a pawn to the ambitions of those around her. Perhaps, they had determined her role in these treasonous events on the very day she was born.

Jane heard the lieutenant ascending towards the room, and stood to smooth her dress.

'My Lady,' he nodded grimly, holding up a chalice, 'I thought some wine might ease your nerves.'

'Thank you,' she mustered; surprised at such kindness.

He nodded once more and quietly took his leave. Jane took a deep gulp of wine, swilling it round her mouth and over her taste buds. She covered her mouth all of a sudden, alarmed. The taste was off, with a sour hint. She hastily emptied the contents of her mouth back into the cup and slammed it down upon the table. She grabbed a handkerchief and wiped the remainder from her tongue and teeth, wary of any residue of tainted wine.

She leaned against the bed to steady herself then released a sharp breath. She trusted no one. Dragging her weary legs to bed, she slid under the heavy duvet despite not having dressed in her nightgown. Her eyes could fight sleep no longer, but her mind was wide awake, paranoid and conjuring up vivid, confusing dreams.

Jane was plagued with a night of fitful sleep and awoke covered in a layer of sweat. She'd dreamed that a river of red streamed from the windows of the Tower. Kneeling beside her bed she prayed for God's guidance in deciphering his cryptic message. There was no time for her to dress, she had urgent matters to attend. She found her way to the desk and ran her finger across the smooth wood and through a coating of its gritty dust.

Jane sat, quill to mouth, thinking of words to describe to her highness, Queen Mary, that she had not, for one second, believed that Mary should not sit upon the throne. She could not help but blame her treasonous actions on Northumberland's ridiculous aspirations. Even her father had been tempted by the man's promises of power.

The Lady Katherine Parr had always held Queen Mary in the highest regards and she was an excellent judge of character. Jane firmly believed the right woman now sat upon the throne. A smile tugged at her lips as she thought of the lady that had bestowed unto her everything; her time, affection and wisdom. She could imagine her stood in one of her striking crimson dresses, a nurturing smile crafted upon her face. A tear ran down Jane's face, staining the page beneath her before she'd even begun to write. She wiped her tear away, dispelling her melancholy, and discarded the tarnished parchment.

*

Jane sighed deeply, finally satisfied with her letter. She signed her name, Jane Dudley, as was expected. After all she was a married woman and had been for almost two months.

Guildford Dudley had been courteous enough towards her, paying her every attention as a husband should. But she was certain; he'd only married her with the selfish ambition to be King. She had denied him of that.

To let such a man be King! A man ruled by his father's political desires and his own greed. Never! They had plotted this for some time, of that she was sure.

**

Jane strolled leisurely, admiring the Queen's herb garden and the wondrous sight of the grand buildings expanding before her. The sun bathed the stonework in glorious light, the old royal walls reflected a heavenly glow. She was sure that she could live as happily here as she could elsewhere. She was afforded plenty of time on the green and to cleanse her soul in the chapel. The lieutenant had also allowed her to sneak her prayer book into his lodgings. She was content with her life presently.

Jane was aware of more than just her guard's eyes upon her figure, holding herself tall against the disapproving stares she listened intently to their raised whispers.

'They say Sir Henry Grey spread word of the rebellion himself.'

Jane halted at the mention of her father's name. *'A rebellion?'* She turned ever-so-slightly towards the gaggle of women, huddled together to share gossip. News travelled fast for a place so far from the common people. Then again, servants knew everything.

'Aye, 'not against the Queen', he'd said 'just her marriage',' replied a deeper voice.

'Why take up against the Queen then? It's treason!'

'There's still some scheme to be had 'ere. Any rebellion against Queen Mary puts that Lady Jane closer in line for the throne.'

'Did you hear?' whispered a new voice 'Queen Mary is bringing her sister, Lady Elizabeth, to be held *here* as a prisoner!'

'No?' Two would-be Queens taking up against Her Highness!'

'Both were wards of Thomas Seymour, you know!'

'Oh! I heard about all that!'

'Shh! Get back to work, the lot of you before I have you flogged.'

Jane, for a moment forgetting she was a lady, grasped her skirts, rushing to her lodgings. She was desperate to escape the voices behind her, desperate to discover the truth for herself, for she could not believe it was true. *Why? Why would my Father rise up against the Queen, knowing that my life is still in her custody? Is his agenda truly more important than my life?'*

The lieutenant awaited her inside. His glum composure betrayed his silence. Jane held a hand to her chest, gasping for breath.

'Oh! Oh no,' she mustered, her chest heaving mightily, 'it is true then?'

She choked back a yell of pure agony as she watched her future, that was once saved, burn before her eyes. Her life was in jeopardy, her future bleak. Suddenly her dream made sense to her, a premonition sent from God. She fell to the cold, hard floor, her knees too weak to support her. Her corset stole much needed air from her body, restraining her breaths, her vision blackened as the floor twisted and turned beneath her. The lieutenant graciously left the room, the door scraping loudly against the wood as he closed it behind him. She vaguely heard him ordering her personal guard to be discreet about 'the Lady's condition', muffling her sobs in the fabrics of her dress.

**

Jane frowned deeply, still attempting to comprehend the shift in her intended fate.

'I'd like a moment, if you please, to say my final prayers,' Jane asked of the lieutenant.

He gave her a sharp nod, his face creased with lines of remorse.

'I will take you to the chapel, my Lady.'

She lifted her skirt as she descended the steps, her shoes clicking as they touched upon the smooth wood. She grasped at the rough wall to steady herself. She could not see beyond the wall of the narrow staircase, or the billowing blue fabric of her dress to see where she was placing her feet. The Lieutenant's hand reached out to aid her as she reached the last step.

*

Jane stepped out from the chapel and into the biting chill of the evening air. She braced herself before being led towards the raised wooden platform. Her hands shook, but not with the cold. Clasping them together, she tried to appear brave.

As she walked towards her final destination, a man wheeled a small wooden cart passed her. She peeked a glance inside, knowing what she might find. There, bobbing, rolling, jumping around was her husband's severed head. Blood oozed from his open wound, his mouth was agape in a silent scream. She carried on walking, but even as the cart passed her she could not tear her eyes away. The man pushing it afforded her a sheepish grimace but as he got further away he began to whistle.

Even though they were gone, her husband's terror-stricken decapitated head followed her to the scaffold, as did the man's creepy tune. The cocky smile had been wiped from his once handsome face. She almost missed it, having grown so accustomed to seeing his smirk. She had been so shaken, preoccupied with the gruesome sight that she barely registered his body being carted closely behind.

The small walk seemed to take an eternity with Jane lost within her own mind. She was helped to climb the steps, her legs too weak to manage on her own. A hollow tap, tap followed her, boring into her as she crossed the platform towards the man who was to take her life.

She was handed the kerchief and took a moment to scan the faces of those around her. Mary held her chin high, jaw set she stared down upon Jane. It needn't have come to this. Mary would feel safe in the knowledge that she had ensured her place as Queen. Her reign would continue on, unthreatened.

The executioner's eyes glistened, his hands gripped his tool to stop his limbs from shaking. Killing was his job, and he would complete it, by order of the Queen. Jane could only imagine what might force a man to kill for a living, the threat of his own death, or perhaps, more gallantly a threat against his precious family.

Her hair was wrapped in cloth so that none would come free and hide her neck where the final blow would be struck. She wrapped the material in her hand round her eyes, blocking the world from her view. It was a mercy for Jane that she could not see the glint of his axe's sharp edge under the setting sun. The blindfold, tight around her face, hid her terror from the eyes of those who looked on, bewitched by the gory event.

She wondered if the blade would hurt, or if she'd be gone before she even noticed the tip of it touching her neck. Would she still feel the pain as her head fell from her body? She shook her head slightly, calming herself, and slowed her breathing. She was a part of God's will and soon she would join him. She fumbled in search of the wooden block, strands of straw sticking sharply beneath her fingernails.

'What shall I do? Where is it?'

A hand grabbed her wrist and led her towards it, where she laid down her head. She grasped the wood tightly, her fingers aching with the force of her grip. Nervous anticipation twisted her stomach, her heart tightened with dread. A small sob escaped her lips, tears staining the filthy rag that covered her eyes.

The swish of the blade slicing the air cut through the silence, deafening the crowd. The chop of the axe trembled through the executioner's body, sheathed in place where Jane's head had been but a moment ago.

He hung his head, mourning another life taken.

*****

CAUSE AND EFFECT
Amanda Staples

THIRD PLACE in the 2016 University Centre Grimsby
International Literary Prize

CAUSE AND EFFECT

FRANK- Thoughts flutter through my mind like bunting buffeted by a breeze. I know someone is there. Where am I? I can't quite...there it is again; a voice I recognise and one I don't. Can't recall the name. Far away in my brain. So tired.

I'm in a bed that's not mine. Sheets feel funny. Can only feel them on one side of my body. Odd smell. Can't move. I can hear my heart but it's pipping not thumping. Can't open my eyes. This is bad. I keep losing my...worms. Nightmare? Someone's there, here. So tired. I can't feel my - what's it called...hand. Try to move a finger. Can't remember how. Too much effort. Try again. Later. Tomorrow. Was I here yesterday? This isn't my bed. I can't move. Am I trapped? Am I dead? In a coffin buried alive? Help! Someone...anyone. I can hear voices.

Is that my boy I can hear? It's been so long since we talked. I'm not sure I know his voice anymore.

Another voice. Someone is moving about.

I hear my Susan. My wonderful wife. So long since I visited your grave. Susan! She's not here. She's not far away though. My Susan.

Man talking. John? That's my boy. If I could just open my eyes. Too much effort.

I feel heavy but light all at once. If I concentrate I can tell I'm lying down, but not in my bed. Susan's here. No. Susan's dead. I'm in a bed I feel on one side more than the other. There's a funny smell and a beeping noise.

Men's voices. Recognise one – John? They're talking about someone dying. I hear a sound like a maraca being shaken slowly. It's coming from me. My heart beat? My breath? I'm dying then. I'm coming, Susan! We'll be together again. If I could just put things right with the boy first; make peace. It's gone on too long. You would've said I was too hard on him. Bad blood's no good.

Stubborn old fool, you'd say. But it's not natural. Don't look at me in that tone of voice, Susan.

Is this how you felt when you slipped away? I blamed him. I admit it. Looking at him is like looking at you. His eyes are your eyes. He's nothing like me. No interest in boxing. Mamby-pamby snivelling pussy cowering in the corner, snot drooling, when all I was trying to do was toughen him up. An accountant and a poof. Christ! A pussy pen pusher and a pansy. Where'd I go wrong? What did I do to deserve him turning out like that?

But I want to say goodbye. How many years has it been? I want to say goodbye for both our sakes. Then I can rest in peace.

Perhaps if I concentrate all my efforts. Focus like I'm in the zone. Like I did for boxing matches. Focus, Frank.

If I can just get a few words out. It's the right thing to do. God knows I haven't behaved like a father for years.

The men aren't talking now. I think I heard one leave. Someone's there. I can hear them fidgeting. John. My boy.

You never even got to see him did you, Susan? He was whisked away from you as you were whisked away from me. Life's so cruel and I blamed him for your death. I wished he'd never been born because you'd still be here and I'd rather have you here than him. Now you'll say that I'm cruel. I know, Susan, I know. I'm sorry. I know I was wrong. He's my son, whatever else he is, he's my flesh and blood.

I want to say something, while my brain is still working. I don't know what words I want to use. Maybe they will just come if I open my mouth.

Focus Frank. Get in the zone.

MATT- I make a fist and shove it into my back and lean into it. Damn these hard plastic hospital chairs. I think about going for a walk. My bum's numb. But every time I mention leaving John alone he panics. Anyway, I need a wee, so I have to move. I push myself up and my bones echo the creaking of the tired orange chair.

'Where are you going?' panicked eyes ask before he does.

'My back's in bits and I'm dying for a wee. And I just need a break, sorry.'

Don't leave me, the eyes beg, but he says, 'Okay,' and slumps further down.

Outside, clutching a polystyrene cup that's supposed to be coffee but tastes nothing like, I lean, relieved, against a wall. I wish I still smoked. Mind you, after what's just happened to Frank, I shouldn't wish that. I push away from the wall and wander around the grounds. It's pretty for a hospital. I pick up a twig and twiddle it in my fingers. I look up at the tree it fell from and see it fighting back against the winter that stripped it bare and clothing itself with bleached-white spring blossom. Life after death. I wonder if he'll die. Frank. The next 48 hours are critical, apparently. I hope he does die. Soon. They come in periodically to check drips, scrawl on charts illegibly to stop us making any sense of it, and look at the monitor. They used to smile, it never reached their eyes. Now we are part of the furniture and they ignore us. I wonder if that's a sign. We are all just waiting for what has now become inevitable.

He's pacing when I get back. Hands are guiltily shoved swiftly into pockets as I open the door so I don't catch him chewing his cuticles until they bleed.

'What's happened?' I ask him, struggling to keep the irritation out of my voice. I distract myself by unravelling my scarf and chucking it on the end of the bed.

'He moved a finger.' John stops pacing and looks at me for an answer. He's simply dreadful in a crisis. And he's emotionally stunted, just like his dad.

I study Frank for a moment, but he doesn't move a millimetre. 'Are you sure?' He looks at me like I'm an imbecile. 'It was probably a muscle spasm, John. They said he's unlikely to come round.'

I pull my coat off and sling it over the back of the chair and watch him. My boyfriend, the emotional train-wreck on legs. Battling with wanting to stay and wanting to flee. Wanting Frank to die and not wanting to admit it to himself. They've never been close but he always hoped. God knows what for. An epiphany? A man like Frank; pig-headed, bigoted, narrow-minded and homophobic - and those are just his good points – doesn't change in my experience. I watch him run a hand through his floppy mop of brown hair as he struggles with himself. His hair sticks up at the back where he messed it up and I have an urge to flatten it down, but don't. Instead I sit down with the newspaper to distract myself.

'I should've come when he had the first stroke,' he says.

'Why?' I don't look up from the crossword. I can imagine his pitiful face. His puppy-dog eyes wet with guilt-soaked tears.

'This pneumonia will take him; it's just a matter of time. He's dying. I left it too late, Matty.'

I scribble letters in the crossword boxes. It's not the correct answer; it's just something to do. I hate it when he calls me Matty. He sounds so needy and childlike; makes me feel like his mother not his lover.

'I don't even know if he wants to be buried or cremated,' John sighs.

'Should we be discussing this in front of him?' I put the paper down and scratch my stubbly chin. Haven't shaved in days. 'They say hearing is the last thing to go.'

John subconsciously raises a finger to his mouth, catches himself just before he starts to chew at it. 'I'm going for a walk,' he says. 'I can't stand this.'

'Get me a bar of chocolate, will you?'

He nods and shuffles out, self-pitying shoulders slumped, hangdog style.

It's just me and Frank now. I wonder if he can hear me. I consider giving him a piece of my mind but really, what's the point?

I return to my paper, flap out the creases and stare at the crossword. Nothing comes. My mind is as full as a binge-eater's belly. I'm a worrier, see. I give the impression of coping calmly and I do, most of the time. I'm like a duck in a pond; serenely swimming across the water, barely creating a ripple but the legs are going like billy-o underneath. I worry about everything. I especially worry about John.

The monitor drove me nuts initially, like a van constantly reversing. Now I hardly notice it, so much so I drift off. I'm startled awake by a sound like a car driving over gravel. It's Frank. He's trying to speak.

Automatically, I lean toward the bed, like I care. The newspaper falls to the floor. I look around for John. He's not back.

'Shit,' I mutter as Frank's weak hand, skin like blue tissue paper, grapples frantically.

'John,' his sandpaper voice finally manages.

I scrape the chair closer, takes Frank's hand; once a boxer's fist, now a thin claw. Frank calms but his eyes remain closed in a frown or grimace. I don't know but part of me hopes it's pain. Frank was perpetually angry. At his friendliest he was gruff. I hope Frank keeps his eyes closed.

'John.' The coarse voice again, searching.

'Yes, dad,' I lie, lowering the pitch of my voice and speaking quietly, compassion taking over for a moment. 'I'm here.'

The death rattle slows, sounds like a motorbike ticking over.

'Son,' Frank coughs. The frown deepens. Spittle gathers like rabid foam round his mouth.

I feel nauseous. Look away. Where the hell is John? This is not my job.

'I want to say,' Frank pauses for breath, I consider ringing John. If I just let it ring out, John would rush back, but I'd have to let go of Frank's hand to reach my phone. 'I never understood you. Don't know why you turned out how you did.'

I fight the urge to run away, to leave the old man to fester in his misery and drown in it. John would never forgive me. For a moment Frank is so still, I think he's dead but the machine's still beeping. Now, in the still silence, its shrillness pierces my ears.

Frank hauls more air into his lungs and starts again. 'If I'd been harder on you, maybe you wouldn't be a poof.'

Momentarily forgetting I am supposed to be John, I start to say something, but stop. I'm glad John's not here and I'm hearing this crap instead.

'Whatever you are, at the end of the day, you're my son. I want you to know –' Frank coughs, spraying spittle. Now I struggle to stay put.

'Yes, Dad?' I manage. I want to hear the belligerent old bugger say it.

'I'm fond of you, son.'

Unbelievable. I let go of Frank's hand. Fond. What the hell kind of word is that? I've had enough now and get up to leave. Let the old man die comfortless and alone.

'John,' Frank struggles on, barely audible, his words slurring. 'Bury me with your mother.'

I hear the monotone on the monitor as I close the door.

John enters the ward as I'm leaving. I halt him with a hand on his shoulder. His frightened eyes question.

'He's gone. I was just coming to find you,' I say, gently. 'You didn't miss anything. He didn't regain consciousness, just slipped away.'

John looks pained and relieved all at once. I brush his cheek tenderly. 'It's okay. I'm here. We've got each other.' I give him my best reassuring smile as I link my arm through his, turning him away from the ward. 'I think you should cremate him. Less fuss. And you don't have to feel guilty about not visiting his grave.'

*****

CREATION

Steve Jackson

CREATION

IT'S AN UNSEASONABLY WET DAY IN MAY. The court building, a bastion of Edwardian red brick, towers against the grey sky. The oversized, mahogany door opens briefly. A small slight figure is thrust out into the rain by a large uniformed official. As the small figure stumbles down the worn Yorkshire stone steps, the large, uniformed official advises him in very unofficial, unsavoury language not to re-appear.

The words reach the small figure, John, heard muffled through the turmoil of his disordered mind, as he struggles to retain his footing on the rain-slicked steps. Once on the pavement, he walks on without a backward glance, hands thrust deep into the pockets of his jacket, his head bowed. He has no hat or coat to protect against the persistent wind and rain. He is, as usual, shabbily dressed. His faded, stained denim jacket, worn, greasy jeans and ragged trainers, once the uniform of his rebellious youth, now seem out of place and time for a man in his late thirties. His hair and beard, once status symbols of his art student youth, are now streaked with grey: long, unkempt and dirty. He looks neither left nor right: someone who no longer expects to be recognised or respected by passers by.

As he walks, his mind is an inferno of seething, impotent rage as it replays the events and language of the courtroom. He can still hear the words of the magistrate, bitter, sarcastic, insulting him from the privileged position of the Bench. His latest artwork, a massive, lurid mural on a concrete wall of the local council building, is to be cleaned off - at his expense. The bill for this work is set to land in his mother's mailbox in the not too distant future. This dismissive insult to his art from the same council who *pay* for artwork elsewhere. Pointless stone carvings and ridiculous 'street furniture', meaningless art drivel, appears everywhere, assailing and insulting the finer senses of the general public. Conversely, his works, designed and developed with care and craft to tell the story of Revelation, the end of the world, are constantly dismissed out of hand as 'utter rubbish.'

However, the warning of a full custodial sentence for any future offences has penetrated even the fog of his mind on this occasion: his mother has threatened him with eviction if he is ever again imprisoned. He walks, still raging inside, until his feet find him in front of the crumbling Victorian house he calls home. He walks through the unkempt garden round to the back, and lets himself in through the basement door.

He still lives in the basement of this, his mother's rambling house: a house which, for both of them has long been a pit of despair. Although his mother owns the whole house, she and her son have nothing to do with each other. She covers his costs and, so far, has rendered him a small allowance to live below, paying his fines when incurred with ever decreasing tolerance. Alcoholic, she has enough money to fund the basic house expenses and a small army of slovenly carers who bring her gin when required. While she ekes out her remaining days upstairs, a whining slave to the twin addictions of alcohol and painkillers, the basement is, for John, both his only home and his malignant cancer of despair. Once occupied by a variety of misfits, the flotsam of 'down on my luck' people who always seem to exist on the fringes of (and at odds with) modern society, he is now the sole occupant. All the others are gone. A few have returned to 'respectable' society. Some, he knows, are still in prison, the outcome of their anti-establishment activities. Most are probably still living on the fringes, somewhere, somehow.

John has no job: he has never worked, seeing himself as a famous artist in waiting. And waiting. He is nowadays always angry, filled with depression, but still sure that his art will one day be understood and respected by the world at large: a belief he must cling to, because there is now nothing else in his world. The main room he lives, works and paints in is at the back of the house, looking out through cracked, cobwebbed windows onto the heavily overgrown garden. This room reflects his chaotic nature, strewn with the detritus of an inspirational painter without inspiration. Paper, canvas, old poster paints, half empty tins of enamels and countless expended aerosols lie everywhere, some thick with dust and plaster debris fallen from the mildewed ceiling. A sordid kitchen area is to the left, rotten with food refuse, with a foul bathroom alongside it. Further towards the front of the house, a mouldering, dimly lit passageway leads to several other rooms, their doorways lost in the gloom. Many of these are without windows. In those whose grimy windows allow a little daylight to enter, various bulky stored items, the leavings of their former occupants, can be glimpsed, covered with rotted plaster from the ceilings.

Picking his way through the rubbish to his bed, he lies down, his mind filled with images of hate. With his latest doomed artwork now to be destroyed, he tries in vain to visualise how he might create its successor, and how he can convey its artistic importance to the world. Eventually, he falls into fitful sleep.

'When the Creator created the world and wished to discover depths out of the concealments, and light out of darkness, at that time they were mingled in one another. For this reason, out of the darkness came forth light, and out of concealment came forth and revealed the deep. One came out of the other.'

He wakes late on that same fateful day with these lines from the Book of Zohar clear in his mind. Somehow, despite all the setbacks and humiliations, despite all the people who have mocked him, despised his artworks, he has continued to believe that it was his destiny to change the world. Suddenly, from this day, this moment, he realises with a surge of passion, the real artwork, the real truth, eluding him for so long, lurking in the canyons of his mind. He is not to be the artist of Revelation, the end of all things: he is to be the artist of Creation, the birth of the new.

He had never before thought of himself as the Creator. His art, his passion, had been in trying to make people see, believe in his vision of the future: dark, apocalyptic, full of fire, chaos, a gigantic fire-storm driving people to see the future, heaven and hell portrayed. So far, his efforts had totally failed to convey this message to anyone. Though he was convinced that they needed his message, his random artworks had failed to make the impression he needed. His artworks at college had been met with faint praise, such as might be given to a student in the hope that they develop further. Epic in scale, using huge quantities of expensive materials, he had painted his grand visions. Soon, marked even by other art students as an oddball, his paintings came to be as mocked and shunned as himself. However, he knew his vision well. He had dreamed it, thought about it: all along, he'd been trying to paint it, capture it – the Apocalypse, the great picture of chaos that would make him known, respected, famous.

John the artist, now fully awake, is at one with his surroundings. He lies as usual on his camp bed in the corner of the room, covered by two grimy blankets but still wearing the wrinkled clothes he has worn for several days. From his bed, he reaches out and rolls an untidy cigarette, which he lights before laying back to smoke and think. He has plenty of time to think: he no longer has any friends, nor any partner or soul-mate in life. As the self-styled artist of the Apocalypse, he is now both mocked and rejected by his contemporaries. From his activities as a 'street artist', he is now well-known to, and well disliked by, both local and city police. His only noted achievements as a street artist are his several minor convictions, including the latest, for graffiti, and one brief spell in prison for resisting arrest.

In detail, his Apocalyptic work, his inspiration so far, is a mishmash of various religious symbols: images of dark times leading to some kind of redemption. At best it is amateurish, gloomy, unattractive. Failed remnants of it litter the room around him as he smokes and contemplates.

Lying on the grimy floor near his bed are the many religious books he has used for his inspiration. Nearest to him is a battered Bible, its pages dog-eared and torn, its cover showing evidence of much use and misuse. For too long now, its last book, Revelation, has been the principal inspiration for his tired attempts at art. Canvases: rejected by all. Street art: scrubbed clean and he, its perpetrator, reviled and prosecuted.

But today, his new inspiration galvanizes his mind like no other.

Rising (the act of getting up, for John, only consists of changing from horizontal to vertical), he picks up the book, and, retreating to a battered, paint-daubed armchair, reads, from his Bible newly seen, the first verses of the first Chapter of the first book, Genesis:

'In the beginning God created the heaven and the earth. And the earth was without form, and void; and darkness was upon the face of the deep. And the Spirit of God moved upon the face of the waters.'

Here is his new beginning. More powerful than any apocalypse, he will paint Creation from its beginning. Not God's Creation but a new one. Vivid, immensely powerful images now fill his mind: colour, light, power, people astounded, amazed by his version of Creation. With this new artwork he will live forever, be famous, be remembered. Those who spurned his former work will be blinded by the new light which will flow from his, HIS personal Creation.

He reads on, to the end of the chapter, savouring the words, feeling their meaning in his soul. God had taken seven days to create the world. He is not God. It might take a little longer. But he believes, more fervently with each passing moment, that now he CAN change the world. Here is his inspiration, his new beginning. His new work will create a new world, one which will so impress all who see it and hear about it, that he will be seen, at last as the great Creator in his own right. It even tells him the words:
'In the beginning God created the heaven and the earth. And the earth was without form, and void; and darkness was upon the face of the deep. And the Spirit of God moved upon the face of the waters.'

He would go once again into the old world, and, like God, create his new artwork world from nothing. With this, his life at last would become meaningful.

However, despite the tumult of ideas rampaging through his mind, he is also able to start thinking of the practical issues involved. In executing his street art previously, he has learned a lot about avoidance from the attention of authority figures. To get everything ready, discreetly: that might take a lot longer than seven days.

He has to think first, where his great artwork will be created. His work will need to be large, grand in scale and composition. It will need to be seen and appreciated immediately by many people, so news of its brilliance will spread and cannot not be suppressed.

However, he is already well aware of how quickly the police and other authority figures will act once he starts work. They will try to stop him, try to keep the old world order, especially when they begin to appreciate the glory of the new. He will have to work quickly, use new methods and materials to execute his work as quickly as possible, like God's earlier creation. This is the first day of creation, the void, the nothingness, and he is ready to create. How this will develop, taking shape and form from nothing, focuses his fevered mind into an all-consuming purpose of its own.

From the inspiration, he starts to think in practical steps. He knows his existing materials well: type, colour, brushes, sprays – but he needs more, newer materials to him, which he has never used before: special, fast. He mind, confused, turbulent, irrational, is still capable of constructive thought when required. He remembers, long after the last of his fellow tenants left, the visit from Special Branch. They had been interested in more than one of the previous occupants, and where they might now be found. John knew nothing, said nothing, and the officials had left. However, some were artists, and many had left various items and trash behind. He's sure that, in amongst those items in the other rooms, there are materials he can use.

Over the next few weeks, he checks out the items stored, with fruitful results. As he builds up his stock of materials for the Great Day, his mind sees colours, light, brought about by his artistic use of his findings. With only a few more, careful purchases, he gradually completes the stockpile of all the things he needs. He shops carefully. He knows the suppliers of bulk paints warn the authorities when he's at work on something new.

The knowledge of how to use some of the materials he's found is alien to him: however, the internet, courtesy of his local library, furnishes that knowledge. He learns, and applies that learning with the thoroughness borne of fanaticism.

Finally, he has everything: a perfect, balanced assembly of all the materials he needs for his forthcoming artwork: his portrayal of Creation, something to remember for all time: a statement, HIS statement of real meaning in a meaningless void.

Now all he needs is an arena: a visual stage on which to present his work, project his Creation into reality. After much consideration, he settles on St. Pancras Station. An ideal place: he'll be carrying a lot of materials, and a heavily laden traveller will not look out of place here. In the rush hour, the concourse at the station will be crowded with people, so his viewing audience will be guaranteed. The huge end wall is not flat, and is punctuated with windows and doorways, but his artwork will use these features to best advantage, he is sure. And, unlike an advertised public event or tourist attraction, there won't be more than the usual attention from police and other more clandestine authorities, so he should not be detected until his artwork is well on the way to full execution.

He has selected the last Friday in June, at five o'clock. From the Friday before, he counts down the seven meaningful days – the mental pressure to achieve on the right day increases, but things are well in hand. He checks and repacks his materials daily. His packs – a large backpack and two holdalls – are arranged so that the materials can be deployed in the right order and colour. He's sure he'll have enough time.

Finally, the first day of Creation. He is ready, the new world awaits. He wakes early. Aware that his usual appearance is likely to generate unwelcome attention, he first bathes and shaves before dressing in the new clothes he has bought for the occasion: a blue shirt, and new jeans. Finally, he checks the packing of all his materials once again with great care. The sound of a car horn indicates the arrival of the taxi he has pre-ordered. Loading the bags, he sets off to his rendezvous with his future.

He has timed his arrival well. As he leaves the taxi, it's just coming up to five. As the taxi drives away, he makes the necessary adjustments to his luggage and sets off, rucksack on his back, and a holdall in each hand. The loads are heavy but he knows he doesn't have far to go. The huge forecourt is a morass of scurrying people, all striving to get the earliest trains home. Buffeted in the crowd, he makes his way to his appointed location, just under the huge concourse clock. Finally, he is in the right place, at exactly the right time to start. He sets down and readies the holdalls, one either side of him.

'In the beginning God created the heaven and the earth. And the earth was without form, and void; and darkness was upon the face of the deep. And the Spirit of God moved upon the face of the waters.'

As he looks around him, he catches the eye of one of the many policemen in the crowd. Peering forward, the policeman seems to recognise him, or is otherwise suspicious. He clutches for his radio, and moves quickly towards John. Others appear among the crowd, moving quickly, spreading out towards him. Inhibited by the thronging crowd, they are unable to close with him quickly. They know him, know his intentions to deface, the damage he can cause. But this time he's got the materials right, the artwork right, and the new world, his new Creation will be seen by all.

As the first policeman reaches him, ready to throw him to the ground, his hand, deep in his pocket, closes on the switch, closes the electrical contacts. He senses the moment as the electric impulse surges down the cables into his rucksack, into the two holdalls, into the bags packed tightly round his body, and activates the plastic explosive charges to commence their decorative, Creative artwork with nails, steel shrapnel, ball bearings and paints of every colour.

'And God said, Let there be light: and there was light.'

*****

MAYBE BABY

Gemma Gilbert

MAYBE BABY

I BARELY SURVIVED the last time I tried to leave. I had two broken ribs and the blows to my abdomen ensured that the baby I didn't know I was carrying didn't stand a chance. Jack behaved better for a while after that but it was too late for me, I didn't love him anymore. How could I love the man who killed my baby. That would make me the monster.

It was almost a day like any other, 'I'm leaving you. You can't stop me this time'. It was so easy in front of the bathroom mirror, I willed myself to be brave but Jack had a way of not hearing anything that he didn't want to. I've got pretty good at hiding how I feel. It's safer that way.

'Baby, why are you hiding up here, you aren't still mad at me are you? You know I didn't mean it.'
Jack always said that, I've lost count of the amount of times I've heard it. I should have shares in concealer with the amount I get through. I should have left a long time ago.

I tried really hard to keep my voice steady. Any trembling, anything other than normal would make Jack mad.

'I know you're sorry; it was my fault anyway. I shouldn't have made you mad.'

I carry on with my makeup. This one is going to take a lot to cover up; the bruise was a particularly bad one. An almost beautiful shade of purple covers my eye and a good part of the right side of my face.

Jack put his hands around my waist and kissed the back of my neck. Any movement and he'd flip; his mood could go either way. I was always on guard.

'I really prefer your hair down Kate.' Jack was looking at me, waiting. It might have sounded like a statement but really it was a command, an instruction.

Quickly I unpinned my chignon. 'Is that better Jack? I'm sorry, sometimes I forget.'

'Better.' Luckily he seems appeased. His whistling echoes behind him as he walks out. My whole body relaxes as the front door slams behind him.

I look at the photograph on my bedside table taken about six months after we met:

I remember how charming he was, so handsome. It was two years before I got to feel the action behind his edge; in the beginning he had seemed so full of mystery.

I didn't know whether to be happy or sad as the test in the supermarket toilet confirmed what I already suspected. I am pregnant. I am afraid.

I could cry except for the fear of ruining my makeup. Time has run out. I have to get away. I have to save this baby. Jack must never know.

I have everything planned; it's taken ten very long days. I've done everything I can to keep Jack happy and thankfully he's been too preoccupied to bother too much with me when I'm behaving carefully.

I should have left a long time ago: I knew I would have to leave or I would end up dead. I didn't care about that prospect for a very long time, death would be better than this life. I have a reason to get strong now and stay strong this time; it's not just about me. Closing the door on that house of horrors I think I feel hope; such an alien emotion.

I sit on the coach at Victoria Station. Always checking that Jack hasn't found out my plan or hasn't had me followed like he sometimes does. I sigh a deep sigh, knowing that I'll always be looking over my shoulder. I used to love the hustle and bustle of London, but now I just feel afraid. There are so many people and I can't focus on them all to see if Jack is coming for me.

With each passing mile I can feel myself relaxing a little more. Gone now are the busy streets and tall buildings. I've been on five coaches so far, an added extra precaution to make it more difficult for Jack to find me. I'm almost there now, just a small seaside town. The houses are quaint and streets are wider. I've rented a small cottage outside the town with a view of the sea. I always wanted to live by the sea. It makes me feel happy and calm, both things I could do with a lot more of in my life. I can't believe I've escaped. Surely it's not that easy.

I haven't seen a soul except for the grocery delivery man; thank goodness for that. Luckily I've been tucking money away for a rainy day most of my life so I can keep myself and the baby without worrying for a while. Even in the beginning something stopped me from telling Jack about my savings. Now it's my saving grace.

A rare trip into town. I'm five months pregnant now. Standing in front of the one baby shop. I somehow slipped.

'Whoa, I've got you.'

As a man caught me, every part of me tensed. But it wasn't Jack.

'Thank you, I'm not sure what happened.'

'It's ok, I'm glad I was able to help. Are you waiting for your boyfriend, can I take you somewhere? You look a bit on the pale side to me'.

Perhaps it was because I actually couldn't remember the last time I had spoken to a real person but I found myself replying before I could stop myself. 'Oh there's no boyfriend. It's just me and my munchkin. I'll be fine, I just need some water.'

'It must be my lucky day, there's a café just a few shops down that has the best cream tea in town and I'm pretty sure they even have water'.

I looked at the man picking up the bag I had dropped. He must have been six foot tall. He had sandy blond hair and he smiled the most amazing smile. I didn't say anything as he tilted his head towards the café in a gently questioning way.

'Please let me buy you a tea or water, whatever you prefer. I feel terrible.'

The café smelt fantastic and for the first time in what seemed like forever I actually didn't feel like throwing up at just the smell of food.

'I'm Harry by the way.'

'Kate. I'm fine really.'

'You do look much better but you'd really be doing me favour sharing a cream tea. I hate eating alone,' He said sheepishly

Adorable, I thought, as he brushed a hand through his wavy blonde hair. It had been so long since anyone showed me any kindness that I just didn't have the strength to argue. Harry shared so many funny stories about his work and moving to the town, I couldn't help but relax, and laugh. Laughter was just the therapy I needed. I couldn't remember when I last felt like this.

'Oh my goodness I haven't laughed this much in, I don't know how long.'

'Well perhaps I can do something about that.'

Harry was so easy to talk to. We touched on the weather, the town, anything easy and light hearted. Harry talked about his job and how he moved to the town a few years ago. He loved it and I was beginning to feel the same way.

It happened so slowly. It didn't scare me. Chance meetings, kind words and a few small but thoughtful gifts, not just for me but for the baby too. After months without any threat from Jack I started to feel safe. I didn't see it coming, falling head over heels in love with Harry after almost four months. It made me realise that I'd never been in love before. It felt natural to call Harry when my labour started. Who else could I call?

Harry burst through the door. 'I'm here, what can I do, what do you need?'

He was so flustered I couldn't help but laugh, or would have if a raging contraction hadn't stopped me. Just breathe I kept telling myself. I couldn't even speak through the contractions anymore.

'How long have they been like this.' asked Harry as he rubbed my lower back. I didn't have time to reply as another contraction ripped through me.

'I don't think I can do this, I think maybe it was a mistake'

Harry chuckled. 'I think maybe it's a bit late to start thinking that, besides you'll be a great mum. Right now it's time to go.'

The drive to the maternity unit seems to take forever, the pains were worse each time but even through this I noticed the printed route planner to the hospital.

Harry was always thoughtful and always prepared.
As I got out of the car and my waters broke, really broke. 'I'm so sorry Harry.' I was mortified and could feel my cheeks burning with embarrassment.

'Kate, I'm in love with you, don't you know that. You and the baby.'
My daughter was born several hours later with Harry by my side.
'What's her name? She's so beautiful.'
'Hope, her name is Hope.'

'I can't believe Hope is six weeks old already, I can't thank you enough for all your help Harry.'

'I love helping, she's such a little darling, and besides I get to spend time with my two favourite girls.'

Harry has been popping in every day, helping with Hope, letting me sleep. At first I would watch him, secretly, to make sure Hope was OK. He is such a lovely man, now I actually sleep. I need it.

My beautiful baby girl is my world, the only good thing to come out of knowing Jack. I keep expecting Harry to ask about Hope's dad but he hasn't so far. I wouldn't be able to tell him the truth, keeping Hope safe has to come first.

'Have you thought about it yet?' Harry asks as he tickles Hope's tiny feet. 'I know it's all happened quickly but it just feels right to me. You two are my family.'

'It's so soon to move in together.'

'I know, but I'm here everyday anyway. It makes sense but more than that it'd make me the happiest man alive.'

Having Harry in my life is like a fairy tale, so despite my reservations I say, 'Lets give it a shot. When do you want to move in?

'As soon as I can get everything packed and moved.'

I can't help but smile, happier than I ever thought possible.

It's a picture of domesticity. I take a moment to admire Harry and smile at the way he runs his hand through his blonde hair when he's concentrating. Hope is sound asleep in her crib and there are boxes littered everywhere. 'I'll help some more when I get back; I just have to run out for nappies, I'm almost out.'

'OK Kate, I'll crack on, why don't you pick up a Chinese on the way back. My treat?'

'You're reading my mind.' I grabbed Hope's coat and blanket.

'It's OK, why don't you leave Hope here, she's sound asleep'.

'Are you sure?' I've never left Hope with him before, never left her at all. My palms are sweaty. I glance into her crib; she is softly snoring. I love to watch her sleep. 'I'll be ten, maybe fifteen minutes at the most.' I kiss his cheek and Harry presses some money into my hand. I shut the door quickly before I change my mind.

I get half way into town before I have to pull over. I can't breathe. Something doesn't feel right. I can't shake the feeling. I take the water out of my bag that I always have. One moment longer and I'm back in the car and heading back home feeling slightly crazy. We can all pop into town together later.

I breathe a sigh of relief as I see Harry's car, he's been my rock.'

I'm already apologising as I open the door. 'I'm back already, I'm sorry, I just thought we could all go to town together later'. I feel silly for worrying even when I'm greeted by an empty room.

'Harry?' I head straight for the crib but Hope isn't there. 'Harry? Hope?' I shout and bound up the stairs smiling, looking for them.

My head hurts and I am trying not to panic. They aren't in the house. 'They must have gone for a walk. Keep calm Kate.' It's not usually a good sign when I'm talking to myself. 'Harry?' I shout outside in case they are in the garden, perhaps they've headed towards the beach. It's all I can think of.

They aren't at the beach or the park, time seems to have stopped and I'm trying desperately not to panic. All I can do is head back to the house and pray they are there waiting for me.

Eight excruciating hours later.

'Kate, you need to calm down so we can go through all of this. You say your boyfriend and daughter are missing?' Police officer Davies hands me a cup of tea; of course tea solves everything. 'We've been through this, I went out, for no more than ten minutes, and when I got back my boyfriend Harry, Harry White, and my daughter, Hope, were missing. I can't find them anywhere. Harry's car is still at my house so something must have happened to them'.
'You've tried calling him?'
My blood is really starting to boil at these stupid questions. 'Of course I have, it says the phone is switched off. Harry never switches it off.'
'Is your pram at home?'
'My pram? I've no idea, what's that got to do with anything?'
'Harry has probably taken your daughter for a walk and just lost track of time, is there someone he could have taken Hope to visit?'
To my horror I realise that I have no idea who Harry would even think of visiting. 'I, I don't know, he doesn't have many friends. He only has us.'
'I'm sure they'll turn up. We could do with some photos of them both and Harry's address and we'll start making enquiries.'
'Officer Harper will take you home now to get them.'
I feel utterly stupid, sitting in the back of a police car as I realise I have no idea what Harry's old address is. He always came to my house or we would meet at our café. Harry often complained about his room mate and so we never went to his place. 'I've got all of Harry's things in my house, our house, he's moving in today.' I'm not sure if I'm saying it to Officer Harper or myself.
Officer Harper doesn't say much. She turns on the kettle but I can see she is taking everything in. Automatically I head towards the fridge for the milk but stop dead in my tracks.
'Something wrong?'
I want to shout, yes something is wrong; my new-born daughter and boyfriend are missing. Instead I say 'My photographs are missing, I had loads on the fridge of Hope, of Harry and they are all gone.'
'Maybe your boyfriend took them off?'
'Maybe.' I hand her the milk anyway.
'Is anything else missing?' Harper asks.

'I don't know.' I start walking around the room. 'My laptop's missing, oh my god, all my photos of Hope are on there.' I can't catch my breath. I run upstairs. I open the drawer of my bedside table. Pressed against the inside of the drawer front is a picture of Hope that I haven't had a chance to frame yet. She is in her bouncy chair in her soft pink dungarees with little flowers on.

Back downstairs, I hand what appears to be the only photo I have of my daughter to Officer Harper. Hope is wearing these dungarees today. I feel like I am losing my mind, at least the photo proves Hope is real.

'I'll make sure you get this back.' Harper takes a photo of the photo and I assume sends it through to the police station. It's a start.

Every second feels like an hour. Officer Harper's presence alternately gives me comfort and irritation. I feel a chill of fear when she asks 'Is there anyone you can think of that would have reason to hurt Harry, or Hope?' It's at that moment that I know.

'Kate, Kate. Sit here before you fall down, you look like you've seen a ghost'. She pushes me towards a chair. I know she's talking to me but it takes a moment to be able to speak. 'Jack. Jack must have them'.

'Jack?, Jack who? Why would he want to hurt them?.'

'Jack Blanchard, he's Hope's father. I ran when I found out I was pregnant. I never told him. I've been hiding ever since, to keep us safe. He'll kill Harry. Harry is no match for him. I've no idea what he'll do with my baby. You have to save them.'

The minutes, hours and days merged together. There was no sign of Hope, Harry or of Jack. Jack had been seen with a baby, he had Hope. Then nothing. He hadn't returned to his house. He just disappeared. I tried not to let myself think of where Harry was; he had to be alive. I had to believe that. I tried to figure out how Jack had found us. Who betrayed us. I knew he would keep Hope hidden to punish me for leaving. What had I done . . .

Three days. For three days I haven't seen my daughter. I've heard nothing about Harry but it looks as though Jack has Hope. He hasn't been home for three days and there are apparently Police Officers waiting there in case he returns.

Officer Harper has been here every day and I can't help but feel like her time would be better spent out looking for them.

Harper goes outside and I retrieve my notebook from under the sofa cushion. I have a list of all the places I could think of where Jack might hide out. I've told the police everything anyway but nothing seems to have happened. I will have to give Officer Harper the slip. I can't just sit here waiting; I have to find Hope.

I take the car and head back to the hellhole I thought I had escaped from. Sitting outside Jack's house. I feel sick, frozen and unable to move. I can't see anyone watching the house but I suppose that's the point.

The car door opens and a hand reaches across to block my scream. 'Kate, it's OK, it's Officer Harper. I figured you would head here, a pretty reckless move on your own.' She removes her hand and I gulp breath after breath for a moment, until I feel almost calm.

'Officer Harper, I didn't recognise you for a moment. You gave me such a fright.'

She's was in her own clothes now, casually dressed. I hadn't even noticed her approach the car.

'You can call me Beth if you like, there is another police car just over there'. She points to the dark Blue sedan hidden from direct view from the house by a white van. I sigh with relief that at least they are watching.

'Get down, Kate, I think someone is coming.' We hunch down in the car as a man saunters past the blue sedan towards the house.

I don't know I'm crying until Beth touches my arm. 'Oh my god, that's Harry'. With my laptop taken and my fridge cleared, I had no photographs of Harry to give to the police. They were working to an artist's interpretation of my descriptions.
Beth stops me from opening the door and running to Harry.

'We have to stay hidden, Kate, he might lead us to Hope.'

'Why does he have black hair? Where is Hope? Is Jack threatening him? Harry must be trying to keep Hope safe, he wouldn't hurt her.'

'Just stay calm, Kate, I promise that we will get to the bottom of this, we will find Hope.'

Harry is only in Jack's house for a couple of minutes. He collects a heavy looking backpack and, oblivious to my presence and the other Police Officers, he saunters past the car on the opposite side of the street, so close I can hear him whistling.

We sit, waiting. The undercover police followed Harry. Beth was told to stay put and to keep me out of sight. I want to run to Harry to feel safe in his arms and ask where my daughter is. He must have a plan to escape with her. Perhaps that's why his hair is black.

The cottage is quiet and empty when we get back. Somehow Harry has disappeared so all is lost again. I don't know what makes me open Harry's box on the table, I want answers and it's as good a place as any to start.

I open the box carefully expecting to find mementos or something personal of Harry's. I peer into the box. I can see nothing through the bubble wrap so I pull at it, imagining some delicate family heirloom or favourite mug for tea. The bubble wrap begins to spill on the floor.

I leave that box and head for another and then the next. There is nothing. Tissue paper and bubble wrap don't count. Beth has stepped onto the porch outside. When she returns she finds me sitting on the front room floor surrounded by empty boxes. Nothing makes sense.

Beth has been called back to the police station, she didn't say why, only that her Sergeant wants to see us both. It's dark by the time we arrive I feel a deep sense of fear.

Inside, I can see and hear Harry from behind some kind of glass looking into an interview room. He doesn't know I'm watching. I confirm it is definitely Harry. Except it isn't. Apparently, his name is Joe.

Joe Arnold to be exact. I think my heart stops in that moment; listening to him explain how Jack had paid him to find me and later to befriend me, all with the intention of taking my baby. It explains the empty boxes.

'Oh my god, what's he done with Hope, that bastard.' Hot, angry tears run down my face. 'How could I have been so stupid.'

The Officer that had been questioning Harry/Joe, slipped silently into the room. He spoke with Beth quietly in the corner. I wasn't listening. I was watching the man that I thought had loved me.

'Kate, Joe is going to help us. He says he knows where Hope is.'

'Why? Why would he help me now?'

'We've offered him a deal. You see, we've been looking for this man in connection with a number of other offences. He helps now and gets a lighter sentence.'

I want to cry. Actually I want to hit Joe repeatedly with a baseball bat. I have to stay calm. I want my daughter back.

The Police are recording everything Joe says and hears. He's been left close to Jack's house. He walks, still whistling, for about 5 minutes to the house where he claims Hope is.

I imagined the scene. Hope, left in the corner of a dingy room with Jack and his friends drinking. Probably playing poker or something. He probably loves the thrill of hiding out while making plans for my fate. Joe has been clear on that. Jack wants me to suffer. Not dead, but to keep the one thing I need from me, to spend a lifetime turning my daughter against me.

I don't listen to their conversations; I'm listening only for Hope. I can hear her crying, then Jack's booming voice.

'Where have you been? Shut her up will you. That thing is driving me crazy'.

Joe must have picked her up. 'She's probably hungry, I'll make her a bottle.'

'Come on sweetheart.'

How little Jack cares for his daughter. Joe, for once is true to his word. He walks through the kitchen, apparently at the back of the house and into the garden. Armed Police usher him and Hope into the nearby van where I was waiting. As Hope is placed in my arms the police swarm the house arresting everyone inside. My beautiful daughter looks at me with wild eyes. Her face stained with tears and her baby pink dungarees covered in dirt. I don't care and neither does she. Hope knows she is safe once again, with me.

We were speeding away from the house when we heard the sound of gunfire. I would later learn that Jack had fired the first shots. He fired without care or mercy, killing his both his friends and a Police Officer. It was Officer Beth Harper who saved my life that day. She shot Jack dead. Never again would we have to run and hide. Thanks to her I had hope, hope for the future and the best kind of hope, my daughter.

*****

THE CAT MYSTERY

Anjali Wierny

THE CAT MYSTERY

'Y OU DID WHAT?' said Graham.

'What's the problem?' Joan said, as she swapped the receiver to her left hand so she could crack open a can of cider with her right.

'You stole their mail, that's the problem!'

'They stole Margot's… *my* cat.'

Silence.

'Is this about Margot?' he asked.

'No!'

She knocked back a gulp of cider.

'Okay.' He hesitated. 'It's just…' He sighed, deeply. 'Look, Steve's…He's probably been… I mean, found… Look, cats are notorious for not giving a shit. I'm sure he's fine and that he left of his own free will.'

She took a swig from her can. Hadn't he heard the bit about the tin? Through the broken gap in the fence there had been, amongst the clumps of hard mud, stones, dead grass and bricks, an empty cat food tin. About a fortnight old: a bit of rust, but not an abundance of rust, she'd noted. It was what TV cops would call 'incriminating evidence': the ex-neighbours, ex by two weeks-ish, hadn't had a cat. At least not then. Not until they'd moved and taken Steve with them. And Joan was supposed to be taking care of him!

Was Graham even listening?

'I still can't believe Margot named her cat Steve, ' Graham said. 'I think it was after Steve from my work. She always said it was after Steve Buscemi, but she didn't even *like* Steve Buscemi.'

He laughed, not even noticing that she hadn't concluded her story. She laughed back anyway, grateful he was even talking to her. If he *knew* what she'd done, then he wouldn't be. *She* didn't even want to talk to her.

But at least she had a chance to save Margot's cat. Joan had realized this morning that the house next door had a low letterbox, which meant it was possible to reach the ex-neighbours un-forwarded letters, which meant she could find out their surnames, which meant she could look up their new address. Excellent detective work. Margot would've appreciated it; Graham just thought she was crazy.

'Wait a sec,' said Graham. 'So, you left the house?'

'What?' said Joan. She looked down at her bobbly grey jumper and the *Star Wars* pyjamas, with a pattern of droids. They seemed to cling to her and every bit that didn't wafted up the smell of three-days of sweat. He hadn't been spying on her, had he? But no, he couldn't have been. If he had, he'd know she still hadn't left the house since…

'No, erm… I got my little brother to do it.'

Graham tutted.

It was definitely best not to tell Graham the rest of her plan.

'Right, that's it. I'm getting you out the house. Come to The Rock, later.'

She imagined going out tonight: usual seats, usual crowd minus one. Clare and Shaz would be high-speed chatting, and Joan waiting for her brain to switch to conversation-autopilot.

Without Margot there, it wouldn't happen.

The windowless walls and their band posters would close in on her. She'd try to think what to say, and she'd think and think until there weren't any ideas left to discard, just a mind filled with the silence between her and whoever.

She'd realize the stupidity of this, and try to relax.

A bit of small talk, a few inane comments…

They'd be too nice to dump her. Worse – they'd let her tag along. She'd smile and nod, thinking that they liked her –

'Nah, I'm sick of The Rock.'

'How, you haven't been for months! Come on, we haven't got pissed for ages.'

'Speak for yourself,' she said. 'Asda delivers.'

'Clare and Shaz really miss ya.'

Yeah, right.

That's why they'd bothered to ring her in the last three months.

'Hey,' she said, changing the subject. 'I saw my dad yesterday and you know what he told me?'

'What?'

'Apparently, once, this German soap star went insane and thought he was the character he played on the show. He started acting like him in real life, and went round signing cheques as Hans Schwarzer, or whatever. That's well weird, innit?'

'Yeah, weird,' said Graham.

And Joan realized she wasn't going to psychoanalyse anyone ever again. Not. Ever. Margot, the only person in the world who really got her, was dead, and Graham's silence filled her with dread.

That was overdramatic. People in films and books were 'filled with dread' or 'wracked with grief'. Huge feelings; overwhelming. Her own watered-down, numbed emotions were nothing compared to the impressions she had of other people's problems.

Graham broke the silence with a laugh. 'I was thinking earlier, about that time we went to Gullies and you got so leathered you fell asleep on the floor –'

'Which time?'

'– and I had to take you home. Your parents were away, so we were all staying over? Margot wouldn't come home yet, cos she was dancing with that guy – Greasy Mullet. Before I went out with her, I mean.'

'Can't remember,' said Joan.

'When Margot slept in the front yard, cos we was both well out of it and couldn't hear her knocking.'

'Oh yeah, I know,' said Joan, heart sinking.

'And the neighbours rung the police cos…'

He stopped, realizing his mistake.

But it was like running downhill – once you've started, you can't stop. Joan finished the anecdote for him: 'Cos they thought she was a dead body.'

For a moment, there was just the sound of their breathing, hoarse and hollow in the phone mics.

Then, finally, Joan continued: 'And she woke up in the garden with the police standing over her…'

'And that one goes into his walkie-talkie…'

They finished in unison with an impression of radio static:

'– *kkkkhhh!* She's alive!'

He forced a laugh. Joan's eyes welled up.

They said their goodbyes and hung up, leaving Joan with an uncomfortable, post failed-conversation feeling. Things hadn't been rounded off properly; didn't seem right. She'd annoyed him with her obsession over Margot's missing cat, bored him with an irrelevant German anecdote and pathetically refused to go to The Rock.

Maybe she *should* go to The Rock. She had to face them all some time. She imagined standing in the beer garden, hovering near Graham as he sat on the fire escape stairs, one knee pulled up to rest his smoking arm on. Her mind would be filled with telling him what she'd *done*, hysterically screaming it, as if the volume would help it to push out of her head and into her mouth. But on the outside, her face would be calm; bland. Sip, sip, sip at a glass of gin, lime and soda. A long, awkward silence.

Eventually, Graham would say he needed the loo and when he came out, he'd go speak to someone else.

There's no way she could get the words out. She knew that. That's why she was planning on writing it. In the back of the *Star Wars* page-a-day diary that she'd gotten Margot for Christmas. The diary, she was sure, would tell Graham everything he needed to know about what Margot had been up to – the affair; everything.

Of course, she hadn't dared to read it, herself yet. Didn't know if she should. She wanted it to invoke a sense of Margot, but what if…?

What if she read something she didn't like. Something Margot could never take back, or explain. Something about Joan.

She ran a finger across the cover of the diary that had only ever got three weeks into January. The rest of the year's pages would have been filled too, if it weren't for her. Who knows with what. Drunken nights out, fall outs, festivals, gigs: life. No one would ever know, now. Now, the only new thing that would ever be written in it was her confession, to Graham, neatly printed on January 23rd, the date that Margot died.

She'd hand it to him. He'd read it and…

Then what? She'd imagined everything – his face falling. Shouting, crying, him punching her in the face.

But, worst of all, that he'd say nothing. He'd be destroyed. His expression of grief, horror, anger, would flash and then it would steel to the stoic realization that he hated Joan and never wanted to speak to her again. He'd just shut his dropped jaw, give her one last look, half hurt, half murder, purse his lips and walk away.

Joan's chest was tight just thinking about it. She downed the rest of the can, tipping her head back to let the last, sweet drop, fall onto her tongue. She sniffed short, sharp breaths that jerked back out of her like her lungs didn't know what to do with the air. No way she was going to The Rock, no way. She was busy anyway. Far too busy.

She had a cat to find.

The problem with leaving the house though, is that your interference with the world outside can cause a chain reaction that ultimately leads to someone's death. She was good at that, after all.

That morning, though, she'd had an epiphany.

Not leaving the house, could be just as tragic. What if her walking across a zebra crossing held a car up by two minutes, which meant that said car didn't run over a person further down the road? Joan could be killing *or* saving people with her every action – there was no way of knowing.

It made it a little easier, putting her hand on the front door handle and pulling it open to face the outside.

She'd imagined a moment where, like a prisoner revelling in freedom, she'd tip her face up to the cold, bright sunlight of April, romanticize the beautiful sight of the sky and the clouds and hear the sound of the wind and the song of the birds as clearly as if it was her first day on Earth.

Instead, she just stepped out and walked three steps down the short grey square of weed-ridden cement slabs, grasped the peeling paint on cold metal of the garden gate and dodged dog dirt as she stepped out onto the terrace street path. It was weirdly normal; just like it would've been on any day of her life *before*.

At the bus stop, the woman without the broken leg asked, 'What have you done to your leg?'

'Don't I know you?' Plaster Cast asked.

'Doris.'

'Doris Cox?'

'No, Smith. Used to be Marley.'

'The Grammar School?'

'No, I didn't move here till the '70s.'

'Oh,' she paused. 'Small world, isn't it?'

Joan listened to their chitchat as she watched Karis and Rachel's curtains twitch, across the street.

At least, Joan thought that they twitched. From this distance, it was difficult to tell if they were moving, or if something were reflecting, or if they were staying still and nothing was reflecting. What did she expect to see, standing opposite the house? The wankers could be skinning Steve, tarring and feathering him in the FRONT ROOM and she wouldn't be able to hear it, let alone see it, let alone stop it.

Joan kind of wished she smoked. She and Margot hated smoking. Still, she could see herself standing on the path, a moody, rebellious sort who the old ladies daren't look at, bringing a cigarette to her lips, inhaling and blowing with a scowl on her face. No non-smoker could look as frustrated as she felt.

Film characters didn't have these problems. The boring bits were edited out and the criminals always, *always* conducted their illegal business in view of an unobstructed window. None of that here. Just curtains. *Closed* curtains, even though it was daytime. The guy in *Rear Window* got a heat-wave; Joan got a cold British spring and soggy socks.

Not-Doris finally revealed, 'It was a motorbike.'

'Oooh dears,' from Doris.

'Hit me coming out the corner shop. Only a young lad. He was so scared, bless him, I told him to get himself off.'

Bless him? BLESS HIM? The little bastard ought to look where he was going. Her eyes welled up, the minutes went by, the house was a house was a house. How were you supposed to tell, from the outside of someone's house, if a person had an illegally-obtained cat inside? Short of Steve literally sauntering out of a cat flap – of which there wasn't one – it was futile.

Joan fingered the diary in her handbag.

For the millionth time, she wondered, What did it say?

The month of January had faded in her own mind. Even the 23rd, sharper as it was, had had its edges blurred by time. The diary, however, was perpetually present. It knew how Margot had spent her last twenty-two days. It knew if Margot had loved Joan as much as Joan had loved Margot. Whether she'd ever secretly bitched about her, after being nice to her face.

Oh, Joan had bitched about Margot, of course. But it was one thing bitching about your best friend and it was another thing them bitching about you. On New Year's Day, for example, the pair of them had woken up in Joan's bedroom, top to tail in the bed. Joan could almost taste the hangover mouth now – like she'd gargled sour bin bag juice – and feel the mascara crust grinding into her eyes as she rubbed them, yawned, stretched…

And remembered.

Oh God.

Margot had pulled, last night.

'*Margot,*' she'd croaked. '*Margot!*'

'*Rrrrngh!*' Margot had grunted, from the other side of the bed.

'*What are you going to tell Graham?*' she'd moaned. And already, her chest had ached at the thought of the betrayal. Already, just after a snog; before it even got serious. And Margot, her darling Margot, had actually said:

'*Tell him? Nothing!*'

'*What?*'

'*You won't tell him, will you?*'

And Joan had reluctantly agreed.

Joan's diary from January 1st was all bitching about Margot. All the things that she hadn't got off her chest in person until the 23rd. Maybe if she'd spoken her mind straight away, Margot might have stopped seeing him. Maybe, it could have been civil. Maybe it wouldn't have had to turn out like it did. Maybe she'd still be alive. Graham would still have his girlfriend, and Joan would still have her best friend.

The bus pulled up.

Shit. She hadn't thought of that.

'After you, dearie,' said not-Doris. 'I don't want you held up behind me.'

'Oh… erm, okay,' said Joan, shuffling towards the bus.

But then she saw Karis and Rachel were walking down the street, away from their house, hand-in-hand. That meant the house was empty.

'Gotta go,' said Joan.

Before she could stop to think, Joan crossed the road and stepped past the low, cement-deprived, weathered brick wall and through the rusty gate. She rushed to the door, whipping out her debit card, and…

Oh. What was she thinking? This wasn't a TV show or a film. The door was one of those white plastic double-glazed ones – there wasn't even a gap to jimmy a card into and she was willing to bet that even lock picking with a hairgrip wasn't anywhere near as easy as it looked on screen. Shit.

Self-conscious, suddenly, it hit her that she was trespassing, and she shot a look down the street. The ex-neighbours, Doris, not-Doris and the bus, were all long gone. She was okay for another minute.

She crouched by the door and paused to psyche herself up. It was too easy to imagine something crawling – or squelching – up through the pavement cracks and into the assailable gap between jean-hem and skin, so she didn't wait too long. She pushed open the letterbox and positioned her eye in the gap.

She grasped the door handle for balance…

And it gave way.

The door was open!

She pushed it and stepped in.

The reality of breaking and entering was nothing like she expected. Something to do with wiping her shoes on the welcome mat; the door closing quietly, the only sound the crunch of the handle as she pushed it up; putting her mobile phone on silent, as if she were going for a job interview or a doctor's appointment. The only thing that made it feel like a crime was the tension – creeping around a dark hallway didn't make her feel like a dangerous predator though; rather, endangered.

Cursing her squelching trainers, Joan made her way towards the kitchen where there might be, if not Steve himself (or herself, she had never really checked), then at least an incriminating bowl of cat food, or a litter tray. It was the standard long-thin terrace style room; worktops and cupboards down one side, sink, window and plastic bin down the other. Out on the tops, kitchen clutter and breakfast dishes – a plate with toast crumbs and margarine-splodged knives; a bowl, its spoon leaning out from the dregs of cereal-sweetened milk. Bottles of cordial, bottles of wine, unopened letters in haphazard piles with leaflets and hand-written notes.

On the floor, just lino, muddy footprint smudges, crumbs and bits of old food – a pasta twist, the corner of a sandwich crust. No sign of a cat food bowl or litter tray. She pulled her sleeves over her hands to cover her fingertips and yanked open the cupboard doors in quick succession. Bowls, plates, pans, cutlery, a sieve, baking trays, condiments, tablets, packets, jars and tins of human food like beans, spaghetti hoops, rice, quinoa, curry sauce, pasta sauce, chopped tomatoes…

No cat food.

She ruffled through the papers, not sure what she was looking for, but found it when she came across the shopping list.

No cat food.

She put the shopping list down. Frowned.

A toilet flushed in the next room, at the back. A woman stepped out, wiping her hands on her dressing gown. Looked up, started; froze.

Oh, so that's why Karis and Rachel hadn't locked the door when they left the house. She'd thought maybe it was fate.

'Who the hell are you?'

'Er. J…emma.'

The woman stepped forward.

Joan's manners kicked in instinctively; she found herself stumbling backwards out of the house and out of the yard, saying, 'Sorry. Just a misunderstanding. Thought it was my Auntie's. Maybe she lives a few doors down. Never mind, eh. Sorry to have bothered you.'

The woman stood in the doorway, arms folded, a wall of pink and white polka-dot fluff. 'Shut the gate behind you, please.'

'Okay,' said Joan, and did.

She walked away briskly without looking back.

There was no denying it, really. The ex-neighbours did *not* have Margot's cat.

Joan got ready. Or tried to. Her favourite top of recent months, homemade, looked like a school textiles project. How could she have been such a fool? Fat over her hips meant a few shorter tops no longer looked good with hipster jeans (all that cider); her long, black t-shirt, which used to look ace with ironically-worn pearls, was too figure hugging, for the same reason. In her 1950s-flared dress she felt too posh; stripes were crap again; and although her short denim skirt still looked good with the yellow Tweetie-pie t-shirt, it was starting to seem too childish.

Jeans it was. But which top? She liked her fitted white shirt, particularly with big, blue plastic beads, but after putting her make-up on she changed her mind: too job interview. Plain black t-shirt: too boyish. Any of her strappy tops: too revealing. Argh!

She poured herself a large, nerve-calming gin with Asda tropical juice and sat down.

She was going to confess. Tonight. At The Rock.

She laid a hand on Margot's diary. Slid her fingers between the pages, touching the paper; her skin on the words that she knew were there. She was desperate to read the entries that followed, but just as desperate not to.

'Not' won out. She'd leave the reading for Graham, who deserved to know what his girlfriend had been thinking; and certainly what she'd been doing, in their last three weeks together. Joan opened the diary well into the future, December, and, so there was no chance of accidentally reading an entry, worked backwards page-by-page until January 23rd. The first date that Margot had not been able to fill in. Then, she wrote:

Dear Graham,

Dear? What was she thinking, it wasn't a job application. She crossed it out:

Hi Graham,

No, wait. Hi? Hi's so casual, so chilled out, like nothing's the matter, like it's one of the notes she'd pass to Margot at the back of a classroom in Maths. Only they'd always write them in German, so no one could read them (except the German teacher). With their limited knowledge of language, the notes were pretty bizarre… *Liebe Margot, Wo ist das Kino? Deine Frau, Joan.*

Liebe Graham,

She must be hysterical.

She pulled her shirt-dress over her head and launched it at the corner. Stupid sleeves were too long. The baggy pale blue top with small pink flowers more festival-garb than party; she still hadn't gotten the gravy stain out of her yellow skirt and even if she had, nothing matched it. Her stripy blouse was only half finished: no buttons, no sleeves. She sighed with frustration, chucked it onto the floor with the rest, turned up Queen's 'Greatest Hits' and plonked back down, finished her gin and poured another.

When her head was finally swimming, she moved, in slow motion. Picked up Margot's crumpled t-shirt and jeans from the floor, removed the knickers and socks that had been slipped off with them, and put on the outer clothes instead of her own.

Margot had left them there, when she slept over, that night. That and the diary. A sleepover, they'd said, like when they were kids.

The button wouldn't stretch to the hole. She sucked in her stomach and pulled until it fit. It pressed in, a tight burn that pushed the gin up into her throat. She swallowed it, and bile, back down.

She returned to January 23rd. Wrote her confession without stopping, before she could think or analyse or worry about the phrasing. Didn't read it back. Closed the diary. Slipped it into her bag.

Sighed.

Okay. Done. But what would she do with herself between arriving at The Rock and getting drunk enough to give the note to Graham? She'd walk in, of course, relaxed, say 'hi' to people. Even people she didn't like or know.

Don't Stop Me Now
I'm having such a good time.

Maybe she'd go to the loos first, check her hair and make-up. Stay there for ten minutes to compose herself. They'd assume she was chatting to someone, not hyperventilating on the toilet seat.

When she came back out, she absolutely would not hover around Graham, hesitating and waiting for him to include her in something. She'd talk to Shaz and Clare and whoever was there. But oh God, what would she say? *This should be fun Graham rang me earlier What time is it? What are you drinking? Cold today, isn't it.* Oh my God. Oh my God. All she'd be able to think of was Margot and the confession, the note in her pocket; there'd only be enough brain power left for dull, idle chitchat.

She stood up, suddenly determined.

She had to. She absolutely had to. It was that, or hide in her bedroom forever, the sole bearer of the truth.

She pulled out her phone and rang a taxi.

They were ahead of her, in the beer garden. Bugger. She'd imagined they'd be inside at their usual table, in the dingy-but-cosy corner furthest from the bar. Not the narrow strip of cement that was barely big enough for its two wobbly garden benches, ashtray buckets and smokers' canopy. Surely it was too cold for outside?

She had two metres to compose herself.

Clare had put on weight and dyed her hair black from blonde – typically for a guy, Graham hadn't bothered to tell her these things. In her little black dress and heels, sexy and trendy, Clare made Joan feel underdressed; Shaz, with her distinctive dreads and thick, patchwork coat, made Joan feel bland.

Graham. Was. Not. There.

At least his not being there gave Joan an opener, she supposed.

She loitered by the table, watching Clare and Shaz whisper. They were so engrossed that she considered clearing her throat to get their attention.

'Joan!' It was Clare's boyfriend, Rob, pointing at her from the doorway, where he was smoking with his footy friends. 'JOAN!'

Clare and Shaz looked up.

'Oh, Joan! I didn't see you,' Clare said. 'I'm off to the bar, want a drink?'

'It's alright, I'll get one in a minute.'

'This is Shaz's sister, Dani,' said Rob, waving his pint free hand in the direction of a trendy blonde who she didn't think she knew, scrunched in next to Shaz. 'Tell her about the time you decked that chav,'

'Not that again,' Joan laughed.

'Dani, Joan, Joan, Dani,' said Shaz.

'Hi.'

'Hi,' said Joan, with a wave.

'Yeah, yeah, yeah,' said Rob. 'So, I heard this crash, and I thought some dickhead was starting a fight. But there's Joan on the floor, decking this guy in trackies –'

'I can't remember that bit.'

'– I had to tear them apart for his own safety! Hahaha.'

Shaz's sister grinned, wide-eyed, either impressed or worried. Joan was just relieved to find herself slipping easily into pub-banter autopilot, even if the topic made her sound like an arse.

'Well, the thing is,' Joan said, mock-sheepish, 'I was talking to Margot, and this guy comes over and goes, *'Are you two lesbians?'* So I was like, *'Piss off and mind your own business'*. But *then*, right, he starts pushing our heads together, trying to make us get off with each other!

'So we get into a big row, cos it's just dead lame how there's always some twat trying to make girls snog. I mean, Margot told me to drop it, but I was just smashed. So me and the chav was right in each other's faces, yelling n tha' – which was stupid, anyway – and he pushed me over –'

'You fell over cos you were so leathered, more like.'

'Yeah, well, anyway, I fell and got a massive carpet burn on my arm.'

She shrugged off her coat and displayed an elbow.

'What?' said Rob.

'Yeah, I can't see anything,' said Shaz's sister, leaning in.

'Oh, well, in the light you can see this white line up my arm.'

'Call that a scar?' said Rob, 'Look at this!'

He pulled his jean leg up and showed everyone the hairless, pink splodge above his knobbly knee.

'Did this playing footy, right, it was dead painful. Black Tom went to tackle me, and —'

'What is this, *Jaws*?' Clare said, putting their drinks on the bench and handing Rob his change.

Joan's chest fluttered.

'Yeah, almost done,' he laughed. 'Go on, Joan, tell Dani the end.'

Joan caught a snippet of Dani telling Shaz about a pair of new shoes... and they were only £25 reduced from... and she'd been looking for a pair to match her...

'Nah!' she said, and sipped her gin through the straw.

Rob downed the end of his pint and picked up the next.

'Cheers sexy,' he said, and kissed Clare on the mouth.

She pushed him off. 'Guys, will you tell him to shave! There's nothing worse than stubble rash on your chin, is there?'

'I tell you what — I'll shave my beard, if you start shaving your arm pits.'

'Rob!' she squealed. 'That's disgusting!'

'I know, that's what I've been saying. It's like going out with a German.'

She shoved him, and he laughed and wandered off to hang out with the football lot. Clare plonked herself on the bench and it tipped a bit.

She leaned in and said, with an almost conspiratorial tone, 'I know he's only joking, but sometimes he takes it too far.' For a moment, Joan thought she meant the casual xenophobia, but... 'I mean, if I had a vest top on, fine, cos everyone could see I'd shaved. I mean, he could at least take that into account couldn't he — that I'm wearing a dress with sleeves?'

'Yeah,' Joan mumbled, wondering why Clare had sat next to Shaz and her sister. There was far more space on her side.

'Bar,' Joan said, climbing out of her seat.

She grinned slightly as she went inside, revelling in the brightness of it all; the pub, the buzz. Strange how she was enjoying the walk to the bar far more than the conversation outside. She frowned as she realised she had barely said two words about anything but herself since she got here. She resolved to take more of an interest in the others when she got back.

Why was it all so bloody difficult with anyone but Margot?

'Double gin, lime and soda, please,' she said.

She took a gulp so she wouldn't spill it on the way back to the bench, then put the straw in. Clinked it against the glass, stirring in the lime.

A hand on the small of her back. Graham stepped up beside her, grinning. 'You left the house!' He sniffed. 'And you showered!'

'I…' she hesitated, just for a second, but apparently she'd hit the drunken confession sweet-spot with her home-poured gins, because next she blurted out: 'I've got something to tell you.'

She pulled the *Star Wars* diary out her bag. Shoved it into his hands.

'What's this?'

He flicked through it.

'Um, thanks?' he said, puzzled. 'I do quite like Darth Vader, I suppose.'

She leaned in to look. The pages were all blank. Nothing.

Margot hadn't even written in the diary. Joan couldn't help but laugh.

'Oh, did you write something in here…' he started, as he reached the only entry – her own, on the 23rd of January.

She snatched it before he could read it and shoved it back into her bag. Suddenly it seemed stupid to do it by letter when they were both standing right there, in front of each other, with mouths and ears.

'Look,' she said, looking at the bar, the floor, anywhere but his eyes. 'The night Margot died. We were having a sleepover. We had an argument…'

'What about?'

She was cheating on you. 'It doesn't matter, now. Thing is, it got so bad that she stormed out in her pyjamas, and that's when she…'

Hit and run. It didn't sound like real life. It brought to mind the screeching of wheels racing off, the camera avoiding the gory, bone-snapping, Margot's inner organs on the tarmac, reality.

Joan downed the last few swigs of gin. 'The last thing I said to her…'

Graham pulled her into a hug.

She gasped. His arms wrapped around her, a little too tight for comfort. Their bodies pressed together, only clothes between them. He pushed her head into his chest, so close that she could hear his heart. She supposed this was when she should sob; let it all go, but it wouldn't be genuine. She only felt numb, like emotions were a fact she could write about in a report, not an experience to be engulfed in.

She realized her arms were still hanging by her sides. She put them up, around his back, one hand flat against his shoulder blades, the other fisted around the empty gin glass.

'You absolute div,' said Graham.

And she felt it all flood out of her. Her essence flow into his, their beings joined in the warmth and shelter of solid comfort. A real hug; one that went straight to the core.

When she pulled back, she noticed that her eyes were wet.

'I'm gonna go home,' she said.

'I'll walk you to a taxi.'

'No, no, it's fine,' she said.

'Okay, if you're sure. I'll see you next week though, yeah?'

'Friday or Saturday?'

'Both, of course,' he grinned.

She forced a grin back. 'I'll let you know.'

She walked home, the paths lit by streetlights, passing cars and the occasional glow from a living room window. Everything was black. The sky, the road, the houses, shops and yards, the one or two people she passed, the snatches of conversation she caught, all muted by night.

'Yeah, I agree. With you all the way –'

' – toaster, but I never got a guarantee –'

' – pure-bred Labrador, but what's wrong with –'

'Ah, get in! Bet she's well up for –'

The air's fresh bite cleared her head a little and her mind wandered to the first time she'd met Margot, back in year seven.

They'd been sat next to each other by the maths teacher and inevitably started whispering to stave off the boredom of algebra. They decided to name their stationery. Joan's pencil was Bob, Margot's was Beatrice, and the rubber, for they only had one between them, was their son. It was rough and grey on one side, soft and white on the other. They added his name in ink: Trevor. Trevor became an obsession of theirs; they joked about his adventures in righting wrongs and how, despite his valuable contribution to school exercise book accuracy, Bob and Beatrice were disappointed that he hadn't aspired to become a sharpener.

It was the first time that anybody had ever been on Joan's wavelength. The only time she'd felt that being weird was something to share, not something to hide.

But they hadn't always agreed on everything.

Joan stopped, suddenly. Turned.

Yes, she had. She'd just passed a bin. She walked back to it, pulling out the diary and holding it in two hands. She squeezed it, like it could give her back a little bit of Margot. She held it up to her face and kissed it. Quickly, because it was a bit strange, kissing a diary in the street in the night. Especially when it had Darth Vader on the cover.

She dropped it through the gap careful not to touch the filthy edges of the bin itself. The diary and the confession clanged against the bottom. Gone.

She walked, faster, cold scratching at her face. She remembered the first gigs that they'd been to, launching into the mosh-pit, crashing and bashing, raising their arms to help stage divers fly. The first boys they'd snogged, and talking about them in the dark at girly sleepovers. Their first drink, at Clare's birthday party; half a light beer each, and trying to walk in a straight line to see if it had affected them. Dancing at Gullies, groaning through hangovers together, arguing about who should get up to make a cup of tea or go to the shop for crisps and orange juice.

She reached her garden gate. Her hand rested on the metal, and she realized that, for the first time in months, she was smiling, not even on purpose, not even to make somebody think she was okay. But because maybe, just maybe, she was; or she would be.

When she looked up, her smile widened. 'Steve!'

He unfurled from where he sat on the doorstep. Slinked over, casual, like it was pure accident to happen across her and rub around her legs. She leaned down to stroke him. His fur soft, smooth, his head pushing against her hand to scratch some itch.

'I found him, Margot,' she whispered.

And Steve purred like he'd never been away.

*****

WORMHOUDT: Escape from Hell

Sharon Dormer

WORMHOUDT: Escape from Hell

JIMMY AND ALFIE HAD BEEN FRIENDS since middle school, growing up together in the small quiet town of Dodwell. There was nothing much to do or see in the sleepy town, but as Jimmy frequently remarked,

'A damn sight more 'appened there, than 'as over 'ere an' no mistake.'

Alfie had to agree. Longing for adventure, they had both joined up soon after war was declared. They were thrilled that they had been posted to 2nd Warwick's Regiment together. However, for months they had been here at the Comines Canal, near the French border with Belgium, and so far, Jerry had been as quiet as a church mouse. Both of them were slowly going out of their minds with boredom. Alfie finished the rolled cigarette that he was enjoying, and turned in the shell scrape he had dug out earlier that week, pulling the rough blanket over him.

'Go to sleep,' he advised. 'It'll most probably be yet another day trudging up and down that bloody canal tomorrow. No use whinging about it either, so just get some kip, eh?'

Jimmy grunted in agreement and snuggled down into his own shell scrape. Despite their discomfort, they both slept soundly.

They woke just before dawn, into a living hell of screeching, shouting, and deafening explosions. Jimmy leapt out from his sheltered hole. The sound of men yelling orders and the screams of the wounded invaded his ears. The wailing of the Stukas as they dived into the camp. Sirens announcing their birthing cry as they dropped their deadly bombs onto the makeshift shelters and trucks. The penetrating screams of the poor souls that were in them at the time filled the ears of everyone in the vicinity. The air was filled with acrid smoke and the stench of burning flesh as the screams of men writhing in agony contrasted the death knell of the Stuka's supernatural, high pitched screeches. Alfie thrust Jimmy's Bren gun at him. Shoving him hard he yelled in his ear over the background roar.

'Shoot the fuckers! Bring them down!'

Jimmy stared, still half asleep, not quite comprehending.

'With a Bren gun? What?'

But Alfie was kneeling up against his shell scrape, aiming his Lee-Enfield at the rear gunner who was firing from the Stuka. He in turn was shooting at the men running like ants from a disturbed nest. Jimmy shook himself awake and pointed his Bren, doing his best to bring them down. He concentrated on aiming for the front aircraft, hoping to maybe bring it down. He lost heart completely when he saw the Panzer tanks approaching the chaos.

'Oh Jesus, Alfie. Look!'

He pointed at the Panzers steadily making progress, firing their shells and adding to the death and destruction already taking place. Alfie stopped what he was doing and stared at the certain doom soon to rain down on them.

'What do we do now?'

'Fuck knows!' Jimmy yelled back. 'All we got is that Boys anti-tank rifle. That's about as much use as spitting in the wind.'

'And that's not all.' Alfie cried. He dropped the binoculars that he was looking through, as the significance of what he had seen sapped the strength he had to hold them. He looked at Jimmy, willing him to be calm. 'It's an SS Division!'

However, the worry of the Panzers approach was forgotten in an instant. Jimmy suddenly fell to the ground screaming. A ragged bloody hole appeared on his shoulder.

Alfie acted instinctively. His best friend had been shot by that damn rear gunner and was bleeding profusely. That was all he could focus on. The rest of the world, in all its hellish confusion, was a slow motion inferno. Working in double quick time, he ripped the rest of Jimmy's tunic away from the wound and reached into his pocket for the field dressing. He applied it to the torn meat of Jimmy's shoulder, whose screams almost eclipsed the roar of the raging battle. Alfie tied the dressing as firmly as he dared. He grinned into his friends face.

'Don't take on so, it'll be fine.'

He squeezed his hand reassuringly.

'Think of it this way, all the girls love a hero, and what says hero more than a wounded soldier. You'll get your dance card marked an' no mistake.'

Jimmy took in some deep, shuddering breaths. The adrenaline was kicking in and he was dealing with the pain. Luckily, the arteries hadn't been damaged. Assuming they made it out of this battle and got to the field hospital in Rosendale he would make it back in one piece. However, it took some doing to stop himself screaming when Alfie half pulled, half dragged him towards Sergeant Collins, who had settled into a fighting stance with the promise of shelter behind him, in the shape of a ramshackle broken down concrete barn.

'Alright lads?' Sergeant Collins asked. He noted Jimmy's shoulder and growled.

'Can you still fight?'

Sergeant Collins was not noted for being sympathetic, and in any case, badly injured men lay all around them. The dead were the lucky ones. At least they were out of it.

Jimmy nodded, grimly. 'I'll have a bloody good go, sir.'

The sergeant nodded. He threw a spare rifle at Alfie and barked at him.

'You! Get a bayonet on the end of that and one for yourself an' all. You just make sure you take as many as them bastards with you as you can. Get it?'

Alfie got it. Just follow orders. He was good at that. Alfie always had a lot of admiration for the Sergeant. He was the one who might order him to his death, but he was also the one who had to live with the decision afterwards. Sometimes it was hard to be the lowest of the low in the ranks, but mainly, it was easy. Just do as you're told. That's all there was to it really. Even now, in battle, with all the death, the fear and the screaming, all he had to think about was following orders. He fixed the bayonets on the end of both the rifles and winked at Jimmy. Steadfast, Jimmy winked back. He was bearing up under the stress and the pain admirably.

For the next eight and a half hours Jimmy, Alfie, Sergeant Collins and the rest of the men fought like demons. They never stopped for a break, or even to treat their wounded. They fought with every ounce of strength they had, getting through each single moment as the hours passed. They gave it everything they could. But in the end... what chance did they have?

The Germans were armed to the teeth, and The SS Leibstandarte was the Fuhrer's personal guard. The Fuhrer's Elite. The whole of the British Expeditionary Force on the other hand had for years been subject to Government cuts. All they had were rifles and bayonets. Supplies arrived infrequently because of the streams of refugees that seem to be a constant in any war.

Jimmy and Alfie could not have known, but back home there was a crisis in the war cabinet. Churchill had only been in power for sixteen days and he was under enormous pressure from Lord Halifax and his followers to surrender completely. Churchill argued against capitulation, citing the bravery and steadfastness of the British troops.

Maybe he had Alfie and Jimmy in his mind.

Jimmy was crying like a baby when the order came to surrender.

'Is it your shoulder, Jimmy?' Alfie asked, as they formed a group for their captors to inspect them.

'Is it fuck!' he replied, spitting dirt and blood from his parched mouth. 'Look around Alfie. Look what the fucking bastards have done.'

Alfie looked. All around him were the signs of German superiority. Broken buildings, trucks and broken men. Yesterday there had been almost five hundred British and French soldiers here, all striving to protect their own little part of the town of Wormhoudt. Now, he counted eighty five men.

He swallowed.

'Yeah, but we held the fuckers off for longer than they thought we would, eh?'

Jimmy nodded. He was concentrating on what was going on at the front. The officer was demanding that the SS guard give help to the wounded and water for the men. The SS guard laughed in his face. He could hear the officer.

'I demand you obey the codes of the Geneva Convention.' He shouted. 'We have men in urgent need of medical attention. My other men need water and food.'

An SS guard walked slowly to one of the wounded men lying in the mud. He turned deliberately to face the captured men. Smiling broadly, he pulled out his service revolver and shot the wounded man in the head.

Jimmy was beaten. He didn't understand why this one man's murder hit him harder than the loss of over four hundred of his comrades during the past nine hours, but it did. All of the fight had drained away from him along with the murdered man's life blood.

'Schnell! Schnell!' cried the guards.

Dejected and afraid, the ragged remains of the men were marched away from the town that they had so heroically defended. They were forced across the green and lush fields. Their mouths dry with fear and their faces drawn in pain and exhaustion, they tramped on while the spring sunshine blazed over their bowed heads.

At one point they came across the remains of a building with one of the walls still intact. The SS pushed them up against the wall, stripped them of their ID tags and laughingly humiliated them. Sergeant Collins remonstrated and tried to fight back, but he was clubbed in the head as a reward and Jimmy and Alfie had to half drag the stunned soldier along with them in an attempt to save him from further harm.

Eventually, they came to a small wooden barn just outside of Wormhoudt. Ordered into the barn, the men huddled together in confusion. Jimmy, Alfie and Sergeant Collins were pushed to the back, barely able to breathe, so tightly packed were they. With their comrades' bodies pressing against them, Jimmy's shoulder was throbbing angrily, but the pain lessened as the adrenaline once more coursed through his veins.

'What's happening, Jimmy?' whispered Alfie. 'What will they do?'

He soon got his answer. Two of the SS guards barged in and took hold of the Captain. He was a decent sort and was wounded in the leg. He struggled as they manhandled him out of the barn into the bright sunshine of the field. In full view of the men, they forced the officer to his knees and bringing their guns to readiness, promptly shot him in the head. Before anyone had a chance to react to what was happening, the enemy entered the barn once more, dragging five other men out with them. They mowed them down before they could fight back. The remaining men in the barn realised that death was upon them and there would be no escape. It came more quickly than even they expected. The SS threw five grenades into the barn and locked the doors behind them. After the explosions, there were no more screams.

When Jimmy awoke, he knew time had passed because it was dark. Painfully, he flexed his muscles, testing to see where he was broken. Miraculously, the only pain was in his shoulder.

He could see outlines of body parts all around him. Men had become ragged hunks of meat. No one had ever told him that death was like this. He could smell the blood of the murdered men and the cordite of the grenades. A hardness settled in his soul that he did not recognise. He concentrated on survival. There was no time to mourn.

'These poor sods 'ain't ever getting up again,' thought Jimmy. Only then did he remember his best friend.

'Alfie, Alfie, where are you mate?' He panicked at first when there was no answer. 'Alfie, for the love of God, where are you?'

'I'm under 'ere,' came the reply.

Jimmy staggered over the dead, pulling at the bloodied pile of mangled bodies until he reached his friend. Alfie was lying under the top half of the remains of Sergeant Collins. The last act that the sergeant had committed in this realm was to throw himself over his young charge. His sacrifice was not in vain however, as Alfie was completely unhurt.

'Is there anyone else?' asked Jimmy.

'I think there was, Jimmy. But they've gone now. I 'eard English and French voices 'bout 'alf an hour ago, but they faded into the distance. The murdering Jerry bastards left ages ago. I think they thought they'd killed the lot of us.'

Jimmy nodded grimly. They both helped each other out of the barn and stood for a while.

'Well, we can't bury 'em,' said Alfie, nodding back at the barn. He looked at Jimmy and chewed his lip.

'I reckon we should just say a prayer for the poor sods, then try to get to the beach at Dunkirk. By my reckoning it's about ten miles to the north of 'ere.'

Jimmy agreed, and so they bent their heads and prayed to a God that both of them so recently had cause to lose faith in. After this, Alfie picked a bunch of wild flowers from the field and left them just inside the door of the barn where the dead bodies lay.

They waited for darkness to fully descend before setting off for what they hoped would be their rescue on Dunkirk beach. The Stukas couldn't fly in the dark so they made good time. The only people they encountered along the way were the ever present lines of thin, ragged refugees. An old man waved them over and gave them half a loaf of bread and some warm goat's milk in a stone flagon. Despite everything, both Jimmy and Alfie wolfed down the nourishment, thanking the old man profusely in very limited French.

In the early hours they finally climbed a large sand dune. They were met with a scene from yet another of hell's domains. There were thousands of men, English, French and Dutch, in vast lines waiting to be rescued by the hundreds of small fishing vessels and cabin cruisers that lined the shore.

Out to sea, like great floating towns, waited destroyers and other larger vessels. All the while the Germans were dropping bombs and shooting at the men. And yet, there was order to the disarray: hope in the chaos.

These were men fighting to save the lives of the trapped armies. Many of the saviours sailors in small boats, were civilians. Lit by the fire of their need to help, they desperately tried to save as many souls as they could.

'Do you think we will ever make it home Jimmy?' Asked Alfie, with defeat glimmering in his eyes.

'Chin up mate.' replied his friend with a smile. 'We've made it this bloody far.'

*****

THE HOUSE BY THE TRACKS
Michael Edwards

THE HOUSE BY THE TRACKS

HELENE SAT IN THE COMPARTMENT of the train watching the World outside drift by. The rhythmic *'Clickity clack-Clickity clack'* of the metal wheels as they passed over the track joints and junction points took her back to her childhood when she would travel on this very same train and this very same line, and to a poem her mother would recite to her on the journey:

The curve of your eyes goes round my heart,
A ring of dance and sweetness,
Aureole of time, nocturnal and sure cradle,
And if I do not know everything that I have lived,
It is because your eyes do not always see me.
Leaves of day foam of dew, reeds, wind, smiles, perfumes;
Wings covering the `world of night.
Boat full of sky and sea,
Hunters of sounds and springs of colours,
Perfumes hatched from a clutch of dawns
Which still lie on the straw of the stars.
As the day depends on innocence, the World depends on your pure eyes.
And my blood flows in their glance.

Helene took out a cigarette from her pocket and lit it. She inhaled deeply into her lungs; the nicotine burned and *'fired* up' her blood. Tipping her head back she exhaled sending a cloud of smoke billowing up towards the compartment ceiling where it hung, motionless, in the still air of the room.

She re-lived the many journeys that she took with her mother; she could not recall a time when they were not together. Perhaps her mother was compensating for the absence of Helene's father who had left before Helene was born; he couldn't cope with being a parent and disappeared, never to be seen again. Helene often wondered what her father looked like; there were no photographs of him in the house and mother never talked about him. She wondered how she would react if they ever met. Every girl needs a Daddy, she thought.

The compartment door was thrown open. 'Tickets please!' A short moustachioed man stood in the doorway with his hand out almost mechanical-like.

Helene slowly took out her ticket and handed it to him in silence for she was irked at being rudely shaken from her memories. The man took the ticket and punched a hole in it with the worn metal machine that hung from his belt and returned it to her without another word. The compartment door was left ajar; Helene got up and slammed it shut.

Returning to her seat by the window she watched once more as the train puffed its way up the line. The train shuddered and slowed until it came to a stop; red light!

Helene watched as puffs of smoke drifted by from the engine a few carriages forward of her compartment. The engine huffed and puffed like a runner who had stopped to catch his breath. The train had stopped close to a row of cottages. Helene could clearly see a young woman standing naked at her curtain-less window, ironing. The woman knew that she could be seen by the passengers of any train that: either passed by or stopped there, but she didn't care for this was her home and she would do in it what she liked.

Helene watched as the young woman ironed and wondered why she was at home in the middle of the day. Did she have a job? And if so, what was it? Had her lover left her perhaps? Did he, or she regret it? Helene enjoyed imagining what lives perfect strangers lived; she was a *people watcher*.

The train shuddered once more as it moved off to continue its journey. Helene looked at the young woman one more time before the train passed. The young woman looked up at Helene and smiled. Helene was not expecting this and it stunned her for a moment. As the train began to move out of sight of the house Helene stood up and moved to the other side of the carriage to keep the young woman in sight for as long as possible. 'Who is she?' Helene thought. Was it just a friendly smile? A smile she gave to anyone who looked? Helene felt that there was a connection between them and that it was more than a friendly smile to a stranger. She dismissed this as being silly; her fertile mind running wild again.

Helene could not get the incident on the train out of her mind and thought back to her many train journeys along this line to see if she could recall ever stopping at this house. Her childhood memory was very selective and she could only recall the events in the carriage with her mother, and little of what was going on outside. She decided to take the train at the same time the next day and hope that the train would stop at the red light again. It did!

There she was; this time sitting at a table drinking from a cup that she held with both hands, sipping from it. The train shuddered to a stop at approximately the same place as the day before (She chose the same carriage). Helene stood up and peered through the window that she had lowered so that she could lean out. The young woman did not look up but continued to sip from her cup, staring into the distance of her mind. The train whistled and shuddered as it began to move off. This noise attracted the attention of the young woman. She turned her head and looked in Helene's direction and smiled. As the train moved off the young woman put down her cup and gave a gentle wave.

That was it! Helene was going to pay a visit. She knew it was crazy but her strong sense of fascination for all things intriguing would not let this matter pass and so she got off at the next station and walked back in the direction of the *'house by the tracks'*

It was not as easy to find the street where the house was situated as she first thought, as the train changed direction several times and her sense of direction was not her strong point. Helene walked for miles before she came across what she was sure was *the* house. She could hear trains chuffing up and down close by. The cottages were just like those she passed by on the train, but which one of the ten terraced houses was *the* one? She thought back to the view from the train and counted. She could see the last house on the left as she looked at the back of the cottages, which would be on her right now. 'Three', she thought. Three from the left so three from her right as she stood in front of them, number eight.

Helene walked hesitantly towards number eight and stood in front of it taking in its features. It looked Victorian; red brick, sash windows and no net curtains, it had to be this house as all the rest had net curtains. 'Now what! 'Do I knock?' As she stood pondering her mad situation her thoughts were distracted by a door opening and closing two doors to her left. A teenaged boy skipped down the steps from the front door and turned towards where Helene was standing. 'Good morning!' chirped the boy. Helene looked down at the boy.

'Excuse me. Who lives here?'

The boy stopped and eyed the lady that stood before him and pondered the question.

'Mr and Mrs. Stevens'. He said eventually.

'Anyone else?' asked Helene.

'Their daughter, Emma'.

'Are they at home now?'

'Emma is. She doesn't go to work anymore.'
'Thank you!'
The boy skipped off whistling.

Left alone Helene pondered her next move. 'What would I say if I knock at the door? She would think I was a loony. 'This is ridiculous,' she thought, and began to walk back to the railway station when the door to number eight opened and framed in the door was the young woman.

'Hello! I was expecting you. Please, come in'

Helene stood, rooted to the pavement for she had not expected this turn of events.

'Errm! Well!' not articulate, but under the circumstances an understandable response.

'It's ok! I haven't escaped from Bedlam!' reassured the young lady with a comforting smile.

'Thank you!' was all that Helene could say as she climbed the steps to the front door pleased that her new friend was wearing clothes this time.

Helene was led into the back room that overlooked the railway lines. It was interesting to see the tracks from this perspective. A train passed by and Helene looked to see if there were any passengers looking at her, there were but they were not looking out of the windows.

'Please. Have a seat!'

Helene sat down at the table by the window.

'Thank you, Emma'

Emma looked puzzled. 'How do you know my name?'

'Your neighbour; a small boy two doors up.'

'Ah! Tom.' Emma smiled. 'Rascal!' she poured coffee into a cup and handed it to her guest. 'Cream and sugar?'

'No. Black is fine, thanks'

Emma joined her guest and sipped from her cup. 'I don't know your name!'

'Oh, sorry! It's Helene.'

'That's nice. Do you spell it the French way? With an E at the end?'

'I do! Clever of you to ask; No one ever does.'

'My mother is French, that's why I asked.'

'I thought I noted an accent. Tom told me your family name is Stevens so I'm guessing your father is not French. Scottish?'

'He wasn't born in Scotland but his ancestors were Scottish though. What about you? With a French spelling name are you of French descent?'

'My mother, is French. I never met my father. He left us when my mother was three months pregnant.'

'Oh. That's terrible! How could a man leave his family like that? I'm so sorry!'

'Thank you, but I don't miss what I never knew! My mother more than made up for not having a father.'

'Is your mother…'. Seeing Helene's reaction to the question Emma didn't finish her sentence.

'No. She died two years ago. I miss her so much, even though I am a grown woman I still need a mother's hug now and then'.

'Well. Just look at us; talking like sisters. When I saw you on the train I felt a connection. I wished that we would meet one day'.

Helene sat up and smiled broadly. 'I'm so pleased to hear you say that because I felt the same and that is why I came to find you like some mad stalking nutcase.' The two girls laughed loudly. 'I have to ask! Why do you do your ironing naked?'

Emma blushed and smiled at the same time. 'Liberation! I feel so trapped here. I have lost my job and have to rely on my parents for support; it's so humiliating. Redundant at 22 and little chance of getting another job.'

'Me too! I know exactly how you feel. I must try ironing naked some time. Does it help?'

Emma laughed. 'No, but it doesn't make things worse.'

Emma got up and opened a drawer. She took out a photograph album and placed it on the table. She drew her chair next to Helene and thumbed through the book. 'These are my parents,' explained Emma, pointing to a handsome couple outside a church in their wedding outfits.

'They are very good looking. You are like your father.' noted Helene.

Emma looked at the photo of her father then at Helene. 'And so do you! In fact, we could be sisters!' A sudden realisation hit the two women at the same time and they looked closely at each other.

'My god! We do!' agreed Helene. 'What are the chances of that?' The answer would soon be revealed. The front door opened and in strode Emma's father. He stood at the door and took in the two women sitting at his dining table. 'Helene?'

*****

BANSHEE'S WARNING
Persephone Clearwater

BANSHEE'S WARNING

A S I WALK THROUGH THE VALLEY of the shadow of death, I fear no evil.

I have walked many valleys, streets and alleys but none quite such as this. Houses stand so close on either side that their rooftops almost appear as though they are touching and the cobble street below remains so narrow that horses and carts could barely squeeze through. The old lantern flame dances from above as it dimly illuminates the old shambles, blood of animals stains the ancient stones that have remained there since the time of the great Roman Empire. As I walk the path for the first time two dogs fight over the waste left by the butcher shops; the stench of rotting animal meat and the copper odour of blood all too potent.

Old meat hooks rest above the windows and doors of the buildings on either side of me, ready and waiting for fresh meat to be left on display for all possible customers. The stench of death surrounds me, emanating from the cobblestones below, reminding me of the thousands of deaths that have occurred on this old street. Sorrow echoes through the dark shadows, carried by the cool winter air as I pass the stone and brick buildings, each of them sturdy, but also fragile in their own way.

The beat of my heart comes to a sudden halt as I pause outside of the old house that had stood for at least one hundred years. With tears welling in my eyes, a sprinkle of rain falls upon my shoulders, leaving a light layer of moisture upon my skin. Clouds roll in above, darkening the once cloudless sky and hiding the stars; a rat runs from the bottom crack of the old oak door, weathered and worn from years of brutal usage.

The householders inside remain unaware of the fate that shall soon be upon them as the candlelight, that touched the poorly fitted window ledge, flickering before being extinguished by the sudden but light breeze.

Using the gentlest grasp that I'm able to muster, I take hold of the woollen cloak that caresses my shoulders and dances in the gentle winds; the lump rising in my throat, trying to escape but it isn't time yet.

I stare at the small entrance of the house, the grain of the wood barely visible in the lantern light but the deep cracks that have formed in the weathering, rotting wood, are all too clear; almost as clear as the cracks in the city core, filled with great wealth but also plagued with great squalor. My legs grow weak and I fall to my knees, my dress touching the filth, drying blood and decaying flesh that covers the old, narrow road.

Finally, I release the cries and wails into the night, knowing that only those of the household, with blood of Irish descent will hear me. In my cries, they will hear my sorrow and the loss that will soon be upon them, through my tears, they will witness the deadly plague that will soon wash over York. My wails echo through the narrow streets, waking the household intended to be woken. Fearfully the man of the house approaches the window, his eyes growing wide and all colour drains from his rosy cheeks as his gaze falls upon the young banshee who cries for him and his family; in his heart, through his blood, he knows the meaning of these mournful screams.

The loose strands of auburn hair that escape the messy bun as it falls to one side, cover my face as they dance, with an elegance that should only belong to the flame of a candle, in the light wind. I wipe my tears as they fall down my cheeks, my body fading into the darkness, slowly fading into nothingness as I vanish from the world of the living, leaving the household with the warning intended for them; knowing that it shall have caused them fear and dread.

Entering the land of the dead once again, where souls pass through as they travel to the other side and those trapped in purgatory remain, guiding the spirits of the living to where it is they are destined to be. Though I enter the shadows only for a brief moment, in the world of the living, a day will already be close to passing. The stars twinkle around me, piercing through the darkness and providing me with enough light as I walk along the path of stardust.

Through another door I pass, and restlessly return to the land of the living, though for myself, only a few moments have passed since I walked the streets of York, in the living world, days have gone by. Though such a short time has passed, the streets appear very different to how they did before, though it is night and most households sleep peacefully in their beds, the stench of death offends my nose, seemingly far more pungent than before. Bodies litter the streets outside the great wall of York. Pus-filled swellings touch the skin upon their necks, armpits and internal haemorrhaging has started to form, producing purple and black blotches. Upon their foreheads are the beads of sweat caused by the fever that is slowly demolishing them inside and dried puke encrusts their clothing, radiating from their skin arises the stench that can only be compared to that of death. The dead lay among the living sufferers, without any feasible way to bury them. In the streets lay the corpses of dogs and cats after being massacred by those that they depended upon that instead, now claim they have brought the black death onto the residents of the city.

I walk through the streets, the smell of posies mixing with that of death as a strange being emerged from the doorway of one of the homes. A long beak piercing through the shadow cast by the black hate from the unusual face of the being cloaked in black, the powerful smell of posies radiating from the being. In a voice flat and emotionless, I speak words so quietly that no animal could possibly hear and the words spoken shall one day become a famous chant to commemorate those who have perished from the plague, 'Ring a ring-o-roses'

The strange creature holds a presence more terrifying than a reaper as it appeared to float rather than walk across the street, remaining as silent as death as it passes through me and to another door. As he passes through, the strong scent of herbs and flowers invades my nose, emanating from within the long beak. It knocks upon the old wood and quickly, it opens to reveal a young woman with deep bags caressing the bottom of her eyes, telling a story of a terrible and fearful night.

'Hello, Doctor. Thank you for coming,' says the woman before welcoming the terrifying being into her home. The creature is a plague doctor, tasked to go from house to house, coming into close contact with the sick and diagnose whether or not, the sickness the ill are suffering with is the fatal black death.

'A pocketful of posies,' I continue to walk the narrow streets, fresh blood touching the old cobble as I pass with sorrow in my heart. Smoke rises to the sky and the smell of burning wood touches my nose as they burn the belongings of the sick in the distance, in a feeble attempt to kill the sickness that plagues the streets of York. Slowly, I approach another building as they empty it of all the possessions within and pile them outside the home, preparing them to burn, 'A-tishoo! A-tishoo!'

They board the doors of another as I pass, the moans and cries from within, agonised and ridden with pain, echo around me as the door comes to a permanent close, trapping them inside and sealing the fate of the household. Briefly, I pause as I watch the cruelty of man at its finest, remaining clear for all to see and yet, the few that walk the streets beside me appear to remain as oblivious to it all as they are to my presence.

So few walk the streets as the plague takes a firm hold over York. Those that have the riches to leave the city to its fate have already gone, others have chosen to remain hidden in their homes, attempting to avoid contact with others so that they may not contract the dreaded sickness that sweeps the streets: the rest have fallen victim to the crisis.

'We all fall down,' I murmur the words as finally, I reach the same household that I'd warned only a few days prior and pause to stare at the home. This time, I shall not remain outside of the home and cry but instead, I enter through the door that the healthy have started to board up, to stop the sick from leaving or stopping anyone from coming into contact with them. The words I have spoken are true, for this is just one of many households that has fallen to the plague. With silent footsteps, I walk up the narrow stairs and approach the door before slowly pushing it open to reveal the young man lying in what almost appears like a drunken stupor.
With blackened fingertips, and an almost corpse like stiffness, he reaches out to me, his desperate brown eyes pleading for mercy. His body so weak and pain-ridden that he wants all to end is all too clear to see within the silent pleas and cries. Beads of sweat touch the forehead of the skeletal man, bloody vomit encrusting the clothing around his neck and mouth, but it is black and purple that paints his skin, caused by the internal haemorrhaging that I know I'll never be able to forget.

My lips twitch into a comforting smile as I silently motion for him to follow with a quick movement of my hand, and slowly his soul glows from within him. It's a gradual process, moving on from life and into the land of the dead as the soul glows and shimmers, slowly cutting the cord that has kept it bound to the body. It's almost an exact replica of giving birth only in reverse, the mother must push the baby from her womb, using her muscles and experiencing some of the worst pain imaginable, for the soul, that will come soon but for now, it must cut the umbilical cord.

The soul begins to shimmer brighter and brighter before finally leaving the body it has been bound to for so many years and out of the corpse, steps a young man. No longer does he appear deathly ill but instead, he looks as healthy as when I first came, to warn him of the passing of his household. His blue eyes shimmer in the light as he approaches, followed by his wife and son.

I turn down the small corridor and glance into the room where the young girl plays happily, she hasn't been touched by the sickness and she won't be. It isn't the destiny of this English Rose to die of the plague for her fate shall be far worse in many years to come. But for now, I leave her to play, knowing she will find a way to escape the house and fend for herself, I have to see that my job is completed as I lead the spirits into the land of the dead.

Surrounded by sparkling stars once again, walking upon a path of stardust, I guide them to the mighty glowing silver gates, where fluffy clouds appear to be on the other side. Never have I seen nor shall I ever see the other side of the gate though I long to. This is where I leave them, in front of a man with a book, where he will decide whether or not they shall pass the gates or fall into fiery depths.

Though I needn't, I return to York, feeling myself attracted to death like a moth to a flame. Perhaps I am just overly curious or fascinated by the process of death that the living don't see, or maybe it is something more. I cannot say.

It has been months now, since the plague began and the reapers remain hard at work before the winter months come and the plague vanishes, almost as quickly as it came. Many have perished from the sickness that invaded the narrow streets and passed through like an unstoppable force. Those who still suffer with the sickness are few and far between, the citizens hope that they shall be the last of the casualties.

Slowly, I walk through the bustling streets, the smell of posies remains strong in the air as the citizens carry them, believing that the sickness is spread through bad smells: though if that were the case, then the city of York would have never stood long enough, for its stench is far worse than anywhere I have ever been. Bodies have been gathered, thrown into pits as those who remain prepare to bury them, their graves remaining in the masses and unmarked as York attempts to finally manage its deceased, though the city struggles to find those willing to do so.

Curiously, I journey to the nearest parish, knowing that one of the final victims of the plague awaits inside, praying for God to have mercy on his soul. The shadow of the reaper casts over my body, hiding the sun from my skin as I approach the door and immediately I know his time is soon to come. The church appears emptier than it should have, the two beds either side of the priest are empty, leaving him alone. The shadow moves and looms over the priest, no longer following my steps and again, I witness the beautiful sight of the soul leaving the body and I can't help but wonder as to where the priest is destined to spend eternity.

Shall he too, be trapped in purgatory? Destined to deliver the souls of the dead to the other side? Whether it be heaven, hell or purgatory! I am not to know.

I return to the outside world, the stench of death, faeces and decomposition offending my nose. These streets will soon prosper again even after the devastation that has swept over the city, despite the cruelty of man that it has revealed. New opportunities shall arise, allowing peasants to become merchants and live lives of better quality. The very thought causes the corners of my lips to twitch, forming a smile. Homes remain boarded and corpses left within to rot and as time passes, I shall remain walking in the shadow of the Reapers, crying with the grievance of death and delivering the souls of the fallen.

*****

TOMORROW IS ANOTHER DAY
Deyanira Andreieff

*Highly Commended for the University Centre Grimsby
International Literary Prize*

TOMORROW IS ANOTHER DAY

I 'M JOLTED AWAKE from a nightmare. I know it was a nightmare but I don't recall the details. I reach out to turn on the radio. I always listen to the radio when I can't sleep. It's totally dark so I grope around for it. My radio set is always on the shelf beside my bed. My fingers are scrabbling on the pillow, on the sheet, then on the wall next to me, but to no avail. I can't even seem to find the shelf. It doesn't feel like home. Where am I? I open my eyes as wide as I can in search of any sliver of light that could help me detect the slightest clue about the place. Nothing. Hold on a minute, I think I hear something. Could it be someone breathing? Or worse, snoring? I think I catch a whiff of lavender? - or is it eucalyptus? - quite pleasant but unfamiliar. What is happening to me? I am frightened but I don't dare to speak, let alone to scream. Try to remember, Mimi, try to remember! Total blank. On second thought, in spite of everything, this situation is not so disagreeable. I am not feeling any pain, no more than usual anyway. It is pleasantly warm in here and the bed is quite comfortable. I curl up, and eventually, I succumb to the tiredness that has enfolded me.

A beam of sunlight compels me to open my eyes. Little people, or they might be animals, are stuck on the walls. They look funny, silly even. A furry blue one with big ears and a round nose is grinning at me. I turn my head and I see roads and tracks on the floor. Wagons of all colours and countless mini cars are jumbled together. A further exploration around the room reveals a little boy on a small mattress nestled under a quilt. I scrutinize him for a while until I become aware of two brown marbles staring at me, and a high-pitch voice says, 'Mimi you're awake!'

'Who are you?' is the only reply I can give.

'My name is Nathan and I'm three years old but I'm gonna be four really soon and then we'll go to Paris!' he says, climbing on my bed.

'Wow, Paris! You are a lucky boy!' I can't help but smile at this sweet little face with tiny teeth and messy morning hair. 'I used to live there you know. The Eiffel Tower is in Paris.'

'And Disneyland!' he yells with excitement, now bouncing up and down.

The poor thing, I don't have the courage to tell him Disneyland is not in France but in California.

After a quick knock, the door opens and a young woman enters the room. She strokes the boy's hair and with a kind expression in her eyes she invites us to the kitchen for breakfast.

This is a relief, I'm craving my morning tea.

'Who are you?' I ask the kind lady as I take hold of the kettle from the counter.

She stops spreading butter on Nathan's toast, turns towards me and answers with a concerned tone, as though I have made a mistake

'Mimi, I'm Lisa. Remember?'

'Oh Lisa! How are you?' Of course I remember her, she's my granddaughter. She looks so grown up though, that's unbelievable!

In order to put the water on to boil I look for some matches, searching in every jar, opening every drawer, checking every container. Lisa gently touches my shoulder and takes the kettle out of my hands. I am not a baby, I can make some tea! But she will take care of it, I am her guest after all.

We are about to leave the house and I'm still looking for my handbag, I'm afraid we are going to be late. I scold Nathan and demand him to give it back to me. I know he stole it, he's always hiding my things. The little boy runs to the bathroom and comes back with my handbag.

'I knew it was him!' I say crossly to his mum, but she just smiles at him. I reproach Lisa for taking the matter too lightly, smiling is not an appropriate response to such behaviour. However, as we are heading for the day centre, while the mischievous boy is frolicking on the pavement in front of us, she blames me for constantly leaving my bag in the bathroom!

Arriving at the centre I'm delighted to see a friend of mine. She is young and beautiful. She has long blonde hair, gold sparkling earrings and a good-natured smile. I hug her because she is my friend. She is at the door with a woman dressed all in white. I overhear my granddaughter informing them that her parents have come back from Italy, so her father will collect me this afternoon. Thereupon, after a tickling peck on my cheek, Lisa says: 'Have a good day, Mimi. Francis is coming to get you today, remember?' Of course I remember Francis, he's my only son! I feel happy.

Sliding my hand under my friend's elbow, I let her lead me into the large living room where many elderly men and women are gathered. One is in an armchair, his eyes well shut but his mouth wide open. Two ladies are piling cubes on a bench. The others sit around the table, three of them are drawing.

I see a bunch of flowers in the middle of the table. I express my desire to paint them. I love flowers. Especially these - pink roses. With my paintbrush I try to recreate their shapes and, by mixing the different pigments, replicate their peculiar colours. As for the scent it is much more difficult! I bend and sniff the roses to absorb their fragrance. It takes me back many decades.

I had just been parachuted into France, to a village near Tours. My mission was to help a group of Resistance fighters by delivering them messages and guns. My right leg was sore from the landing and I was scared, obviously. Although I had been taught how to kill with my bare hands and how to escape from handcuffs with a hairpin, I wanted to experience neither one nor the other. I needed to pass as local. My contact had been required to wait for me at the church so I kept walking in the sombre streets, pretending to know exactly where I was, focusing on the steeple, bearing in mind that one agent had been uncovered because she had looked right instead of left when crossing the road. As I approached the rendezvous, I could feel beads of perspiration trickling down my back. And when I somehow reached the church square, I spotted a tall dark-haired young man with grey overalls and a beige overcoat leaning on the church wall.

As soon as he saw me he plastered a broad smile on his face, waved at me with one hand and proffered a pink rose with the other. At once I understood he was supposed to be my boyfriend. Summoning up one last effort I ran towards him, arms open wide, as if we were reunited after a long separation. He gave me the flower and held me tight in his arms, and, resting my head on his shoulder, smiling at this comforting pose, I smelled the distinctive perfume of the rose.

His code name was Max. He was American but he had spent his childhood in France, thus he had been one of the first OSS agents operating with the Free French forces. For a time we worked together, but one day he lost contact with our group.

'Mimi, your painting is remarkable!' I am upset now that my resurfacing memory has been interrupted so I leave the table and withdraw into a sulk. At the back of the room, I notice a big aquarium with fishes, stones and plants of many colors. Filled with curiosity I make my way towards it. I stay hours contemplating the animals swimming and gliding through the water, their tails moving from side to side.

Unexpectedly I hear some music. One of the ladies stands up, and starts swinging and humming the tune. As I approach, we hold hands, and together, we sway to the melody. I am 18 again… I have just received my calling-up papers. I had decided to join the WAAF and I had applied for special duties. My sister and I decided to celebrate. We dressed up in our best clothes and even applied patches of rouge to our lips and cheeks. The dance hall was vast, sumptuous and - thanks to the music and the hubbub of voices - cheerful at the same time. There were groups of men and women in uniform laughing with civilians, young boys flirting with older girls, but I was fascinated by the dance floor. It was filled with people swing-dancing! My sister and I joined in. For a couple of hours we were able to forget the tumult of the previous days: the wail of air raid sirens, the whistle of falling bombs, the 'ack-ack' of anti-aircraft guns, the boom of collapsing buildings, the howling of hopeless people, the ringing of emergency vehicles. For the last song I was delighted to slow dance with a tall gentleman in an officer uniform. Hand in hand, our bodies, barely touching, gently, smoothly undulated to the rhythm.

We'll meet again
Don't know where
Don't know when
But I know we'll meet again some sunny day.

I am hauled back to the present by a mix of mouth-watering aromas.

'Would you like to help set the table?' asks my friend. Of course I wish to help - I'm a polite person and we should always help when invited to.

'Shall I put the flowers on the table?' I love flowers. They always add some joy to a place.

After my soup I am waiting for dessert. There is still mashed potato and minced meat to come but they don't appeal to me. The obese woman, on the other hand, can't stop devouring all that she is offered. No wonder she is so fat. Someone should tell her that she is ugly and that she disgusts everyone. To avoid staring at her I choose to check the contents of my handbag. I first find a comb, which I use to tidy my hair, then I take out my fountain pen and a notebook. I see a blue pack of paper handkerchiefs and I set about opening it when I catch sight of a small coin purse, so I start to count the money inside, one penny at a time. When I am tired of calculating I continue with my inspection and I recognise my beloved pearl necklace and emerald brooch. I hide them in the zipped compartment. I don't want anybody to examine them! I take out a lipstick instead.

After the delectable lemon sponge cake my friend suggests that we read the newspaper all together. She displays the pages on the table. She reads an article, shows a picture and then asks us what we think of it. Among different stories there is one about a bomb blast at a market in a foreign country. It explains how the terrorists have placed explosives in a telephone box. An image comes to my mind.

On a clear June night I was preparing some explosive charges that we intended to attach to railway tracks and telegraph poles. It was a few months after Max had disappeared. Secret messages had been broadcast warning us of the forthcoming Allied invasion. We had been instructed to double our efforts to execute acts of sabotage.

We were getting ready for one of them when we learned about the landing of a special forces team that was going to help us pave the way for the liberation of France. We were so excited, we ran to the appointed place. I raised my head and looked up into this vision of countless parachuted containers falling from the sky. I didn't even pay attention to the three soldiers. We quickly but carefully collected the boxes and put them in the carts to take everything to the headquarters as soon as possible.

Once there, we set about opening them. I had never seen so many weapons, helmets, camouflage jackets, radios and all sorts of equipment and supplies. There were even some biscuits, chocolate and candy bars! I was capering about and laughing with joy when I felt a hand on my waist. I instantly turned around. Embarrassed at my childish behaviour, a blush spread across my cheeks. My heart beat even faster when I laid my eyes on him; he was more handsome than I remembered.

'Merriment suits you!' said Max with his charming smile.

We married on 8th May the next year, our wedding festivities were very special. The streets of Paris were full of people celebrating the end of the war, everybody was cheering, singing and hugging and we jokily pretended that this jolly spirit was in our honour.

A voice rouses me from my reverie. 'Your son is here, Mimi.'

I stand up in a buoyant mood and make my way to the entrance accompanied by my dear friend.

I see an old man wearing jeans and a brown leather jacket. He opens his arms. His face rings a bell.

'Who are you again?'

'I am Francis.' He says.

According to the doctor I had been too frail, thin and tired to become pregnant immediately after we married, therefore, when it finally happened we were immensely happy. I was at my desk, on a hot summer afternoon, fountain pen in my hand, thinking about what to write in my notebook, when my husband came back from work earlier than usual with a broad grin on his face.

'I have very good news! My contract here in France with the agency has come to an end.'

My puzzled look compelled him to continue.

'It means that I can go back to the United States and have a normal life! I am now officially a free ordinary civilian! There is just one thing we must do before…'

It was something I never guessed about my husband. I knew Max was an alias but I didn't know we had married under his nom de guerre. Now that the war was over he was about to regain his real name and I was going to lose mine, for the second time. Suddenly a hot wave of disbelief engulfed me and everything became blurred, he seized me in his arms as I was on the verge of fainting and carried me to the sofa. He stroked my hair and my face. For two years I had been Mrs Francis and I already missed it.

I spent the following months getting used to my new identity. Therefore when I gave birth in November, it was obvious that my son was a Francis.

Such memories certainly put a smile on my face. The man motions me closer with a charming smile, that he inherited from his father, and hugs me tight.

'Of course, you are Francis,' I say in a whisper.

As we are leaving, my friend runs after us and gives me a paper.

'This is yours,' she says with a smile before returning to the centre.

'Wow this is a very colourful painting! Did you do it?' Francis asks. 'What is it?' The sheet is daubed with blotches of different reds and pinks.

'I don't know, somebody gave it to me.'

We take a stroll in a beautiful garden, I want to pick up flowers but Francis is cross and says that these flowers are not supposed to be taken. It's a pity because I love flowers and a bouquet would be beautiful on the kitchen table.

Once we are at home my son leads me directly to my bedroom, which I inspect immediately. A jacket and a skirt rest on a chair beside a closet and below the window is a table with a lamp, a book and a couple of framed photographs. There is one of my husband when he was young, with Francis on his shoulders. There is one of my dear granddaughter Lisa. She must be eight or nine. I wonder where she is now – maybe in Italy with her cousins - I haven't seen her for a while.

I sit down on the soft bed and I meticulously examine my handbag. I start to remove the items, inspecting them one by one. All at once I hear the front door shut and a gleeful voice, Barbara is just back from work. I love Barbara. She is Francis' wife and Lisa's mother. She is a bright jovial woman with a forceful personality probably derived from her Italian origins. I rush down the hall to welcome her and she is also happy to see me. Francis wants me to take a bath but I am not in the mood and Barbara stands up for me so we soon sit down for supper. He presses me to take some pills that are supposed to be good for my health.

'But I'm not sick!' I argue, showing my annoyance. 'I don't want your poison!'

'It's not poison, Mimi, it's medicine that will help you sleep.' Francis is starting to lose his patience.

'I will have plenty of time to sleep when I am dead, thank you, son!'

Barbara, elbowing her husband, once again sides with me and we resume our dinner in a friendly atmosphere as they recount their holiday in Italy.

After cleaning and tidying up the kitchen the three of us settle down in front of the television for the evening film, unfortunately it's too long and not easy to follow so we all decide to retire for the night. The scene of disarray in my bedroom bewilders me: my handbag is open and empty, and my valuables are strewn all over the bed. I scrupulously put everything back in my bag where they ought to be. Before getting into bed I have a call of nature. I open the door across from my bedroom but a dark brown wood desk and an antique leather armchair face me along with piles of cardboard boxes in the corner. I am obviously in the wrong place. I desperately roam around in the corridors and I set about opening all the doors, turning on all the lights, in search of the water closet. After what seems like an eternity I find Francis and Barbara lying on their bed, reading by the light of their bedside lamps. My son frowns and instantly gets up.

'Is something wrong, Mimi?' He has a puzzled look on his face. I move my shoulders in a light shrug, not daring to vocalize what I have to say.

Embarrassed, I finally confess,'I was looking for the loo…'

'Come on,' he says taking my arm, 'I'll show you where it is.'

Shame paralyses me. Francis is standing in front of me with a perplexed look. Mortified, I feel a teardrop fall on my cheek.

'It's too late.' I mumble lowering my head.

'Don't worry, you're wearing a diaper.'

I feel warm tears welling up now and I shout with a brittle voice 'A diaper? But I'm not a baby!'

'Oh, Mimi!' His voice is breaking a little as well. He wraps his arms around me, hugging me very tight and I, losing any rest of dignity, let myself cry over what age has done to me.

In the kitchen, we sit grinning at each other over the rims of our teacups. I finally accept to swallow the drugs he has handed me. They're for my own good. For a little while we talk about life, about our lives, happy moments. I start to feel sleepy and it is time to call it a night.

I climb into bed and my son tucks me in as I used to do for him many years ago. He lays a kiss on my forehead as I did when he was a child.

'Night night, Mimi.'

'Night night, Francis.'

'Sleep tight,' he utters in a soft reassuring tone, and, with his comforting, charming smile that he inherited from his dad, while he is carefully closing the door, I hear him whisper the very words that I've always murmured in his ear, every night before he went to sleep:

'Tomorrow is another day.'

Tonight I don't want to switch on the radio, I curl up under the eiderdown, close my eyes, and with a melancholic but truly content smile, I hark back to my precious song, its powerful words and its beautiful melody, until I finally fall asleep.

We'll meet again
    Don't know where
    Don't know when
    But I know we'll meet again some sunny day.

*****

MONEY

Laurence Short

MONEY

AS GAVIN MORTIMER SHOT HIS RIVAL in the head he snarled: 'The game is over, you lost the bet.'

He holstered his weapon, and added, 'I'm not sorry about your damn luck!'

'We've actually succeeded, Gavin,' commented Bruce.

The smell of gunpowder floated in the church back room. However, the smell of victory was oh so pungent.

A few days earlier… The night was crisp, cold and foggy as the factions met at the church. This was considered a neutral ground, ironically: a supposed place of peace that had brought about many wars over the years. This time it was the beginning of the demise of one of the two rival groups. None of their members were religious, though their leaders each considered themselves a kind of 'god'. The leader of the Barton faction was Gavin Mortimer, with his second-in-command, Bruce Holloway. Emily Silverberg was leader of the Scunthorpe faction with Ralph Taylor her second-in-command.

'A good evening to you, my old friend,' said Gavin.

'Let's skip the niceties, shall we?' Emily replied.

'As you wish then, sweetheart.'

'I'd rather you didn't call me that. Let's get down to business.'

'Yes, let's.'

With that, they started negotiations that would never truly be completely agreed by either side. Arguments by both sides began and lasted for some time, but as the night wore on both sides decided on a bet of some kind. Both factions came to favour this idea – they just had to agree on what the risk and the reward would be.

As dawn approached, a bet finally became the collective decision. Discussion of the stakes of the win and loss of the bet commenced. The final agreements were as follows: the loser would be unapologetically killed by the remaining leader; the winning faction would take over the losing faction's territory, to be overseen by the losing faction's second-in-command. There weren't any declarations to be signed, or any other formality: there was a handshake and the usual code of respect to be followed.

Emily and Ralph exited the church heading towards their car, where they quietly exchanged a few words before departing.

'You realise how crucial this bet is to each faction's survival?' Emily said. 'It's paramount.'

'Yes, I know,' replied Ralph.

They pulled out from the church car park in their black limousine, which was fitted with tinted, bulletproof glass and reinforced wheels and rims. Emily and Ralph were plotting how they would win the bet that would end the factions' warfare. They figured they had five days. They didn't have any time to spare, as they knew Gavin and his crony would be doing the very same thing. Each faction would go about it in a different way, but ultimately, there would only be one faction controlling both territories.

Back at the church Gavin and Bruce were conversing about the events that had just happened.

'This isn't about old sins but about claiming the absolute future of the gun and drug trade,' Gavin stated.

'The old sins are better off kept in the past after this bet is all over,' remarked Bruce.

'There shouldn't be any backlash from the outcome,' Gavin said.

They left in their black SUV en route to their headquarters: the old and supposedly abandoned Reeds Hotel. A once respected establishment that was damaged by flooding a few winters back, it had been bought cheaply by Gavin Mortimer due to those unfortunate circumstances, and then renovated.

There were always two guards positioned outside the main gate to the path that led onto Reeds Hotel. There was a sign on the gate that stated 'Guard dogs' (of which there were none, just guards with guns instead). It was a good vantage point. Nearby there were a few places to discard dead bodies: the woods, the River Humber and the dump, only a few minutes away. For a consideration, the workers at the dump looked the other way when a body was to be abandoned, as long as it didn't happen too often. It was a bendy, narrow, gravelly road to the Reeds Hotel, with lights on both sides every few metres. Before you reached the Hotel there was an old hut that looked dusty and was almost concealed in cobwebs. Inside, however, it was immaculate, and filled with the latest gun shipment. The entry door to the hut was reinforced steel and had a passcode. The lack of guards positioned there made it look unimportant and trivial.

This time Gavin made sure they stopped outside before finally reaching the hotel. Gavin and Bruce entered the hut and pondered over which weapons would be the most useful for the crucial next few days. There was a good selection of guns, from those with ranged, scoped silencers to the heavy type (mini-gun). They picked a few of the aforementioned guns for themselves and the rest of their faction.

Both Gavin and Bruce preferred guns; similarly, Emily Silverberg's preference of weapons was guns, as they were quicker and not too messy. Ralph Taylor favoured knives of all different sizes. He once killed someone with a one-inch knife and he dismembered a traitor with a twenty-eight-inch machete. Ralph had his own area of expertise that he liked to use when he could, or when Emily sent him on special assignments. Ralph didn't want to be the faction's leader at the beginning; he still didn't want to be, but he did want his piece of this action, and suitable payment.

Once, one of the Scunthorpe faction's local gunrunners got a bit too big for his boots; thinking he could do his own little side business with the faction's wares. Ralph sent his underlings to get him and bring him back to his house. Upon arrival he was taken to the basement. When he was stripped to his boxers, then had his legs and arms chained to the back wall, Ralph took his jacket off and rolled his sleeves up.

'I'll hazard a guess that you know why you're in this room, yes?' Ralph asked.

'I.. I didn't think it would cut into the profit all that much.'

'Is that right?' Ralph says as he turned his phone off.

He pulled out a folding knife from his back pocket, 'Well, this will cut into you.'

'No, please.. please don't… NOOOO,' the gunrunner cried.

The gunrunner's ears each hit the floor with a bloody splat, like cold cuts from a butcher's.

'What can I do to make this stop?'

'Stop? It's already too late for you, but that's fortunate for me.'

Ralph went to his knife cabinet to select the next device to inflict agony and suffering. He prolonged the selecting period, then picked the knife he knew he would choose all along: a customised pure silver pocketknife with a black leather coated handle.

'Are you familiar with 'lingchi'?' Ralph mused.

'N-no, what is that?'

'It also goes by the name of, 'death by a thousand cuts"

Emily had given the order for this move without hesitation, as she wanted to prove a point at this vital time; if anyone stepped out of line there would be no forgiveness. She'd been present a number of times for Ralph's undertakings and only on two occasions did she have to leave the room. Once, she sent her lover, who had repeatedly cheated on her, to Ralph's basement.

Emily owned The Refined Butterfly nightclub in Scunthorpe, where she operated all the daily commerce. She didn't have a high opinion of the drug trade, but it made a respectable amount of money. Emily's topmost qualm was with sex trafficking. She had heard that it was happening in Scunthorpe, but she didn't know who was behind such an unwholesome operation. Emily had her office in the back of the nightclub, elegantly styled and organised in a precise manner.

On the second day Emily had been ringing her contacts all morning with the hope that she could make the leading transaction. *The bet: who could sell the biggest gun and drug shipment in a five-day period, without the other faction playing havoc with business proceedings or dealing in the other's territory.* Emily wasn't worried. She could set up a meet for Tuesday and then have the deal done by Thursday. This would give her a day to plan the future of her territories, once victorious. Emily decided to phone Ralph to learn the progress of his latest assignment. Her call went straight to voicemail.

'Ralph, I'll take it your assignment is still on-going? Come to The Refined Butterfly when you've finished,' requested Emily.

She hoped he wouldn't be too much longer, as he was needed back at the nightclub to be brought up to speed. Emily took her handgun out of its holster and made certain it was fully loaded with safety off. She did this sometimes without thinking. Emily now waited for Ralph to return to discuss their on-going progress.

Back at Ralph's house he was cleaning the blood and dismembered body parts from the basement floor. He was ecstatic with how the assignment went this time, as he hadn't had the pleasure of torturing someone in a while. The poor bastard had tried to hold on, but to no avail. Whilst Ralph was seemingly lost in his blissfulness, a noise from above disrupted his thoughts. He stood up and went to the knife cabinet. Selecting a weapon to protect himself in case of intruders, he moved to the stairs to listen intently. He pondered over who it could be. Friends of the gunrunner he'd tortured to death? Perhaps. Ralph realised that if he didn't go up soon, eventually they would come down to the basement. He still had the element of surprise on his side.

There were intruders in Ralph's home, but it was actually Bruce and his band of goons.

'Check the rest of the ground floor, I'm going upstairs,' Bruce whispered.

'Sure thing, boss.'

'Remember, we're not here to kill him. We need him alive,' Bruce stated.

Bruce slowly climbed the stairs, holding tightly on to his stun gun. They were not there to execute Ralph, but to kidnap him instead. Ralph was a strategic component to the Barton faction's grand plan. Bruce had brought two goons as backup. He wondered if he should have brought more men, as Bruce knew that Ralph wasn't one to be taken lightly for your own sake. He entered the bedroom, and saw at a glance that it appeared empty. Even so, he checked under the bed and in the wardrobe in case Ralph was aware of their presence. When he was sure this area was safe he made his way to the other rooms.

Ralph was now in the kitchen doorway after swiftly getting out of the basement. He spotted one of the intruders. As quietly and rapidly as possible he came up behind him, grabbed his mouth with his left hand, then thrust the knife under his chin with his right hand. Ralph felt the man shake from shock. He pushed the knife to the hilt into the man's head, then he removed it and plunged it into the dying man's throat. When he withdrew the knife, blood sprayed like an erupting volcano. He sat the corpse down against one of the cupboards and surveyed the room. Ralph remained as silent as possible, but something was audible from another room. This game of cat and mouse was not over yet. Ralph had the home advantage, but he was uncertain how many there were inside. He slunk into the living room, where he spotted the second intruder standing within a few feet of him.

'We're not here to murder you ... ' murmured the intruder.

With absolute precision, Ralph sharply threw his knife in the direction of the invader. The knife went in the man's groin region, making him drop to his knees and release the grip of the gun. Ralph dashed over, pulled out his folding knife and drove it into the man's cranium with a blunt thud. However, as Ralph straightened himself he felt a pinch in his neck, followed by a sensation of burning as the electrical current raced through him. He dropped to the floor, where his would-be capturer lay dead. His vision hazed and his world faded to darkness.

The third day got under way with Ralph waking up in what he surmised must be the Reeds Hotel. He realised he'd been gagged and tied to a chair. Now he had no weapons or any form of communication, and no idea who might know he was here. Ralph wondered how long it would take Emily to discover that his assignment was in fact finished, and that he'd been kidnapped by Bruce. Bruce walked into the room with a gigantic smirk on his face and removed the masking tape from Ralph's mouth. The inevitable question time had come. Gavin was the interrogator.

'Hello Ralph. Don't worry we're not going to do to you what you do to others,' Gavin said, gesturing a cutting motion.

'In fact, we have a deal for you.'

'You don't embrace my proficiency for torture, Mr Mortimer, but let's hear this deal,' Ralph retorted.

'Very well, I'll tell you,' Gavin uttered.

'Yes, humour me.'

Gavin told him the grand plan and what would be his part in it. Gavin wanted him to goad Emily into attacking Bruce whilst doing a business deal, which would make her spontaneously forfeit the bet. The reason she would attempt to eradicate Bruce would be because of his dealings in sex trafficking. The outcome would be that Ralph would oversee her territory, but would have to pay fifty percent of profits to the Barton faction even though he'd be governing it for them.

'Fascinating covenant. What if in the subsequent year it goes sixty to forty in my favour?' Ralph queried.

'I knew you wouldn't consent so effortlessly, but…'

Ralph interjected: 'You're asking me to give permission for my leader's death sentence, I need it to be worth the betrayal and then some.'

'Understandably. You can run Scunthorpe as you wish but you have to give us fifty percent in year one, then you can pay forty in the subsequent year,' Gavin specified.

'I want this agreement on paper rather than the spoken word,' Ralph demanded.

'Considering the circumstances, I think that is a fair request,' Gavin responded.

Later in the day…Ralph had been taken home by four of Gavin's subordinates, as they wanted to play it very safely this time. Now Ralph was free again he headed to the basement. When Ralph entered he suddenly remembered he hadn't completely cleaned the mess from his latest torture, but that would have to be a lesser priority for now. Ralph armed himself and turned his phone on. He noticed he had missed calls from Emily: no surprise there. Before getting in the car he checked the perimeter to see if anybody was on surveillance. Ralph sat in the car, procrastinating for a while before calling Emily.

'Ralph, what in heaven's name have you been up to?' sighed Emily.

'Hello, I was just very involved in the assignment,' Ralph said.

'Can you get to the nightclub immediately!'

'Yes, I'm actually on my way now,' responded Ralph.

Emily was sitting in her chair at The Refined Butterfly, which was symbolic for her throne as she sat atop of her empire. Whilst she was waiting for Ralph to get back in contact, Emily had made her business deal for a winning transaction on Thursday afternoon. Now she had to wait for Ralph to arrive. While waiting, she anxiously checked her gun for the third time. She knew how close triumph was, and how fundamental tomorrow truly would be. A sound was emanating from somewhere, but she could not quite work out where it was coming from. Snapping back into the real world, she realised that it was someone knocking on the door. Hopefully, it was Ralph on the other side.

'Come in,' Emily reluctantly said.

As Ralph opened and closed the door he said, 'Sorry Emily, I should have contacted you earlier, but I went on an undertaking of my own.'

'Well, I can now inform you on the latest business,' said Emily.

Emily put her gun back in its holster and stood up saying, 'Pray tell what this expedition was?'

'I picked up a lead on the sex trafficking operation,' Ralph divulged.

'You're not fucking kidding me, are you?' Emily shrieked.

'No, not even in the slightest,' Ralph clarified.

'Then tell me what you've discovered,' Emily demanded.

Ralph went on to tell her what he'd found out about the ongoing sex trafficking in Scunthorpe. He told Emily that Bruce Holloway was in charge of the dealings, and had been for some time. Ralph started to embellish some 'facts' about Bruce's operation. He told her that Bruce had sixteen-year-old girls as part of the selection. He also added bits about the living conditions and how many times they might be used in a day. In reality, Bruce never used girls under the age of eighteen, but the living conditions weren't great. Ralph furthermore told Emily that Bruce operated in Scunthorpe, although he primarily worked out of Barton.

'I'm aware of a deal taking place tomorrow morning,' Ralph informed her.

'Let's take this fucker down!' Emily commanded.

Day four had now become the key day. Emily and Ralph were waiting outside Bruce's warehouse. They had seen Bruce enter and were now waiting for the business deal to go ahead. Emily was so filled with rage that she could wait no longer, and burst in. Aiming at Bruce she went to shoot, but as she did, Ralph knocked into her and she only hit Bruce in the right shoulder. As she recovered her balance, guns from all directions were pointing at her, even Ralph's. She realised that something was seriously amiss.

The bet had been won.

*****

207

THE ULTIMATE GOAL
Abi Thompson

THE ULTIMATE GOAL

OF COURSE NOBODY WOULD believe it actually happened. Nothing like that happened; ever. Not in the real world anyway, maybe in storybooks or films but not actual real life; my life anyway!

It was a normal kind of day for me. Weekday morning routine: get up, get dressed, gel my hair and have breakfast. Then the usual conversation with Mum about whether I'd had a nice sleep and what I'd dreamt about or maybe even, if I was *really* lucky, she would tell me all about her crazy dream; like I actually cared. I just wanted to have my breakfast in peace. Then Dad would trudge downstairs, coughing up the phlegm that has collected in his throat overnight, trying to whistle in between. I preferred the weekends when Dad would be out at Golf and Mum would be having her usual lay in watching the Coronation Street omnibus in bed. That's when I really enjoyed my breakfast, when I was alone.

As usual Mum would go and get ready for work. I would always have the same old conversation about what was going on at school that day and what subjects were my favourite. Then the dreaded daily question: have you decided what you want to be when you grow up yet? I actually had no idea why she kept asking me the same question everyday like it was important. I was ten for god's sake!

I gave her the same answer most days: a footballer, like every normal ten year old wants to be. Of course if I was feeling in a silly kind of mood I'd come out with something ridiculous, just to annoy her. My favourite one was telling her I wanted to become a florist! That one really made me laugh, she wasn't impressed though. Don't know why she didn't believe me.

I'm Joe by the way. As you can probably tell my parents drive me insane. They just nag me about the same thing every day. I don't think it's a big deal what I want to be when I grow up. I'm quite happy just doing whatever at the minute. I'm only ten; I've got the rest of my life to make stupid decisions.

Anyway, as I was saying, my days were usually the same; especially weekdays. On this particular day I set off for school as normal, around 8:30. I grabbed my coat and hat and slung my bag over my shoulder. I gave my parents a grunt and closed the door behind me. It was a chilly autumn morning. I could feel the leaves crunching beneath my feet as I walked across the lawn. The cold air froze the inside of my nostrils as I breathed in. I pulled the zip on my coat all the way up to cover my bare neck and buried my chin.

My friend Tom lived down the street from me, we usually walked to school together. As I walked towards his house I could see him coming out of his front door and jogging down his path to meet me. His mousy brown hair was stuck up at the back, as if he'd slept against a wall. That was the thing with Tom; he never really cared about what he looked like. His collar on his shirt was always stuck up on one side and down on the other. He took no pride in his appearance; I always had to sort him out on the way. I, on the other hand, wouldn't dream of leaving the house if I hadn't gelled my hair. If it wasn't perfect, I wasn't moving!

Anyway, I'm going off again, I was trying to tell you about my day. So when I got to school I sat down in my normal place. I had to sit between two 'sensible' girls because apparently I was easily distracted. What my teacher wasn't aware of, however, was that his lessons were extremely boring and rather than moving me he should've just tried to be a bit more interesting.

After maths my friends and I headed out onto the playground. It had been dry for a few days so we were allowed to go onto the field to play football. Best part of the day so far! I loved playing football with the boys in my class. It was always really competitive as we were a pretty talented bunch. We had a football match for the school team tomorrow, I needed the practice. I usually played left wing (it helped being left footed) and tried to score all of the goals. I admit I can be rather greedy when I get the ball but who isn't? That was my favourite part of the day, any day for that matter. If I was playing football I was happy!

So after school that day I walked home with Tom. We didn't really speak much as I had tackled him at afternoon play and he was a bit grumpy about it still, he always sulked. He gave me a grunt as he headed down his path towards his front door. As I carried on walking home I couldn't stop thinking about the match this afternoon. I played brilliantly, like I'd never played before. My dreams of becoming a footballer became more of an ambition every day. I knew my Mum wouldn't take me seriously, if only she was interested.

That night when my Dad came home from work we all sat down at the table together for dinner - Mum had cooked her famous 'Chicken Casserole' (which was more like chicken vomit). We got speaking about our days: Mum had been doing the usual filing and photocopying and Dad had spent most on the day on the phone planning business meetings. Then they asked me about my day. I told them how great it was and how my team won the football match at playtime and lunchtime and how many goals I scored and how brilliant I was at football.

'Joe I was talking about your lessons – did you do well in your lessons today?' Mum said it in such a patronising tone. She didn't care about football and she totally didn't understand how passionate I was about it. So I told her.

'Mum you just don't get it! I don't care about Maths; I only need it to add up how many goals I score. And as for English, well, I don't need to spell to become a pro footballer, do I!'

Well that certainly put her in her place. I stormed up the stairs and slammed my bedroom door. I threw myself on my bed and looked around my room. My walls were top to toe in baby blue Manchester City wallpaper: my favourite team. I had a giant poster of Aguero next to my bed; he was my hero. As I lay there staring around my room I must've drifted off to sleep. I dreamt about football and scoring the winning goal for Man City against Man United in the FA cup final. Wow – that would've been amazing!

A knock on the door woke me up, it was my Mum (hopefully coming to apologise). I turned towards her rubbing my eyes. She was holding a glass of milk and a plate of biscuits, as if I was five.

'I'm sorry Joe. I didn't mean to upset you earlier.'
I thought she actually meant it until she said,

'I just don't want you getting your hopes up about becoming a footballer.'
If only she hadn't said that. I imagined flipping the plate of biscuits out of her hand and pouring the glass of milk over her head…but I didn't. Instead I politely told her to get out of my room unless she had something nice to say. She infuriated me. She's never even been to watch me play football, how would she even know if it would happen or not.

Mum gently placed the milk and plate of biscuits on my bedside table. As she walked out of my room she stopped and turned towards me.

'When's your next match?'

'Tomorrow,' I snorted.

'Ok love. Do you want me to come watch you?'

I couldn't believe she actually just said that. She must've read my mind (I hope she didn't hear my thoughts about the milk and biscuits).

'If you want,' I said.

She smiled and closed the door behind her. Although I was a bit mad at her she was finally going to come and watch me play and see how good I actually am. Maybe she will take me a bit more seriously from now on about my dream. I really couldn't believe she was going to come and watch; it was a miracle!

The next morning I woke up and did the usual routine, I'm sure I don't need to go over it all again. I felt different though, I was quite happy to sit and have breakfast with Mum. I was excited about the game and couldn't wait for her to come and watch me. As usual I walked down my street to meet Tom. He was in a better mood that morning and had forgotten what had happened yesterday. We were both so excited about the match that night.

School dragged as normal. Maths was boring, English was boring and Science was boring. Let's just say school was totally and utterly boring! When the bell went I rushed down to the cloakroom to collect my kit from the P.E. teacher and got changed. I was playing left wing, my usual position, and I was feeling on top form. As we were all getting changed our teacher said,

'Listen up everyone. I've got something really exciting and important to tell you!'

We all stopped chatting and listened to what she had to say.

'There is a scout coming from the local team to come and watch you all play. He's going to see if any of you are good enough to have trials to play for his under 12's team. So you better make sure you play your best but don't worry about it, I know how brilliant you all are. Tom, don't sulk and Joe, don't be greedy! And make sure you show off that left foot of yours! Right everyone, you've got 5 minutes!'

OH MY GOD! Now I was even more excited about playing. Not only can I show off to my Mum but a football scout as well!

I quickly put my shin pads on and pulled my thick red socks up. I pulled them over my knees and carefully folded them back down to sit neatly at the top of the shin pad. I looked over at Tom who was grinning like a Cheshire cat.

'Can you believe it Tom?'

'I know mate, let's show him our skills!'

We jogged onto the field with the rest of the team. We began warming up as the other team approached. I felt butterflies in the pit of my stomach; it was the first time I had ever felt nervous. The referee blew the whistle and as we made our way to our starting positions I saw my Mum walking towards the side line; she actually came! This day couldn't get any better.

Throughout the game I was conscious of playing my best but most of all passing. As I weaved in and out of the other team's defenders I saw on opportunity to score. My head told me to go for the shot but I knew I had to pass. I cut the ball across from the right into the centre to set Tom up and with that he gave it a powerful kick. As the ball head for the top left corner it missed and hit the crossbar. It rebounded back in my direction. This was my opportunity. I jumped up and headed it. It flew straight past the goalie and in the back of the net! I jumped in the air and ran towards the centre of the pitch, my team running and cheering behind me. It was such a great goal. I glanced over to my Mum, she was smiling and clapping; she must've been proud.

We ended up winning the game 1-0 so my goal was the only goal. As we ran off the pitch, chanting, our P.E. teacher and a man approached us. He was tall and thin. He was dressed head to toe in a black tracksuit and a woolly black hat. His trainers gleamed white against the muddy ground; he looked important.

'Well played lads!' His voice was deep yet cheery. 'I'm guessing you all know why I'm here?'

We all nodded, scared to say anything.

'Good. Well a few of you boys stood out for me. There was a lot of great passing between you and some top teamwork. You'll hear from me by letter if I want you to come for a trial but you did really impress me. You're a talented bunch.'

I couldn't believe what I was hearing. He actually liked us and we impressed him; what an achievement. Not one of us could stop smiling; it was so exciting. I couldn't wait to get home and tell my Dad about it.

When Mum and I got home she told me how proud she was of me, which I already knew anyway: why wouldn't she be? She said I was brilliant! I was sat at the table day dreaming about the match, did I really score the only goal? I was pretty brilliant. Mum was cooking my favourite tea, Spaghetti Bolognese, as a treat for being such a top footballer. A loud bang snapped me out of my day dream, Dad was home. I rushed to the door, smiling from ear to ear.

'Hey Joe, you look like you've had a good day.'

'You'll never guess what happened, Dad. Well, the scout was here to watch our team play football, he really liked us all and said how good we all were and guess what else, I scored the only goal! I went to pass it to Tom so he could score but he missed and it hit the crossbar and came back towards me so I headed it and it went flying past the goalie and straight in the back of the net!'

I could hardly catch my breath.

'Wow, Joe, that's great news, well done mate. Don't be getting your hopes up though.'

Was he for real? Of course I was going to get my hopes up; it's what I'd always wanted. He obviously didn't have a clue what he was talking about. Dads! I just smiled at him to humour him as he walked past me and into the kitchen.

A few days passed and I couldn't contain my excitement. Every day when I arrived home from school I checked the post. I still hadn't heard anything though. I was trying not to worry but Tom had already had a letter saying they wanted him for trials. Why hadn't I heard anything? I didn't understand. It was finally on Friday that I found a letter. I rushed in from school and saw it on the kitchen side addressed to 'The parents/Guardians of Joe Hamilton'. It was definitely the letter I'd been waiting for. I saw that it was already open so I turned the envelope over and slid the letter out. It read: 'To the parents of blah blah…' I skimmed further down the letter, to the important bit. My mouth dropped open, it felt like my jaw had hit the floor. I couldn't believe what I was reading. They didn't want me for a trial. Were they actually being serious? My whole dream had come crashing down in front of my eyes on this stupid piece of paper. I shouted my Mum to come downstairs; I think I was in shock. There was no way that he wouldn't want me to have a trial, I was the best player in the match he watched. He was obviously the biggest idiot in town.

Mum eventually made it down the stairs and asked me what was wrong. I slammed the letter down on the unit and burst into tears, I was absolutely gutted.

'Joe, what's wrong? Did you read the letter?' She said it with such excitement; like she was happy that I was unsuccessful (I suppose that she didn't really care anyway, that's what she wanted, for me to give up on football). 'Why are you crying?'

'Why do you think I'm crying? They don't want me, they think I'm rubbish.'

'What? Have you read the letter properly?'

Mum handed me the letter. I wiped the tears away from my eyes and scanned over it. It still said I was unsuccessful; Mum was pure evil making me re-live it. I carried on reading further down the letter and saw the word 'however'. However? I knew that was a word for 'but' and 'but' is always the opposite of whatever someone has been talking about. So it was bad 'but' now it's going to be good kind of thing. I carried on reading. It said 'however we would like to offer Joe a temporary contract for six months and place in our under twelves team.'

I felt the smile creep onto my face and I looked at my Mum who was beaming with happiness. I wrapped my arms around her and we both screamed.

'Oh wow Mum, how ace is that? I can't believe it. I don't even need a trial!'

'Yes, Joe, it's absolutely brilliant. I am so proud of you, you know.' She took my arms from around her body and grabbed my hands. 'I've never seen you so happy. Maybe you will be a professional footballer one day, who knows.'

She actually believed in me for the first time ever and she was right to as well. You'll see.

*****

SECLUDED 1916
Heather Buckby

SECLUDED 1916

THE BUILDING COMES INTO SIGHT, causing my stomach to writhe. Never have I felt so frightened as I do now, as if reality has just touched upon me. Every night I've been waiting for this moment, and I've suffered from dreadful nightmares. The process of getting here was just as unbearable as arriving now. Every day, whilst walking the streets, I see people stare and glower at me. I have been judged as if I were a criminal, but no ordinary criminal... you would think I had committed murder. It wasn't a Tribunal it was a judge, jury and executioner; introduced to assess my conviction and sincerity. Sometimes I wonder if I should have made other choices, then I wouldn't be here. But I had to stand my ground, and protest our immorality. For that reason my own voice will be silenced.

My thoughts cluster as my wife taps my back, insisting I continue my slow walk towards what looks like a vast heathen temple. I stand still, my feet refusing to take me to where I know I have no option but to go. They wanted to shut me away from society and now they have gotten their wish, and I have no choice but to obey, my rights curtailed.

At the gates there stands a crowd of women, with white feathers grasped firmly in their flailing hands. As I pass through them their hatred turns to shouting and screaming, almost mocking cheering, confident that after today I will never return. This is because, in their eyes, I am the monstrosity to be excluded from society, and I know this from the whispers I hear while I walk down the streets, whilst my family are too ashamed to be by my side. Now everyone is leaving me here to suffer for my crimes alone. I presume you must call this a crime, from both sides. I committed crimes against the defence of my country and in return the country will incarcerate me and most possibly commit almost unbearable torture upon my mentality. This place will decrease my sanity not cure it. My wife says this is paranoia and that I have manic episodes, but she hasn't been listening to what the people are actually whispering. I have heard so many stories of what happens to my kind in prison. I hear they get something called 'field punishment', where they're tied up maybe to a fence, or to ropes, with their arms extended, and their feet tied together, and just left there.

My eyes are scanning my new home, and from what I can see this also can only be described as a prison. The premises themselves are huge, tall fences barricading the large grounds. The trees stand perfectly cut, structured singularly around the fencing, almost like tall soldiers guarding it; no one enters and no one leaves. As I'm walking down the long, narrow pathway, I'm gazing up at the building, it has hundreds of windows, created most probably for the eyes of the insane to peer into reality.

'I'm going to leave you from here.' Isabella comes to a halt.

I contain a sigh. 'That's fine. I understand, darling.'

'I just can't bear to see where I'm leaving you, knowing you'll be here alone.'

I merely kiss her on the forehead and smile. 'I'll be okay, don't worry. I'll write.'

I say this although I know it's a lie. I won't be given the privilege of having pen and paper in my possession. But saying this at least gives her some remote reassurance. I'm trying so hard not to blame her and my family. I'm being sent here on the grounds of having 'Chronic Mania' which I know I don't have, but my family insisted that I was to be given a good examination by the physician here, and it didn't seem to take long until he came to his conclusion. My father, who convinced the doctor that I'm suffering from depression and paranoia, had started all this. That was it! I was diagnosed with Chronic Mania. I don't know how he did it, sitting there watching me as my sanity was basically sentenced to death. He lied through his teeth because he was disgusted that I wouldn't oppose evil with evil, repelled by my own right of choosing not to fight in this war.

My breath is becoming shorter whilst my chest is tightening, as my feet reach the gigantic front doors. My own mind is pleading not to go in, but I have no other choice, if I didn't do it myself it would be done against my will, which when I envision being dragged in whilst I kick and scream, I feel it would be subjecting myself to even more humiliation. Once I walk into the hallway I shiver, then my body shudders at the unpleasant smell, a mixture of chemicals and corrosion. My eyes close tightly as my humanity is stripped from me, I'll just have to get used to it, now I shall have to live by the law. I am now a number with no name, no voice, and my life is in their hands. How long will I be here? My political past leads me to think I may never see daylight again. My mind can't comprehend how large the opening hallway is and its numerous corridors. The walls are all glazed brown bricks. This I think is quite a morbid tone, but then I guess it suits the building's intentions.

There is a stream of nurses walking determinedly back and forth. I take a deep breath as I notice one of them approaching me, her face isn't inviting, with looks of stone.

'Charles Baker, is it?' she says scanning me with her emotionless eyes. 'Yes, it is!'

'Would you like to follow me? I shall show you where you will be staying.'

Before she finishes her sentence she begins to walk away. The building is as big as it looks on the outside. As we walk around all I can see is endless corridors, and other parts of the building from out of the small barred windows. My luggage is becoming heavy as we trudge up flights of stairs, but I know that I would not long be burdened by it, as I know it won't be long until most of it is removed from my keep.

I haven't seen many patients, which comes as a surprise, it's making me feel more unnerved, and the ones that I have seen completely ignored my existence, their eyes don't even flicker as they hobble past me with their heads hanging down, hair matted from not being washed, their limbs seeming lifeless.

The nurse finally marches down a particular corridor. I'm examining every speck, I only presume this is going to lead to where I will sleep, and this place I know will be easy to get lost in. To my left are huge, arched windows, I can just see grey sky through the opaque glass. Ornaments are scattered around the walls, none of which have any purpose but just seem to be obscure objects. But it's when I look to my right that my heart finally drops, seeing the rooms forces my fate into reality that bit more. Dark wooden doors, with two open panels of black wire instead of glass windows, and a similar decorative circle at the top of the door filled with black wire again. I focus my mind on the paintings that are evenly spaced throughout the corridor, then I glare back at the statue of a stone lion that is perched by every two doors. I can see this place becoming rather repetitive very quickly. Finally she stops and I feel far from eager to see into where she is pointing.

'Here we are, this will be your room. I will let you settle in whilst I attend to other matters. You have approximately fifteen minutes until it will be time for dinner, so I will collect you and show you where the dining area is.'

My body shivers as I walk through the door, then the nurse quickly slams the door shut behind me. There is no handle on the inside. My stomach knots, this really is imprisonment. The room is dark, with only a glimmer of light seeping through the holes in the black wire windows. There is no outside window. I place my bag on the bed, a low metal frame with a thin mattress and a rough blanket. I shan't be sleeping well tonight, not that my own bed is that of a royal, but I wouldn't lend this bed to someone who is homeless. I'm circling the room, unable to concede how small it is in here, nothing to see, and nothing to occupy my mind. My fingertips brush against the walls, they're bare, undecorated and the rough brick chafes against my skin. Sudden bangs against my door.

'Mr. Charles! Are you ready for your meal?' the nurse shouts from outside the door.

I stand back as she throws it open. I can't even reply to her, I'm not ready at all. I just want to go home. I'm following her back along the corridor, this time I look at nothing; it is only the same as that I've seen before and what I will see for many days to come, and the foreseeable future. Once we enter the main hallway I can hear what sounds like crowds of unruly animals, people shrieking and moaning as they are guided to their destination. Some are resisting and are being escorted by multiple nurses. I see the physician stood in the small, white windows of the offices above the entrance, he's watching us all, examining our every movement. Some of the patients are staring at me, making me feel completely uncomfortable. Will I be welcomed or will I expect hurls of abuse?

As soon as I enter the dining hall my mind can't even gather thoughts it is that loud: some patients are rocking backwards and forwards in their seats, wailing with anxiousness or anger, some are sat perched on their chairs, sitting upright as if they were at a conducted meeting whilst others are roaming around the tables, their eyes dulled with medication, their minds like bottomless pits. They don't sit down until the nurses seat them.

I'm seated at a round table. I glance at the people who will be accompanying me through the meal; I examine them, trying to see if they would be capable of having a conversation, but something isn't right... None of them lift their heads up, their eyes are locked looking down and focusing on the table, the noise in the room is slowly decreasing as the food is being brought out. I daren't make conversation first, it seems that this isn't acceptable or someone would have spoken and enquired about my reasoning for being here. So I keep silent just like everyone else.

The plate is thrown in front of me, and I look down at the mashed up food, looking like someone had vomited and poured it onto a plate and called it a meal. No knives, no forks. I suppose I can understand that... here. Once everyone has received their plates there is a pause until they all dig straight in. I hesitate, moving it about with a spoon like I'm a ten-year-old child all over again, until I gather the courage to lift the spoon with a small amount and force it into my mouth. As the rough texture hits the roof of my mouth, my jaw clenches, the taste is vile, I'd rather eat animal excreta than this, but when I look at the faces of other patients I can see the elation in their eyes, like this is a treat for them. If the rest of the food tastes like this I'll very quickly become a skeleton. I consume all of it though. I know that's the most sensible option.

Once I have finished eating, one of the nurses approaches me.

'I'll show you back to your room now, but we will walk via the main lounge and show you where most of the residents spend their time in comfort,' her face is expressionless and her voice is monotone.

As we walk back through the entrance I notice a lot of the patients from the dining area have wandered in here too, walking around in aimless circles, one is crouched beside the large stairway, rocking back and forth. The nurse nudges me for my attention then glances at her watch.

'At around half seven you will be expected to be ready to attend this room, for your medications. So you have two hours to rest.'

I am being quickly escorted back to my cell; it's far from a room. Whilst I walk the narrow spiral staircase, musty air hits me, I'm sure there's a vile aroma of stagnant water in this corridor. She unlocks my door and steps aside whilst I enter. I decide to lay on my bed, just staring at the ceiling and thinking to myself, but all of my thoughts are empty of meaning. Part of me is wishing I could find a way to escape: with the mixture of sanity and intelligence I already have a higher likelihood of succeeding, well, in comparison to the rest of the patients anyway. My eyes begin to involuntarily close, more from mental exhaustion than anything else, then an abrupt bang of the door opening. I can see the white clothing of a nurse, another one I haven't met. But this one doesn't speak to me, just physically gestures with her head to come out and for which way to go.

I follow and join the queue in the main hall. One by one the patients ahead of me grab a small cup from the nurses, gulp the contents down, then limply walk away again. I really don't want to take these medicines, but I know how that would result. When it comes to my turn I force myself to swallow them, without even looking to see what was there, but I can feel several. I hear someone shouting, it's a patient screaming sentences that don't even make sense. It isn't long until he is carried away. The towering clock starts to chime. It's eight o'clock.

All the nurses take a patient each and begin to guide them away; one grabs my arm, I am quickly led away. Now, I am sat back on the hard mattress of my bed. So this is the basic routine? I have memorised every object and so now the only thing I can do is try to occupy my mind. Without warning, the lights are turned out. I'm left in darkness. I rub my trouser lining, where a small penknife is hidden, waiting. I have a lot of time and so much thinking I need to do.

*****

SEHNSUCHT
John Ashbrook

*Highly Commended for the University Centre Grimsby
International Literary Prize*

SEHNSUCHT

D AD WAS DYING TO BE A SUPERHERO; it was all he'd ever really talked about, until mom shushed him. The truth was though, he was never going to be leaping from the rooftops in skin-tight clothes and rescuing beautiful women from evil German bad guys, because Oldma and Oldpa hadn't been gunned down in front of him, space aliens hadn't come down and given him superpowers and he hadn't been bitten by anything radioactive, so he became an accountant instead.

After five days in a suit and tie, his adventures came at the weekend. When he'd hung out the clean flag on the pole on the front lawn, he would set off on a 'quest' to bravely visit the local grocery stores, drug stores and newsstands in search of the latest issues of his favorite superhero comic books. Sometimes it took him hours to find everything he wanted and, while he was away, Mom would never rest, she'd dust and push the Hoover around or bake cookies and tell me time and again that she was just glad he was out of the house.

When Dad returned from his mission, he would head straight up to his library in the attic so he could read his comic books in peace and quiet and, as he put it, 'keep them away from the sticky fingers of children'. I was never sure who these 'children' were, as I was the only child in the house: nine years old and under strict instructions from Mom never to read comic books less they make me 'foolish like y'r father'.

So, both Mom and Dad were very clear that I shouldn't read his comic books, which shows that they really didn't know me at all. Saying 'no' to me just made me long for something that I otherwise probably wouldn't have been that bothered by. I would lie in bed, in the dark, looking up at the ceiling as though I could see them through it.

Which is why I made it my business to sneak up there every chance I got. Sometimes, when Dad was out, Mom would drink and take pills and sleep a lot, so it was easy for me to accidentally lower the stairs to the attic and find myself up there among the shelves.

It was always warm and comforting up there, rich with the smell of dry, aging paper. Or maybe it was just dust. Either way, it was magic to me. The flimsy, vibrantly-colored volumes were standing upright in cut-down Cheerio boxes, all the Avengers were together, as were all the Captain Americas, and so on. I knew he kept them all in the right order so, when I read them, I was careful to put them back where I found them. I also made sure my fingers weren't sticky.

I would get a rush of excitement just from the covers, their flaming reds and bright yellows glowing out of the paper at me. Each of them would depict a moment of conflict, the hero in pitched battle hovering over the New York streets (it was always New York, for some reason), or being zapped by a ray gun that could turn him into a pillar of salt. Sometimes this scene wouldn't appear in the story at all - which I didn't much mind - or sometimes it gave away the ending - which *did* annoy me. I hated being able to guess the ending.

The overall impression I got from the stories was that New York was a really exciting place, full of colorful people doing amazing things every day. There must have been something in the water there, I thought, because we didn't have superheroes like that here in Potwin.

'Why don't we have superheroes in Kansas, dad?' I asked when we were out in the yard playing catch. Dad caught my slow pitch then straightened up and I saw the glint of a smile, probably because I'd shown an interest in his specialist subject (Mom was out shopping, so it was safe to talk about it). He thought about it for a moment and then said: 'Maybe it's 'cause you can't leap over a tall building in a single bound ... If you don't have any tall buildings.'

I guess that made sense. He tossed the ball back underarm and I asked, 'What would your superhero name be, Dad?'

'Well, I've considered this quite a bit.' I thought he might, 'and I can't decide.' Oh. 'Y'see, the problem is that there aren't any superheroes called Donald.'

'It would've been okay if your *second* name had started with a 'D' too.'

'What, like 'Matt Murdoch' or 'Reed Richards' or 'Sue Storm'?'
'Zackly.'

He raised his catcher's mitt and I gave him my hardball, aimed straight at his face. He ducked and the ball flew over the fence. We watched it come to a halt in the middle of Mr. Dangerfield's lawn and dad nervously glanced over at our nightmare neighbor's house. Dad's foot hovered for a moment, he was considering stepping over the picket fence to get the ball back, but that could mean being attacked by Mr. Dangerfield's ratty little terrier again. Dad's foot returned to the ground and he turned to me, ball suddenly forgotten:

'I could be Don *Dangerous*.'

'Yeah! Or Dangerous Don?'

He liked that. A lot. He was grinning so much I could see his gold tooth near the back. That glint of gold was always a good sign. We agreed then, Dangerous Don it was, and I even got to help him design the costume. My felt pens and crayons had never been turned to a more important use. We worked closely together and, very soon, the design was finished, gauntlets, knee-boots and all. He asked me to draw both the front and the back of the costume in as much detail as I could. It was a rare occasion when we worked together as equals. It had hardly ever happened before. It would never happen again.

That night, I heard him and Mom arguing. Something about 'savings' and 'what about the new car?' It was troubling to hear them argue, but boring that it was about money again, so I turned over and wished myself to sleep.

The next morning, Dad was gone.

Mom said she didn't know where he was and didn't care. I pretended I didn't care either and watched some TV. Then, in the afternoon, when she did her usual laying down thing, I quietly snuck upstairs to the attic, in search of clues.

Dad had left some comic books scattered across the carpeted floor. This was very unusual. He always put them away when he was done with them. Always. There was a Sgt Fury, a couple of Invaders, a Süperman, a Daredevil and a Fantastic Four. An odd mix. I flicked through them, they didn't seem to have anything in common, the stories and bad guys were all different, the writers and artists were different. Then I noticed that they all had the same advert on the back cover.

It was a cartoon drawing of a dad pulling a sheet off a big shiny statue. The dad's face and the statue's face were the same. The little boy and the mom he was showing the statue to were laughing and clapping. The advert was for a company called 'Real Life Heroes'. They made full size statues of superheroes, based on your design, and they'd even take your face and make the hero look like you. It cost $999 (cape extra).

Wow, a statue of a superhero. The notion set my mind racing.

Later, when it got to teatime and there was still no Dad, I went to ask Mom about it and found her still in the bedroom, crying. I hugged her and told her I loved her, which helped and made her smile. Then I told her it would all be okay 'cause Dad would be back soon, but that *didn't* help, she started crying again.

I slumped down to the kitchen and poured some Golden Grahams into a bowl for myself. This didn't feel right: eating breakfast as the sun went down. As I munched, I considered the photo on the wall over the kitchen table. It was a photo of Oldpa, Dad's dad; he looked very proud, standing there in his uniform. I hadn't thought about it before, but Oldpa *then* looked just like Dad did *now*. Apart from the uniform, of course. Oldpa wore that in all the photos we had of him, including the wedding photo and, my favorite, the one of him smoking and sitting on a pile of rubble in some town in Germany.

His medals were on display too, in a glass case on the dresser in the front room, where Dad would polish them every spring and autumn.

There were pictures of Oldpa with Oldma, and of Oldpa with his eldest son, my uncle Gary; but none of Oldpa with Dad. Mom had a picture of uncle Gary, saluting and smiling in his own blue uniform and white cap; she had this in a silver frame beside her bed in her room and she slept facing it. I'd never met uncle Gary, because he'd died before I was born, not long before Mom and Dad got married, so they say. He didn't look much like Dad though, uncle Gary, he had blue eyes for one thing, like I do.

I put my bowl in the sink and went to bed.

Eight o' clock the following morning, the doorbell rang, making Crypto bark. It was a man, drawn and chapped in the early morning chill, with a delivery for us. He muttered as he eyed-up our doorframe, that they'd need to bring it round the back.

When I first saw it, I understood why they hadn't tried to bring it through the front door. It was over six feet tall, four feet wide in every direction and was wrapped in a cardboard sarcophagus. The delivery man and his younger colleague grunted and grumbled to each other as they pushed their upright trolley to-and-fro around the tricky bend into our yard. They clearly adored their company's commitment to door-to-door service.

Mom stood in the shadowed doorway, watching them from a distance, but I danced impatiently around the box as they cut the straps, unfolded the cardboard sleeve and set about slicing through the taped seals until the two halves of the polystyrene block parted with a sound like a drawn breath, and the statue was revealed.

It was Dangerous Don in every detail. The two letter D's were stretched across his domed chest. His thick, muscly arms ended in the gauntlets I'd drawn, one pressed against his waist, the other proudly saluting. His head was held high, square chin thrust defiantly out.

He was completely gold.

The statue had a good four or five inches on my actual dad, and two or three inches of muscle all the way round. Then, of course, there was that cubic chin. When Dad came back, I'd have to carefully compare its rigid lines to the soft curves of his real chins.

That apart, the statue was the spit of Dangerous Don; they'd done a fantastic job of capturing Dad's face, wide grin and all. He'd rarely looked happier.

I spent a while sitting on the lawn gazing up in awe at the magnificent life size effigy then, gradually, the shine wore off. I went in and watched The Muppets while Mom slept upstairs, then took my ball out. As the sun dipped down, reflections slowly swept around the statue, like the hands of a clock and Crypto peed up against its leg.

He wasn't real good at catch, my dad, but he was better than the statue. I bounced the ball off its massive chin. Crypto jumped, caught the ball in mid air and ran in with it. I ran in with him, leaving the statue in the gathering dark.

Mom was up now, watching the TV, so I stood in the doorway, sort of hovering, not knowing whether to ask about Dad, to see if she was as concerned as I was. But she was sitting with her back to me, watching a soap opera; it had lots of people with too much makeup on shouting at each other, much as Mom and Dad had. So I went to my room and played with my Action Man instead.

Next morning, Dad's shiny statue was dripping with dew. The neighborhood houses were faint shapes in the grey mist, and Mom was standing on the damp lawn, watching the statue and smoking. She only smoked when she was *really* upset. She'd been to the store and bought some, special. I was relieved that, this time at least, it wasn't me she was upset at. I stood next to her and her free hand dropped from the crook of her elbow to gently wrap round mine. I tingled with joy at this touch.

She breathed out her own cloud of mist, pointed her cigarette at the statue and told me: 'That cost more than our new car would've.'

'But our old car's nice, Mom.'

'A new 'un woulda been nicer.'

After a brief think, I asked: 'Is Dad in trouble?'

She didn't answer, just squeezed my hand. Then she leaned forward, squinting at the gold statue. 'It's cracked.'

I followed her gaze and there it was: The square line of the chin had a very obvious crack on it. Right where my ball had hit it. My hair tightened on my scalp. Oh no, I was in trouble after all! Frozen to the spot, I watched as she slid her fingernail into the crack and the gold just flaked away like eggshell. Underneath was something white, like you'd see under actual eggshell. She touched it tentatively with her nail and it crumbled. It was powdery. A few grains stuck to the tip of her finger, which she sampled with the tip of her tongue.

'Salt.'

I looked up at mom, she frowned down at me, mystified by the salt and seemingly not bothered about what caused the crack. Relieved, I dragged over one of the lawn chairs, climbed on it and prodded the hole in the golden chin myself. I scratched the powdery surface and salt showered down. Then, from beneath this, grains of a different color, a light brown, like that sugar mom put in her coffee. Further down, the grains were darker brown, like that British treacle toffee dad had brought home once, rich and deep and sticky.

I stuck this in my mouth, expecting something sweet but, instead, I got an unpleasant tang like the taste of my fillings when they first put them in.

Looking at my screwed-up face, Mom asked, 'Still salt?'

'No. Don't know what it is.'

I prodded my finger into the hole I'd created, worming into the made-up chin they'd added to my dad's face until, when I was knuckle deep, I found something hard and tacky that I couldn't push past. I pulled out my finger and we both looked closely at it.

There was something like brown jelly on the tip, it was the sort of brown that looks like red. The sort of brown that looks like red that I sometimes get on my fingertip when I've been picking my nose.

Mom stopped breathing.

She grabbed me by the shoulders, lifted me off the chair and spun me around, then marched me into the house and away from the statue. She kept saying 'no' lots. No-no-no-no-no.

The next bit I saw at a distance through my bedroom window. Mom dashed out of the kitchen with a knife and stepped up on the chair, so her head was blocking my view of the statue's. Her elbows pumped in and out, like she was running on the spot, and jagged lumps of gold-plated salt fell away, bouncing across the grass. Crypto gobbled one up, then spat it out again.

Finally mom stopped. The knife fell from her hand and she just stood there, like a statue herself. Not seeing what she was seeing was agony until, slowly, she turned and looked up at my window, as though she'd known I'd been there all along. Her eyes were ringed with red, she looked older, more like her mom, my nanna, than ever before. I couldn't understand that look on her face, I'd never seen it before. Not sure anyone had.

She stepped down and I saw Dangerous Don's face. The gold skin had been hacked away and beneath it, packed safely in the red-stained salt, was a bloody skull. Threads of raw meat still hung from the cheek bones, while the empty eye sockets were oozing and dark. But, like all skulls, this one looked genuinely happy. To this day, I cannot imagine a look of greater delight and satisfaction. I cannot imagine a wider full-toothed grin, with that familiar glint of gold near the back.

*****

'Women want love to be a novel, men a short story.'

Daphne du Maurier

HAMMOND HOUSE

Authors for Authors

Ethical publishing company and members organisation providing help and support towards a successful career in writing.

Membership Benefits

Author profile page

Publish your work

Submit articles

Literary Prizes and Competitions

Member's forum

Service providers

www.hammondhousepublishing.com

2016

International Literary Prize

The inaugural year of this prestigious literary prize saw a record number of entries spread across five continents.

WINNER   The Deaths and Deaths of
Winston Witherstone- *Marian Harrison*

2nd Place   The Beekeeper - *Joe Fuller*
3rd Place   Cause and Effect - *Amanda Staples*

HIGHLY COMMENDED
Meeting your Maker - *Olivia Waelde*
Ode to a Loving Husband - *Amy Naylor*
Tomorrow is Another Day - *Deyanira Andreieff*
Sehnsucht - *John Ashbrook*
After the Fall - *Jemma Hough*

SHORTLISTED
Dialogue - *Ian McDonald*
Vivian - Katy Southall
The Goths Cross - *J.A. Grierson*
The Jigsaw - *David Brennen*

JUDGES- Peter True and Anjali Wierny

HAMMOND HOUSE

2017

International Literary Prize
1st Prize £600
2nd £100   3rd £50

Worldwide Publication
for the top 25 stories

Theme: ETERNAL
Short Story of 2000 - 5000 Words
Entries open 1st January 2017
Submission deadline 30th September 2017

OTHER 2017 COMPETITIONS

International Poetry Prize
Screenwriting Competition

www.hammondhousepublishing.com

University Centre Grimsby

The University Centre Grimsby, as part of the Grimsby Institute, is built on high expectations, a focus on learning, commitment to achievement and an engaged, practical education for all students.

A wide range of degree level courses are available including BA (hons) Professional Writing.

www.grimsby.ac.uk

KENWICK PARK ESTATE
Golf Hotel and Spa

Country house hotel in 320 acres of woodlands, parks, and manicured grounds with woodland lodges, club spa, evergreen spa, tennis courts and championship golf course. The perfect place to relax and recuperate

www.kenwick-park.co.uk